# No Chance

Gareth Alun Thomas

First published in 2025 by Blossom Spring Publishing
No Chance © 2025 Gareth Alun Thomas
ISBN 978-1-917938-20-4
E: admin@blossomspringpublishing.com
W: www.blossomspringpublishing.com

# Acknowledgements

A special thank you to my two daughters: Ellie, for encouraging me to carry on writing when I was on the verge of giving up; and Rebecca, for all her help and advice, and putting her English degree to good use. To my son, Dan, for providing me with many distractions from writing this book, including borrowing money and making me laugh – well, I needed a break sometimes!

Thanks to Amanda, my wife, for her words of encouragement and support. "It's no Sidney Sheldon," made me laugh.

Thanks to all my friends and family who took the trouble to proofread the book, including Timblick, Huw, Richard and Tinhead.

A big thank you to Amanda Ellison at Blossom Spring Publishers for patiently editing my book and correcting my many mistakes. Thanks also to Laura Cosby for her cover design.

Finally, thank you to Blossom Spring Publishers for helping me achieve my ambition of seeing my work in print.

# Acknowledgements

# Preface

Following the deaths of my parents, within three months of each other, my two brothers and I had to clear the family home before putting it on the market. It was during this process that I came across the diary I had kept when I went interrailing with a group of friends in the summer of 1985. I used this diary as a template to write my first novel and, although the journeys were all genuine, the story itself is a work of fiction.

# No Chance

# Chapter 1

## 1985: Swansea University Disco

Right, here we go. Let the good times roll.

I had consumed just the right amount of alcohol: enough to give me confidence, not so much as to induce vomiting. My bladder had recently been emptied – although I could do with going again. *Please don't let me down, bladder. Not this time.*

Did I have time to quickly nip to the toilet? No. I was in position now. It was too late. It was all systems go.

I was standing on the edge of the dance floor, watching the throng of third-year students dancing to Madonna's 'Into the Groove'. My friend, Bob Cousins, was DJing tonight and he'd assured me that, not long after the Madonna song, he'd play one slow song – the last song of the night.

This would be my window to approach a girl for a dance. I just had to find one. A girl, that is – not a window.

A group of girls, dancing, screamed in delight as 'Happy Birthday' by Altered Images began. They were pushing and shoving who was obviously the birthday girl to the centre of the dance floor, and she was looking suitably embarrassed.

My attention wasn't on her, though – it was on another girl, dancing with wild abandon, totally immersed in the music. She wasn't restricting herself to the confines of the dance floor and was instead dancing almost manically around the perimeter of the room, weaving her way between the dancers and onlookers.

The song ended, and Bob Cousins was struggling with

the music. *Come on, Cousins, sort your act out. Do not blow it for me, you half-wit.* There was an awkward pause before the mesmerising saxophone of George Michael's 'Careless Whisper' began. Bob Cousins gave me the thumbs-up from his deck. I started to panic slightly – I knew I had only three to four minutes to achieve my objective: find a girl. Anyone.

Just as I searched the dance floor, a girl grabbed my hand as she stumbled into me. It was the nomadic dancing girl I had been watching. She led me back into the crowd of dancers. She threw her arms around my neck and pulled me closer. I couldn't believe it: I was actually holding a girl, and a beautiful girl at that. The music was too loud for conversation, so I focused on holding on to her as tightly as I could manage. It was the slow song, after all. This was expected. It did feel good. I could smell her hair, her perfume and a slight aroma of cigarette smoke – though, to be fair, I don't think the smoke smell was coming from her. I started to think about attempting a kiss – probably a bit ambitious, to be honest – and tilted my head slightly to look at her face. She had her eyes closed. A good sign, I hoped, but wait ... was she *asleep*? I hoped she wasn't, but as the song came to an end, she continued to hold me tight. The lights were on now; the disco had finished, but still the girl held on. Not that I was complaining. Two girls approached us and peeled the girl's arms from my body.

"Come on, Ruby, the disco has finished! Let's get you to bed," said one of her concerned friends.

Ruby still had her eyes closed as her friends tried to move her. She was drunk. Very drunk. She was so drunk that the two girls had to support her after peeling her off me while walking her away. She opened her eyes, looked at me and smiled. I had just been keeping her upright all this time. I could have been anyone. But that smile, those beautiful brown eyes – it was magical. And, at the age of twenty-one, I was in love.

# Chapter 2

## Ruby

The next morning Ruby woke up with a thumping headache. She was lying on top of her bed and was fully clothed. She was still wearing her shoes. There was vomit in her waste bin. And on the floor next to it. She didn't remember being sick last night or how she had got back to her room, although she had a vague recollection of her friends carrying her up the stairs.

She started to recall the night before, how she and her friends started drinking earlier in the student bar at lunchtime. It was only meant to be a quick drink. She remembered then going to the pub on the way back to her student accommodation. They had drunk wine – and more wine. She remembered eating crisps. Somebody had given her a cigarette, but she hadn't liked it. Then it was the disco, and then dancing, and yet more dancing. And then that boy she had fallen into on the dance floor …

He had supported her until the end. She couldn't remember much more, except he was skinny and a bit clingy. Never again, she thought, and got up to rush to the toilet.

# Chapter 3

## Will

Wow, what a night! And that smile at the end. That smile. Ruby. Ruby was her name, and I was in love. I couldn't stop smiling as I recalled the night's events. I had held a girl for the first time since New Year's Eve 1984.

Life was good.

Over the next few days I looked out for Ruby. Mainly through the window of my university room, which was on the third floor and offered a good viewpoint to students walking back to their accommodation. The girls' block was behind the boys' accommodation, so they would all walk past our building. I did see her, fleetingly, a few times. She wore quirky clothes: colourful jeans and an old-man suit jacket over a patterned T-shirt. Big men's jackets were fashionable for girls at the time, usually bought from charity shops and paired with chunky Dr Martens boots. Ruby usually wore a hat of some sort; today she wore a black beret, covering her long brown hair, which fell in curls just above the shoulders. The looking through the window and obsessing went on for a few days before, finally, our paths crossed. I was walking through the park on the way back from the shop, and she was walking in the opposite direction. She was by herself, which was good for me. I was carrying an egg mayonnaise sandwich, which, for some reason, I tried to hide. Why would I be embarrassed by an egg mayonnaise sandwich? I suppose they do smell a bit.

"Hi," I muttered shyly as we drew alongside each other.

"Hi," she said, smiling sheepishly. She stopped now

and turned to face me.

"Sorry about last week – I was a bit drunk. I suffered the next day, big style," Ruby continued.

"No worries. I was glad to help." I had to concentrate on not staring too hard; she was so lovely.

"It's Ruby, by the way."

"Oh, yeah, I know," I said. "Hi, Ruby Bytheway. That's an unusual surname. I'm Will."

Ruby chose to ignore my poor joke. Not a good start.

"Hi, Will."

"I enjoyed your dancing the other night."

"Oh, yeah, sorry – I get carried away sometimes."

I wished *I* could carry her away, preferably to my bedroom. *Keep those thoughts to yourself, William.* I could almost hear my mother talking.

We both smiled a bit awkwardly.

"Anyway, thanks again for the other night. I think you held me up during that last song," Ruby continued.

"Oh, yeah, no worries. Glad to help."

I couldn't think of anything else to say to prolong the conversation.

"Well, see you, Will, I've got stuff to do, people to see, essays to write, coffee to drink …"

She winked at me. Why was she winking at me?

Should I ask her for a coffee? *Go on, Will – ask her for a coffee. Ask her. Ask her.* But it was too late: she had already started to walk away. *Good one, Will. You could have kept her talking for a bit longer.*

My heart was racing, though, and my stomach felt weird – like the time I went on the Grand National ride at Blackpool Theme Park. I think it was what's known as butterflies in the stomach or something, although I had never experienced it before.

# Chapter 4

## The Mumbles Run

The following Friday, a group of us were going on a pub crawl around Mumbles, an area of Swansea near the seafront, popular with students. There were ten pubs in Mumbles, and the idea was to have a drink – a pint or a shot – in each one. Maybe I would bump into Ruby in one of the pubs. There was a good chance: most students seemed to go to Mumbles on a Friday night. My friend Pete was the only one I knew who had completed the challenge. On that occasion, he had celebrated by eating a daffodil, which he had pulled out of a flowerbed before vomiting over my shoes outside the White Rose. The White Rose was the last pub of the Mumbles Run. People started calling him 'Pete the Drink' for a while, after his exploits. But the nickname didn't stick. Pete was the first person I met at university – his room was next door to mine – and we'd been friends ever since. Nevertheless, we were different people: Pete was obsessed with football and dubious heavy metal music, while I liked The Smiths and romantic comedies – though I kept the latter to myself! We bonded over our love for the pub and our unsuccessful pursuit of the opposite sex. I was tall and skinny and usually wore donkey jackets, Sta-Prest trousers and Doc Martens. I sometimes wore a blue mohair jumper I had got my mum to knit for me. I had to pay for the wool myself, though. Pete was shorter and, as he liked to describe himself, chunky. I would have called him fat – though not to his face. He preferred to wear denim jackets, often with denim jeans and trainers.

"Are you ready for this, Evans?" Pete always called

me by my surname.

"Yeah, I'm all set. Is Phil coming?"

Phil was Pete's mate from his course, computer studies. He was taller than Pete – most people were – and came from Harrogate, I think. I found him a bit boring because when the two of them got together they talked obsessively about football. While I would watch football, like the World Cup or the FA Cup final, I found the relentless cycle of Saturday fixtures a bit tedious, especially the pub analysis afterwards. I mean, why did it matter? There would be another game next week!

"Yeah, he's already started – he's with the others."

The others included Simon Tigwell, known as Tigsy, and John Pitcher, who was notoriously tight and had consequently earned the moniker of Mothball. I didn't really understand the reference, but Pete said it was so rare to see John's wallet that, when it *did* make an appearance, mothballs would fall out of his pocket. I was scared to admit I didn't know what mothballs were, either.

The evening passed in a blur, and by the time I got to the last pub I was feeling ill. I had managed to leave a few of my drinks without the others noticing; I was skilled at drink-hiding and often pretended I had consumed a drink in every pub, to save face. But still, I'd drunk way too much. Ruby was in the pub with a group of girls. They were standing by the fruit machine, so I would have an excuse to walk over in that direction. I was drunk enough to be able to walk over and start a conversation. I walked over confidently.

"Hi, again." I was slurring badly. *Compose yourself, Will. Compose yourself.*

"Oh, hi …" She looked a bit annoyed to see me, but I

could've been wrong.

"We've just done the Mumbles Run." I was conscious I was still slurring.

"Oh, nice. I've done that a few times – never completed it, though."

"Nor me. I'm just a lightweight, really … Eh, have you had a good day, Ruby? What have you been up to?"

My heart started to beat quickly. She looked amazing tonight, just wearing a pair of tight black leggings and a simple green T-shirt, which she had matched with a pair of green earrings. She was also wearing green eyeshadow, which seemed to accentuate her stunning brown eyes.

"Well, no, not really. I tried all day to finish my essay but got nowhere, and I stubbed my toe getting out of the shower."

Ruby glanced over her shoulder at her friends, who were watching our painful exchange. I thought she was anxious to join them.

"Oh, sorry to hear that. Sounds painful. Listen, I've got a joke," I said, recalling a joke Pete had told me earlier in the evening. I was talking quickly now, keen to make her laugh. Establish a connection. "What's old, pink and wrinkly and hangs out your pyjamas?"

"I don't know," Ruby replied quickly.

"Your mother."

I started to laugh, hoping Ruby would too. I had laughed when Pete had told the joke earlier. But she wasn't laughing. She wasn't even smiling.

"To be honest, Will, I don't find that joke very funny. My mum died last year."

"Oh, sorry – I didn't know. Well, obviously I didn't know. I should have gone with the other joke I heard tonight: what's green and sings at the bottom of the garden? Elvis Parsley … So, how did she die?"

"I'm sorry, I'd rather not talk about it, if you don't mind. I don't know you very well, and it's all rather personal. I've got to go, sorry. See you, Will."

Ruby turned her back on me and started talking to her friends again.

Well, that wasn't very good. I had simultaneously managed to upset her and possibly offend her in the space of a few minutes. *Good stuff, Will.* In my defence, though, how was I to know her mother had died? But all I could think about were her eyes: those beautiful brown eyes. My stomach lurched again. Butterflies again, or too much beer. Probably both. I headed for the toilet. Pete was outside the toilet, eating a daffodil he had extracted from the pub garden.

"Oi, Evans! I saw you talking to Ruby. You've got no chance there. Apparently, she's got her eye on Tom Bellows from the fourth floor."

Tom Bellows. Who was Tom Bellows? Cool name, though.

# Chapter 5

## Tom Bellows

Tom Bellows, it turned out, was doing a postgrad in maths – so that would make him a year above us. He was skinny, too, but his face, unlike mine, was acne-free. He too wore a donkey jacket – most students did – and he put gel in his hair, which was jet black. His hair, not the gel. The gel made his hair look like it was wet all the time. Pete pointed him out to me the next day; he was with Ruby. He was good-looking, if you liked that sort of thing.

"I told you: got no chance there, Evans. No chance."

He laughed, throwing back his head while doing so.

I didn't see Ruby for a few days, until the Saturday night disco. 'Careless Whisper' was playing again. That song seemed to be played relentlessly everywhere I went. I did like the song, though – but liking George Michael probably wasn't considered cool. I was drunk again. I scanned the room for Ruby and saw her dancing with Tom Bellows. That should have been me. They weren't just dancing, but kissing. It was as if George Michael was taunting me, his lyrics lamenting a love that could have lasted, a dance that might have spanned a lifetime, and the torment of having no one to share it with.

If only Ruby were listening. Pete was right: I had no chance. I went back to my room and took out my favourite record at the time: 'Heaven Knows I'm Miserable Now' by The Smiths. The lyrics seemed to sum up my mood perfectly: a brief, tipsy spell of contentment giving way to bleak self-pity. Morrissey wailed, while a tear cascaded down my acne-marked face. To be fair, I was probably unhappy in the haze of my drunkenness, and even more miserable right in this moment – and it was all down to Tom Bellows.

*

Tom Bellows couldn't understand why he wasn't happy. He was in his final year of university and doing well in his course. In fact, he found the work easy; he had always been good at maths. He had a girlfriend who was cute, sexy and funny. Yet he wanted more. He blamed Charlie, his best mate from home. Charlie had said the only thing he was taking to university was a suitcase full of condoms. Yes, he'd hooked up – but maybe it was too soon to be tied down. Wasn't this the time to be enjoying himself? Before his final year, Charlie had said he expected his bed to be broken by Christmas, given the number of girls he'd be pulling. Tom secretly thought Charlie was gay, but that was for another day. Tom thought about his plans for the day. Getting up would be a good start – it was already 9.30 a.m. He didn't have any lectures that morning, so he decided to go and see Ruby. He knew she was free.

About an hour later they were sitting together on a bench in the park by the student residence. The bench had one of those little metal plaques stuck to the back support: 'To the memory of Sam Pritchard – he loved this place.'

To be fair, it was a nice bench: it had shelter from the nearby oak tree and a sea view, with the Mumbles pier visible in the distance. *How much time had Sam Pritchard spent sitting on this bench?* Come to think of it, why was he sitting on a bench close to the student residence? Probably some kind of pervert spying on young girls. Or young boys. But if he was a pervert, why would somebody dedicate a bench to him? Tom really had to stop overthinking things. He wondered if, when he died, he would have a plaque on a wooden bench. Ruby had joined him now. Tom knew he wanted to break up with Ruby, but he wasn't absolutely sure why. He wondered if it was something to do with not settling down, sowing his wild oats. Seeing what else was out there. Playing the field, as Charlie had told him to do.

"The thing is, Ruby – don't you think we should have a bit more fun while we can? Do you think we should slow things down?"

Ruby looked upset. She had not expected this conversation when she woke up this morning, but smiled as she replied, "Slow what down, Tom? We're just having a bit of fun, aren't we?"

Ruby thought it was more than fun. To her, anyway. She really liked Tom.

"I'm glad we're on the same page, Ruby. It's a big world out there. We can still be friends, obviously, but maybe we should give this relationship thing a bit of a break."

# Chapter 6

## Ruby

Back in her room, later that afternoon, Ruby was crying. She hadn't expected this response. She hadn't expected to fall for Tom Bellows this hard, but she had – and now he wanted to "slow things down" and "give this relationship a bit of a break". What did that even mean? Would he want her back after a break? And if so, how long would this break be?

She wished she hadn't started to cry on that bench in the park. He didn't cry. He didn't even look upset. Still, she had her finals coming up and she knew she should concentrate on those. Though it would be harder to concentrate now. That much she knew. How had she let a boy get under her skin and upset her so much?

# Chapter 7

# Will

I didn't see Ruby for a few weeks, despite my best efforts to find her. *When I do see her again, I must try not to upset her.* I was obsessively walking through the park, hoping to see her. I did buy a lot of egg mayonnaise sandwiches during that period, but our paths never crossed. My exams were over. I had studied biochemistry. Biochemistry was one of the first courses to finish. I'd hated every minute of the course. And my acne was flaring up again.

The leavers' ball would be the last time we would all be together before we made our way out into the world. Bob Cousins was on the entertainment committee and had managed to book the iconic 1980s group Darts. The concert was fantastic. Most people had drunk too much, and emotions were high. The night was drawing to a close, and people were hugging and crying. Tomorrow was leaving day at the halls of residence. I finally found myself in front of Ruby, and we hugged too. It felt good.

She was looking beautiful, as usual. She was wearing a simple classic black ballgown. This time she had gone for black eyeshadow. The butterflies had returned.

"I can't believe our time at university is all over – it's so sad," said Ruby.

"I know, the three years have flown by. Mind you, it's not *really* three years if you take out all of the holidays; it probably equates to nearer two years."

I was boring *myself* by this stage. *Up your game, Will.*

"Have you got anything lined up?" asked Ruby.

"Eh, no, not yet. I may have an interview at some

enzyme production company, though I hate biochemistry. I'm not sure I want to work in that area. What about you?"

"Oh, I've got a job back in Birmingham – a trainee accountancy post."

"Oh, that's good. Well done. Lucky for some."

*Well done* was my go-to phrase. I'd used it on numerous occasions over the years, but today it felt shallow, insipid almost.

"Anyway, Will, see you again. Good luck!"

"Wait, I don't have your address." I wanted to say this, but of course I didn't.

But then again, she hadn't asked for *my* address.

And with that, she disappeared out of my life. I wasn't sure if I would ever see her again. Probably not. Pete appeared from somewhere.

"Unlucky, Evans."

"What do you mean?"

"Your chance is gone, mate – three years and you've got nowhere."

"Well, to be fair, I only knew her this year and at least I got further than you ever got, in three years, with any girl, ever."

Pete, who was very drunk, was laughing almost uncontrollably.

"You blew it, Evans."

Deep down, I knew he was right. My chance was gone. I *had* blown it. Ruby had gone out of my life. I would have to find another Ruby – if I could.

# Chapter 8

## July 1985: Cardiff

University was over. I was back in my hometown. I didn't have a job lined up but was applying frantically. Rejection letters came through my door on a regular basis. I had started to accumulate them in a folder marked 'Jobless'. Every day I watched from the kitchen window as the postman trudged down the drive carrying my latest rejection. Two letters for me this morning. The first letter was a 'regret to inform you' letter from a company that analyses horse blood after a race, to rule out doping. I didn't even remember applying for that job and, besides, it would have been based in Cheltenham, wherever that was. The second letter was in a small, grubby white envelope. This one looked more intriguing: I tore it open quickly. This time it wasn't a job rejection – it was from Pete.

Oi, Evans! Got a job yet, you loser? If you haven't, a group of us are going interrailing in August, if you're up for it? So far, it's me, Tigsy, Mothball, Ruby and Tigsy's girlfriend Gwen. I expect you will want to go as Ruby is coming (no chance). The price of the ticket is £109, plus spending money for beer and condoms. Let me know by the end of next week if you are up for it. Pete.

I had to ask my older brother what interrailing was, and he explained it was a train ticket that allowed you unlimited train travel across Europe for four weeks. His friend Billy Williams had done it the year before but had to come home early after he'd jumped into a swimming pool that had no water in it and broke his arm.

As soon as I read that Ruby was going, I knew I had to be on that trip. I had just enough in my account to cover the ticket as my gran, who'd died a few months ago, had left me £200 in her will. So, the next day, I went to the main train station in Cardiff, where you could purchase the ticket. It was on! My pursuit of Ruby had reached its second chapter. Let's hope the second chapter would be better than the first. I was excited at the thought of seeing Ruby again.

Pete had arranged for his uncle to take us to London, where we would meet the others at Victoria train station for the start of the trip. For the last few days I had scrambled around getting supplies and packing clothes for the thirty-plus days of the holiday, which I then tried to stuff into a rucksack. I'd borrowed the rucksack from my mate Kevin, one of the Dobson brothers. Kevin Dobson was a keen runner, and he used to jog to the local swimming pool, swim thirty-two lengths and then jog back, carrying all his stuff in the rucksack I had managed to acquire for the trip. It was a cheap, old red rucksack, but my finances would not stretch to a new one. It smelled slightly of Kevin Dobson's sweat, and my mum told me to leave it outside for a while to "air" – whatever that meant.

My dad had tried, at great length, to talk me out of the trip: "The party's over now, Will. You need to concentrate now on getting a job, not gallivanting around Europe. You shouldn't be wasting your time any more. Did you look in the local paper for any jobs with the council?"

I had been looking in the local paper for jobs with the council every day, but there didn't seem to be much on offer for a lovesick, acne-ridden, twenty-one-year-old biochemistry graduate.

Besides, I had made my mind up – and it was only for four weeks. I had the rest of my life to find a job – but only four weeks to make Ruby like me.

# Chapter 9

## Interrailing

On the sixteenth of August, Pete's uncle beeped his horn outside my house in Cardiff, and I left to begin my pursuit of Ruby. My mum and dad waved me off, and my two brothers were both making obscene hand gestures from the dining room window. I hadn't given much thought to where we would be heading; I would leave that to the others. There was a Labrador in the car too. Dog hairs were everywhere, but he was a friendly thing and rested his head on my lap. There was some elaborate story of a messy divorce and shared custody of the dog, Buster. The uncle was passing over the dog to his ex-wife for an allotted three-month period. Luckily for us, his ex-wife lived in London, not far from Victoria train station, so Pete had arranged a free lift for us.

"Looking forward to seeing Ruby again, Evans? Please don't embarrass yourself by dribbling every time you see her."

"Well, yes, obviously I'm looking forward to seeing her – and the others too. But the only dribbling this holiday will come from you, any time you spot some alcohol."

"Ha ha, good one, Evans – but you've got no chance with Ruby, so I wouldn't waste your time, though she's split up from Tom Bellows, I heard. I may take a crack myself."

"In your dreams, Pete. You're the one with no chance there."

I hadn't expected that, though. What if Pete *did* pursue Ruby? The whole point of me going on this trip was to try and establish some kind of romantic relationship, and now it looked like I had competition. I was happy to hear that she had split up from Tom Bellows, though. I wondered why they had broken up.

We arranged to meet by the clock at Victoria train station for 9 p.m. Everyone had arrived by the time Pete and I turned up. Ruby looked even better than I remembered, and she smiled as she saw us. She was wearing three-quarter-length blue trousers with white trainers and a red T-shirt. Her brown hair was tied back into a ponytail. She was already looking like she had seen a lot of the sun during the summer as she had a lovely tan. My stomach lurched with that butterfly sensation again. Tigsy and Gwen were holding hands, and Mothball was checking the contents of his wallet, living up to his nickname. We'd arranged a rough itinerary, which would initially require us to get the train to Dover from Victoria and then the ferry crossing to Calais. I had to say something quickly to Ruby, to settle my nerves.

"Your rucksack is small, Ruby. Are you sure you've packed enough for the trip?"

*Not good, Will. Not good. Memo to self: must do better.* Though, to be fair, the rucksack *was* small – and expensive-looking. I bet it wasn't borrowed either, like mine. Or it didn't smell of Kevin Dobson's sweat, the smell of which still remained, even after the airing.

"You should be used to seeing small packages, Evans – every day, when you put your pants on in the morning," laughed Pete.

Annoyingly, I could feel myself going red and saw that Ruby was laughing too, as were the others. I'd forgotten how annoying Pete could be at times. It could be a long thirty days in his company, with nowhere to escape.

We headed for the platform. Pete was talking to Ruby. I had a plan to stick with Pete so I could keep an eye on him. I didn't want him trying it on with Ruby. I had to keep my eye on the ball, to use a football metaphor.

"Did you have a good summer, Will?" Gwen asked.

"Oh, yeah, it was OK, though it was strange going back home after university. What about you?"

"It was good, thanks. Me and Tigsy both got summer jobs in the wrapping paper factory near me – saving up money for the trip. Tigsy's got a place teacher training in September, and I'm going to work for my dad for a while, in the family business."

I tried to rack my brains to remember what the family business was, as I knew Tigsy had told me once, but all I could recall was that it was something to do with cheese distribution.

"That's good. I've got nothing sorted yet, just a file full of rejection letters. My dad's been nagging me to not go on this trip. He said I should have stayed home and looked for a job instead."

Tigsy started to sing about looking for a job then finding a job, only to be now miserable, happily mimicking Morrissey, lead singer of The Smiths. It seemed mandatory as a student to know the lyrics of The Smiths' back catalogue, and I had lyrics of some of their songs on my bedroom wall. I wondered if Ruby like The Smiths.

We finally boarded the train, and I managed to acquire a seat opposite Ruby. I was off to a good start.

"How was your summer? I bet you didn't expect to see my ugly face again," I shyly muttered.

"Yes, that face is enough to scare anyone. It was pretty grim, really. My summer, not your face. You probably heard Tom dumped me before the end of term. I spent the whole summer wallowing in a sea of self-pity."

I didn't know if Ruby was joking or whether she just had a dry, self-deprecating sense of humour.

"Yeah, I was sorry to hear that – and about your pity party – but you know that saying: there are plenty more fish in the sea."

"Yeah, but I don't think I want to go fishing any more."

"You don't have to be fishing to catch a fish."

Ruby looked at me blankly. OK, what was I even saying? I'm not sure I understood myself. Nerves were getting the better of me. *Focus, Will. Focus.*

I had always been terrible at talking to girls. Growing up with two brothers I hadn't had much practice. I didn't know how their minds worked and watched in envy when people like Mothball talked effortlessly to the opposite sex. Though he did have an older sister, in my defence – so he would be practised in the art of 'girl talk'. Usually, I could only talk to girls under the influence of alcohol, and this would involve me firing questions at them so I didn't have to talk much. I was definitely a listener as opposed to a talker. The better-looking the girl, the worse I was at talking to them.

It was quite late now – coming up to 1 a.m. – as the train sped towards Dover. Ruby had closed her eyes. I looked at the window and the reflection allowed me to stare at her without anyone realising I was looking at her. She was even more beautiful as she slept. Her hair was no longer in a ponytail and now her dark brown hair fell down to her shoulders, adding to her appeal.

"Oi, you pervert! Stop dreaming about Ruby and get this down you."

Pete passed a flask of what he described as his "special cocktail". It was a mixture of vodka, squash and Strongbow and it tasted vile. But I took a big slurp, and soon I was dreaming about Ruby.

We arrived at Dover and walked onto the ferry for the crossing to Calais. The plan was to find a seat on the ferry and sleep, but they were all taken so we had to find a space on the floor. We were all tired, and the crossing passed in a flash. It probably was more comfortable on the floor as opposed to sleeping on a seat, as at least you could stretch out on the floor.

We arrived at Calais at around 3 a.m. and had to hang around Calais boat terminal for about an hour before we were able to get the bus to Calais railway station. It was freezing, and I was starting to regret only wearing two layers. I did have a light jacket, but it was right at the bottom of my rucksack, and I didn't have the energy to unpack all my clothes to get it. Besides, it had been a monumental struggle to fit all my clothes in, so I didn't relish the thought of attempting that again. Maybe the shorts I was wearing were a mistake, though, as my legs were freezing. Further plans were made for the holiday. I was feeling a mixture of tiredness with excitement at spending the next four weeks in Ruby's company, during which time I was hoping my feelings for her would be reciprocated. We eventually boarded the 6.13 a.m. train from Calais to Paris, and in just under three hours the train pulled into Paris Gare du Nord Station. The first big city and first country of the trip: France.

# Chapter 10

## Tom

Tom Bellows was listening to The Smiths in his bedsit in Salisbury. Morrissey was singing about getting his hands on some mammary glands or something. Tom thought he also needed to get his hands on some mammary glands soon – it had been a while.

His thoughts turned to Ruby. He had hurt her when they had split up at the end of term. He knew that. He was starting to regret his decision as he often thought about her. Well, he thought about her every day. That infectious laugh and that smile. Those brown eyes. He had not heard from her for a while, though he knew she had gone interrailing for a few weeks. Well, he had heard it from Ruby herself; she had asked him to come with her. As friends. Tom was tempted to go, even though they had broken up, but after graduating with a first-class honours degree and a further postgraduate qualification in maths, he had secured a position as a trainee actuary for a large financial company. As a result, he had moved down to Salisbury to start the next chapter in his life. It was a great job with a competitive salary, and he had done well to get it. In fact, there had been over two hundred applicants for only six positions, but in a perverse sort of way Tom knew he would get one. He usually got what he wanted in life.

So why was he feeling a detachment from everything? He felt empty inside, like he was just going through the motions. The light was on, but nobody was home. He knew why: he was missing Ruby.

Ruby was the missing piece to the puzzle. He wanted her back in his life.

# Chapter 11

## Paris

We arrived in Paris and made our way to a cafe where I bought a strong coffee and a croissant. I needed to try to talk to Ruby more. So far, she seemed to be talking a lot to Pete. I wondered if he was serious about "trying to bed her", as he had eloquently phrased it – ever the wordsmith. Though he seemed to be getting on well with Ruby so far this trip. My plan to stick with him so I could keep an eye on him was going well. I was unable to eat much when Ruby was around. She made my stomach flip and made me feel queasy. All I was able to eat for lunch was a couple of nectarines and half a French stick, or baguettes as they were known. Though my lovesick diet was good for my holiday budget, as I was on limited funds for the trip. And the French stick was immense. What was it with French bread that made it taste so good? Why couldn't we get French sticks like that in Wales?

Before the trip, Pete and the others had arranged to meet Beth, an American student from our hall – who was on holiday with her friend Penny and Penny's mother – at 2 p.m. on the seventeenth of August. The meeting point was to be the Eiffel Tower. Beth was a beautiful girl, blonde and bubbly and great fun. I had once spent a rainy afternoon in halls playing Trivial Pursuit with her, Pete and her boyfriend at the time – whose name escapes me. Ricky, Richard ... something beginning with 'R'. We got to the Eiffel Tower at 1.50 p.m., not realising beforehand how big it was and how many people would be there, making it difficult to find Beth. But, after about twenty-five minutes of searching, we finally came across them.

Beth was wearing cut-off denim shorts, sandals and an 'I love New York' T-shirt. She looked gorgeous.

She hugged everyone, including me, and my body tensed in awkwardness as I wasn't used to physical affection. I was brought up in a non-tactile household and couldn't remember ever hugging my parents – or anyone, really.

"Hey, why are you so stiff, Will?" Beth laughed.

"Don't worry, Beth, he's always stiff when a girl hugs him!" laughed Pete.

Everyone laughed, including Penny's mother, as my face turned bright red.

We were all going to go up the Eiffel Tower, but when everyone saw how much it cost we were not so keen to spend so much on day one of the holiday. I was on a daily budget like everyone else, but because of my poor appetite around Ruby I hadn't spent much on food so far, so I could just about afford to go to the second-stage viewing platform. After much discussion, it was decided that I would go to the second stage with Beth, who was a little afraid of heights, and Penny and her mother would go to the top. We would meet all the others later, outside the lift entrance, in a few hours' time. It was a magnificent day, warm with a gentle breeze, and for the first time on the trip I became aware of my surroundings. The Eiffel Tower really was an impressive structure, and as we got off the lift at the second stage I took in the glorious sight of Paris in the summer sun.

"C'est magnifique," laughed Beth, in a terrible French accent.

"I know – it's an incredible view, isn't it?"

"Are you talking about me or the Paris landscape?"

"Ha ha, both I think."

*Smooth, Will. Smooth.*

"And there was me thinking you only had eyes for Ruby."

"What do you mean?"

But even as I spoke, I could feel my face reddening.

"Pete told me you have the hots for Ruby, and you only came on this holiday because she was coming. I suppose she's a pretty girl, if you like that sort of thing."

"Eh, well … eh, yeah, I do like her. I suppose, but I don't think she has any feelings for me in that way, and she wasn't the *only* reason I came on this holiday."

"So you *are* taking four weeks to pursue her. Do you think you'll wear her down eventually?"

"I'll keep you updated. Did you know I had a dream about you a few weeks ago?"

"Oi, you dirty boy – hope it was clean and I remained fully clothed."

"Of course. Who do you think I am – Pete? No, I was at a train station, and you were getting onto a train. I was on the platform as the train pulled away. I was crying, or laughing; I wasn't sure."

"Probably the former," laughed Beth. She had a lovely laugh. Infectious.

"I think it was the former. I remember feeling sad when I woke up. Probably something to do with you going back to America."

Beth was easy to talk to. There were no awkward gaps in the conversation, and no alcohol involved for me to reach this level of communication. Maybe I was getting better at talking to girls.

We walked around the second floor, competing to recognise the various Paris landmarks. The Arc de Triomphe (one point for me), the Grand Palais (Beth), the

Louvre (Beth), Notre-Dame de Paris (Beth), and even the Sacré-Coeur Basilica (Beth). I wasn't very good at that game, to be fair, but I was staggered by the beauty of the French capital and would have like to have stayed longer. It was my first time at the Eiffel Tower and next time I would go to the top. Paris was spread out in all directions. It was a huge city.

"What are your plans, Beth, now you've graduated?"

"Well, after our holiday I'm going back to the USA to start looking for a job. You should come and visit – I could show you the Big Apple."

"Oh, wow – I would love that. But after this holiday I don't think I'll be able to afford it, and I've got my dad on my back, nagging me about finding a job."

"That's a shame, Will, but if the situation changes let me know."

"I will."

I looked at Beth, and she winked back at me. What was that about? It reminded me when Ruby had winked at me in the park in Swansea, when I was carrying my egg mayonnaise sandwich. I hadn't known what that meant either.

I thought back to the first time I had met Beth, when we had played Trivial Pursuit. She was going out with a boy from our corridor, the one whose name I couldn't remember. They came out of his room and bumped into Pete, who already knew Beth from his course. He said hello and asked her what she was carrying. It was the new game everyone was talking about at the time: Trivial Pursuit. It was essentially a general knowledge game where you competed to answer questions to get wedges to fill your counter. Each counter had space for six wedges. There were various categories, such as History and Science & Nature. Pete asked Beth if he could have a game, and the three of them knocked on my door to ask if I wanted to play too. We all sat down on the floor of my room and played the game all afternoon. I remember making Beth laugh a lot, probably as a result of some of my answers. It was the American version of the game that Beth had, and Pete and I were useless at some of the questions about American presidents and all the sport questions about baseball and American football. I loved Beth's accent. I think she was the first American I had ever known. Predictably, I was quite smitten with her, but I knew she was taken, so tried to bury those thoughts. She was cute, though, and Pete agreed she was a 'hottie'. We became friends after that, and sometimes I would walk back from university with her. I would often look out for her at the end of my lectures, hoping she would be around to walk back with to the halls of residence. It was a shame she already had a boyfriend, but in a way it made things less awkward between us – and my 'girl talk' was definitely improving.

It was time to take the lift down, as we had to meet up with the others soon. Ruby and Pete were eating ice creams and laughing at what seemed like a private joke.

It was time for Beth to leave; Penny and her mother had booked a hotel in Nice, and they had a train to catch. This time I was prepared as Beth gave me a hug. I hugged her back strongly. It was nice to hug someone. Very nice.

"That's better – not so stiff this time, Will." I was waiting for another comment from Pete at this point, but luckily I think he was out of earshot.

"Thanks. I'm trying to get used to this physical contact nonsense."

"Well, you *are* getting better at it. Keep in touch, Will. Write to me, will you?"

Beth passed a piece of paper with her address in the USA on it.

"Oh, eh, thanks," I stuttered. "I will."

Beth had made the effort to give me her address, in contrast to Ruby.

And with that, they walked away, and I thought again of the dream in which I was on the platform, crying as the train pulled away.

"Wait, Beth!"

Beth turned around to face me.

"What is it, Will?"

"My address! I haven't given you, my address!"

"It's OK, Will. I got your address from Pete at that end of term."

"Oh, great! Hopefully I'll be in touch soon – that's if I'm not married to Ruby. I'll send you an invite to the wedding."

I winked at Beth as I said it. It sounded ridiculous, even to me.

I expected Beth to walk away, but she walked towards me and took my hand in hers and kissed me on the cheek.

"I'll look forward to it, Will – not the wedding, obviously, but you are keeping in touch."

I was sad to see Beth go; I really enjoyed her company. It was a shame she wasn't coming with us. The rest of the day was spent walking around Paris, which was tiring, with our rucksacks. Pete said we should start leaving the rucksacks in luggage storage from now on. We were still learning this interrailing game. We ended up at the Arc de Triomphe and Pete, Ruby and I used our student discount cards to get cheap admission. We had to walk up 284 steps to get to the top, but it was worth it for the view, both of Paris and of Ruby, whose face had gone slightly red due to the exertion of the climb. Pete was puffing hard too, which was good to see.

"Struggling to breathe, are you, Pete? I thought you would be fitter since university, but you may have confused the 'I' with an 'A'."

"What are you on about, Evans?"

"You should be fitter, but instead you're fatter."

I started to laugh at what I thought was clever wordplay. It was a shame that Ruby hadn't heard, but she was busy taking photos of the Paris skyline.

"Oh, Evans, you are hilarious. Got a job as a standup comedian lined up, have you? Skinny git."

I was secretly pleased at my joke, though – but it would have been better if Ruby had heard and laughed.

*

In the evening we ended up in the Latin Quarter of Paris, home to the Sorbonne University and famous for its student cafes and book shops. Even though we couldn't really afford it, we ended up in an Italian restaurant. We were all glad to sit down and enjoyed the food, even though we couldn't stretch to a bottle of wine. The wine was very expensive. I ordered a plate of spaghetti bolognese. I was annoyed to see Ruby and Pete were sharing a pizza.

Pete had worked out a plan for the trip, which would involve a lot of overnight trains. This way, he figured we wouldn't have to pay for any accommodation – since we would be sleeping on trains – and when we woke up we'd be at our destination, sometimes in another country. That was the theory, anyway. We boarded the train at 10.40 p.m., destination Toulouse. We managed to get two carriages between us, so Ruby, Pete and I took one, while Mothball, Tigsy and Gwen took the other. Pete slept on the floor between the seats, so I was able to get a few hours' sleep. Opposite me, Ruby slept almost immediately as soon as she sat down, so I was unable to engage in any conversation, although surreptitious staring at Ruby was possible when both Pete and Ruby fell asleep. I still hadn't managed to have a meaningful conversation with her yet, though.

# Chapter 12

## To the South

The train got to Toulouse at 7 a.m., and we departed the train full of optimism for the day ahead. The plan was to head to place called Adge, which was on the coast, as two of Ruby's friends – Sarah and Tracey – were staying there at a campsite for the summer. We had to get two taxis to the campsite from the station and try and sneak past reception. The campsite was quiet when we arrived, and we walked confidently past the reception without being challenged. Sarah and Tracey were away on a trip to Spain but had left instructions on where the caravan and, more importantly, the key would be. The campsite was right by the beach and so, after leaving our rucksacks, we headed out for a swim in the beautiful, warm sea.

The sun was strong, and I had forgotten to bring any suncream, but I figured I would be OK for a few hours if I kept my T-shirt on. Besides, I was a bit self-conscious about taking my top off and exposing my pale, skinny, white body and acne-covered back.

After a short swim, surprisingly I found myself alone on the beach with Ruby. The others had gone in search of an ice cream. Ruby looked amazing in a red bikini, and I had to make a conscious effort not to stare at her for too long.

"So, how are you enjoying the holiday so far, Ruby?" A good opening gambit, I mused.

"Yeah, it's great – it's just what I needed after what I've been through."

"What. you mean with Tom?"

"Yes, with Tom. And my mum dying. It's been a

horrible time for me."

I needed to say something to keep the conversation going before the others came back. *Think quick, Will. Think quick.*

"And what about your dad, how is he coping now?"

Not bad. Not too bad, I thought. Ruby seemed to hesitate at first, as if she was reluctant to answer.

"He's just taking it day by day. He's throwing himself into his work and keeps himself busy. I didn't think he had enough time off work myself, but he was keen to go back almost straight after the funeral. He said it was his way of coping and taking his mind of it. He's taken up a new hobby – he bought himself a guitar and found a guitar teacher. He has always talked about playing the guitar. He is terrible at it, though. He hides his grief, though I think he cries when he's out walking the dog, as his eyes always look red when he comes back. And our poor dog, Bluebell, has never been walked so much. He tries to pretend it's his allergies, but I know he is lying. Also, if there's anything remotely sad on TV, he's in floods of tears, which again he tries to hide."

Ruby went quiet for a bit. Maybe she was conscious she was talking too much. I could see she was hurting.

"What did your mum die of, if you don't mind me asking?"

There was a pause in the conversation. Maybe I was being too intrusive.

"Eh, no, I don't mind. It was something called a subarachnoid haemorrhage – a type of stroke that causes bleeding in the brain. It happened at her desk in work. Her colleagues were quick to call an ambulance, but she died a few hours later in the casualty department. It was such a shock. I think, in a way, it's worse than when you have a long illness. It was all so sudden. I was out walking the dog and when I got home my auntie was in the house, and she only would normally visit at Christmas, so I knew something was up. She was comforting my dad. The pair of them were in floods of tears. It was awful, the whole thing."

I could see Ruby was getting upset. I wanted to comfort her, hold her, tell her it would be OK. But it would not be OK: her mum had died, and any words of comfort would do little to appease her grief. But maybe I should have hugged her or something. Maybe it would have been too awkward, with Ruby in her red bikini. Maybe if I hugged her, I would get 'too excited'. What should I do?

"I'm so sorry, Ruby. What a horrible thing to happen. And she was so young too."

"It's not your fault, Will. I didn't cope very well at first. I wasn't able to eat anything for a few days; I felt sick all the time and had no appetite. It was terrible. My dad was worrying about me not eating, at the same time as trying to process his own grief. It was selfish of me, really. The only thing I ate in the first few days was a Bounty bar."

"No, Ruby, it wasn't selfish at all, just your way of coping at a really difficult situation. I read somewhere that grief never goes away, you just learn to live with it. At least you managed to get a Bounty bar down you."

"I suppose that's true. I almost didn't come back for my final year. I was going to have a year out, but my dad persuaded me to go back. He said it would be what mum would have wanted. He was right about that: my mum was proud of me getting into university. I can't look at a Bounty bar now, though – or eat one. Too many bad memories come flooding back."

Ruby was crying now. Tears cascaded down her beautiful face. She looked so vulnerable, so sad. I knew I should go over and comfort her, but I did nothing, my sense of awkwardness kicking in.

"Your mum was right to be proud of you," I offered clumsily.

"I know. Thanks, Will – I think it helps to talk about it. Tom was a big help in that respect."

Good old Tom Bellows, I thought guiltily.

"So what happened between you two?"

Ruby seemed to hesitate slightly again before she answered.

"I don't know, really. I thought things were great between us. And then one day, out of the blue, he told me that it was getting too serious and we should be taking a break."

"He must need his head examining," I said.

Ruby laughed. It was nice to hear laughter, after the crying.

"Thanks for saying that, Will. He really hurt me. That's why this trip has come at the right time for me. And besides, I've always loved travelling. I would really like to go to Istanbul, though I'm not sure that's on the itinerary that Pete has set. Plus, it is a long way, I suppose."

"Who made Pete the boss? If you want to go to Istanbul, go to Istanbul. I'll come with you."

"Ha ha, I might hold you to that. Look, here they come now."

I looked down the beach, and there was Pete and the others holding ice creams. Pete was giving me the finger as he approached. I was annoyed they were back so soon, as I was finally having a meaningful conversation with Ruby.

My one-to-one with Ruby was over for now. I would have to wait for my next opportunity to get her alone again. Surely, she would start to like me soon.

Hopefully, Ruby wouldn't be able to resist me once I gave her the full Will Evans charm offensive, whatever that was. But I must remember never to eat a Bounty bar in her presence …

Istanbul: I had try and get some information about the place as, to be honest, I didn't have a clue where it was, or which country it was in – but, in my mind, it was where I was heading. I was pretty certain it was in Turkey. I think. I had heard the song 'Istanbul not Constantinople', referring to the renaming of the city. That was where my knowledge ended.

That evening there was a disco at the campsite clubhouse. Pete had managed to get hold of some cheap wine and a bottle of vodka, and immediately drank himself into a stupor. We had to carry him back to the caravan – after he'd managed to spoil the night – as he was so drunk he almost got into a fight with a small Belgian bloke while arguing about football. So, reluctantly, we had to escort him back to the caravans. The girls slept in one caravan and the rest of us crashed out in another empty caravan that Tigsy had manged to break into. It was lucky the campsite was so big, and there didn't seem to be any campsite security. Also, there were many empty caravans. I pulled up my sleeping bag around my neck and tried to sleep as I watched Pete urinating into the sink while simultaneously eating a piece of cheese. He quickly finished urinating, swallowed the cheese and then vomited into the sink with a final flourish. It was quite the performance.

After our chat on the beach, I was hoping Ruby and me would become closer, but it seemed like she was avoiding me for the next couple of days. Ruby seemed happier with female company and, with Sarah, Tracey and Gwen, formed a tight little unit. We went to the beach again and then spent a day at Aqualand, a water park full of gigantic water slides and assault courses. It was the last day at the campsite, as Sarah and Tracey were heading home. So we said our goodbyes and got a taxi to Adge, from where we got the train to Avignon.

# Chapter 13

## To Strasbourg

I remembered how, in primary school, we used to sing a song about Avignon. 'Sur le Pont d'Avignon' was a popular French nursery rhyme and children's song that has been sung for centuries.

"We should find the bridge at Avignon and take a photo," I suggested.

"No chance. We've only got an hour before the train to Strasbourg we won't have time, sorry," Pete replied.

"Yeah, and we still need to get some supplies for the train," added Tigsy.

To be honest, I didn't even know why we were going to Strasbourg. But Pete had it all figured out. He carried a big red book everywhere: the *Thomas Cook European Timetable*. It listed railway and shipping services across the continent, and he consulted it religiously. I was impressed and a little surprised to see Ruby had her own copy too. Where had they got them from?

According to Pete, Avignon to Strasbourg was 718 km and would take about five hours on the train. Though, after a while, Pete's descriptions of the distances involved were starting to bore me. The train to Strasbourg was hot and no air conditioning, but we were able to get one double seat each, so we all settled down for a nap. The train stopped at Lyon (230 km from Avignon, according to Pete) for an hour and Ruby, Pete and I got off the train to stretch our legs, while the others looked after our rucksacks. Ruby was a little distant, but she may have been tired. We got back onto the train, and I slept all the way to Strasbourg eventually arriving at 7.50 p.m. We made our way to the youth hostel where we would be staying the night. When we weren't sleeping on the trains. youth hostels were a cheap alternative, though usually they would involve sleeping in bunk beds with a number of other travellers in the same room. They were cheap, though, and usually included breakfast, which was a bonus. The males and females had separate accommodation, so Ruby went off with Gwen – with another chance to talk to her gone for the night.

# Chapter 14

## To Germany

The following morning, Tigsy and Gwen went off exploring by themselves. Sometimes it was difficult as a group of six travelling to please everyone, and usually people had different ideas of where they wanted to go and what they wanted to do. The rest of us set off to find Strasbourg Cathedral. Strasbourg, as Pete pointed out is on the French-German border and is famous for its wines and Roman ruins. We didn't have long in Strasbourg, though, as Pete had another train journey planned – this time from Strasbourg to Mannheim in Germany, a distance of 138 km. *Enough of the distances, Pete.* At Mannheim we booked into the youth hostel for two nights, which included breakfast. The following day we took the short train journey to Heidelberg, and we headed off to see Heidelberg Castle. Again, I had never heard of Heidelberg or its castle, but it was impressive to say the least.

"Heidelberg Castle is a symbol of Romanticism," droned Pete.

I don't know who he was trying to impress with his boring observations, but he was getting on my nerves. According to the guidebook Pete had managed to acquire, Heidelberg was famous for its castle, the Philosophers' Walk and the baroque Old Town, as well as the university and the Student Jail. The Student Jail is where students were sent for misdemeanours, such as night-time carousing. I wondered, if Pete had been around then, if he would have been banged up for physical abuse to a daffodil. After a brief visit to see the Student Jail we walked up the mountain side to Philosophers' Point and a Nazi amphitheatre, which, grudgingly, I had to admit was worth the long walk. Ruby seemed to be spending her time with Gwen; they seemed to be getting on well of late, so I kept a low profile and concentrated on the scenery. I was a bit sunburned from the beach at Adge but was pleased to see the redness turning a rusty brown colour. I hoped all the vitamin D would start to attack my acne.

Back in Heidelberg Square, I tripped over an iron bar on the pavement and cut my leg in front of two policemen, who seemed to find the whole incident amusing, as did the others. Ruby was stung by a wasp but turned down my offer of antiseptic cream from a dirty tube I had found at the bottom of my rucksack. Talking of my rucksack, one of the straps had broken when I had tripped over the iron bar, so carrying it was difficult. Kevin Dobson wouldn't be happy.

# Chapter 15

## Ruby

Ruby couldn't decide whether she was enjoying herself on the trip so far. She hadn't realised how tough it would be, sleeping on trains, struggling to find a toilet, carrying a heavy rucksack, not being able to wash much and feeling dirty all the time. The distances involved between each destination were a lot more intense than she had envisaged. Admittedly, she wanted to get to Istanbul because she remembered her mum had been there when she was a girl and always spoke fondly of the trip. However, when she looked at the map, she realised it might be a stretch too far. The lack of quality sleep on the trains were already making her more emotional than normal. She felt that tears were always not that far away.

She regretted that moment with Will on the beach at Adge. She had shown her vulnerable side and didn't think she knew Will well enough to show that side of her. She didn't know what to make of Will. He was obviously kind and funny and sometimes she had the impression he liked her. It would be really embarrassing if he made a pass at her or something, though she knew she wasn't ready for another relationship. Tom had hurt her badly. She had hoped the trip would allow her to move on from Tom, but she still thought of him on a daily basis. Will wasn't as good-looking as Tom; she thought it was the acne. *I wonder why he never did anything about it?*

# Chapter 16

## Train to Munich

We were on another train, this time from Mannheim to Munich. It was only a short trip for us about three hours. I was in the train toilet. It was disgusting. I was looking at myself in the small broken mirror over the tiny sink. My skin was bad. Really bad. Acne was my nemesis. Over the years, I think I'd tried every remedy or treatment there was for the condition, but nothing seemed to help. I remember my mum had made me go to the GP about it. My teenage years had been blighted by chronic shyness and acne.

The GP was the father of an old friend of mine. Dr Watkins. I had known him for years.

I remember he asked what I had come to see him about. I said it was my acne, and he had switched on his table lamp and moved the flexible arm of the lamp to illuminate my face.

"Yes, it's bloody awful," he proclaimed, before prescribing some useless white paste, which I had religiously applied to my face every night before bed. The only thing that made any difference was squeezing them as this made the offending spot heal more quickly. All the advice was to never squeeze spots, but in my mind this advice was given by experts who probably had never experienced the condition. And who wanted to walk around with a great yellow pustule on their face? If you tried to squeeze a spot that wasn't ready to be expelled, this was when the trouble started – and this did make it worse. But over the years I had become proficient in the art of evacuating a small eruption on my face. I think this trip was making my skin worse; it must be the lack of sleep and poor diet, but I hoped when we got more sun my skin would improve.

We eventually arrived at Munich Station and headed out to explore the city. We found a supermarket and bought some bread rolls and some German ham, which we ate in a German beer garden. They were selling steins of strong German lager which, according to Pete, was the equivalent of two pints of lager. We all decided to buy one, and I remember buying another two, which were consumed over about three hours in the German sun. The next thing I remember was waking up on the platform of Munich Station on my own. I couldn't remember getting there or where the others were. I was woken by a German bloke who dropped a tour guide on my face at about 4 a.m. He was laughing with his two friends as he walked away. I located the others, who were sleeping further down the platform, and went back to an alcohol-induced sleep before we were all woken at 6.30 a.m. by a guard. He told us we weren't allowed to sleep on the platform and to move on.

We split into two groups that morning. Gwen, Tigsy and Mothball wanted to see the concentration camp at Dachau, which was about 22 km out of Munich. Secretly, I wanted to go there too as I had enjoyed history at school and thought the trip would be educational, though probably a sombre experience. Pete and Ruby wanted to go and see the Olympic Stadium so, sticking to my plan, I pretended I wanted to see the stadium too. The stadium was built for the 1972 Summer Olympics and, admittedly, would be easier to get to than Dachau, and cheaper – according to Pete. I was surprised Mothball wasn't going. Also, the swimming pool would give me a good opportunity to shower and catch another glimpse of Ruby in her bikini.

The Olympic Stadium turned out to be an imposing structure, and we had the chance to swim in the same pool in which the great American swimmer Mark Spitz won his seven gold medals at the 1972 Summer Olympics.

"I can't believe we are swimming in the same pool that Mike Spitz won all those swimming medals," offered Ruby.

I wanted to correct Ruby and tell her it was Mark Spitz, not Mike Spitz, but I didn't have it in me to correct her. Ever the pleaser. And it was difficult to contradict her while she was wearing her red bikini.

"Eh, yeah, he was a great swimmer, Mike Spitz," I replied, trying not to embarrass Ruby.

"What are you two on about, you stupid twats? It's Mark Spitz, not Mike Spitz," said Pete, and he threw his head back and laughed in that annoying way of his.

To be honest, I couldn't care less what his first name was – he could have been called Bartholomew Spitz for all I cared. All I could think about was how nice Ruby was looking in the pool today. I think Pete noticed her too, as I caught him a couple of times, staring at her.

"Put your tongue away, Pete," I bravely said, as I saw Pete watching Ruby swimming down the pool.

"You can talk, Evans; your tongue has practically been on the floor this whole trip. Women don't like to be gawped at, you know."

"Yeah, I'm not going to take advise from you on women."

"Just keep gawping then, Evans – let's see where that gets you, shall we?"

After a few hours at the stadium we stopped off for some food. We were all struggling a bit for money, so Pete and I shared some fishcakes and chips while Ruby had some fried squid. It was nice to feel clean again. Who knew when we would get the next opportunity to shower?

"We'd better make our way to the station," said Pete, as once again he was arranging the itinerary, usually based around overnight trains or cheap accommodation. We were due to meet the others at the station, and soon we had boarded the 4.15 p.m. train from Munich to Innsbruck, the so-called scenic route. The journey would be short – just under two hours – and we were onto our third country: Austria, after France and Germany.

# Chapter 17

## To Austria

The train was hot and stuffy, and the one toilet had a sign: 'außer Betrieb'. Tigsy said that meant it was out of order. Luckily, I had used the toilets at the platform in Munich, but Pete had not and was, in his words, "desperate for a piss". It got so bad he was forced to ignore the sign and push his way into the toilet. A few minutes later, he was out.

"Out of order, my ass! It's just clogged with a big German turd!" He laughed out loud, throwing his head back as usual.

"Don't you mean Austrian turd?" I ventured.

"No, we haven't crossed the border yet, so technically Pete is correct," said Mothball.

"Anyway, it's been mixed with some Welsh shit now too – my guts are well dodgy."

"Eh, that's gross! Too much information, Pete," said Gwen.

"Though, to be fair, the smell is coming up the carriage. I'm moving down the train," said Mothball.

We eventually got to Innsbruck, where we had to take a bus to the campsite that Pete had booked. The campsite we had booked turned out to be right next to a youth hostel, which cost only a bit more to stay the night. So we abandoned plans to stay at the campsite and opted for a concrete roof over our heads rather than canvas. We all had youth hostel cards, giving us access to cheap accommodation all over Europe. It would mean Gwen and Ruby going into the female block again, though, and everyone else going into the male block. At least I could have a break from my obsessing, and possible gawping at Ruby.

We were up early the next morning. I had slept badly: an overweight Austrian bloke in the bunk above me had a terrible case of flatulence. He was sleep farting all night. It was funny at first, but at 4 a.m. it wasn't so amusing. He seriously needed an appointment with a gastroenterologist. We had the breakfast included at the youth hostel, which consisted of hot chocolate, two rolls, jam and some liver pate with a piece of bread. An unusual combination, but it did the job and set us up for the day, as I'd heard people often say. We left the youth hostel about 10 a.m. and walked to Innsbruck Station, where we got a train to Seefeld. The scenery was beautiful on this journey, and I had the added bonus of sitting next to Ruby. She was in good form, doing an impression of Gwen, who had developed a reputation for being a bit of a moaner on this holiday.

She was always moaning about something: the trains, her rucksack, the food, the cost of everything. To be honest, she wasn't really cut out for this type of holiday, but I think she had just come along to please Tigsy. Pete referred to her as the 'fun sponge', sucking the fun out of everything. She didn't drink any alcohol either, so was never keen to chip in and buy some for the train journeys.

Seefeld was a very picturesque place with huge mountain lakes. The guidebook said it was a great destination for families and couples. I imagined myself walking around the lake, holding hands with Ruby.

We had planned to spend the day in Seefeld and then catch the overnight train to Zagreb in Yugoslavia, but Pete had checked the timetable and said the train wasn't due to leave until midnight. As a result, we decided to change our plans and got the train back to Innsbruck and then got on another train to Verona in Italy.

# Chapter 18

## Verona

We finally got to Verona at around 9 p.m. It was raining for the first time on the trip, which was a bit of a shock. We were all tired and hungry. We managed to find a reasonable Italian restaurant and, after a quick meal (spaghetti bolognese for me – did I even need to look at the menu?), we made our way back to the train station, still were not sure where we would be spending the night.

It was at this point that my pursuit of Ruby moved up a notch. Pete and Mothball announced, out of the blue, that they had experienced enough culture on the trip and were off to Corfu. Pete's friend – Phil from Harrogate – was there for the summer, staying at a mega-cheap campsite called Camp Vatos, and their plan was to head there. I fully expected Ruby to go with them as she'd been looking for a bit down lately, so that would mean me going there too, but, surprisingly, she said she wanted to get to Istanbul.

"What about you, Will? Are you coming with us to Corfu?" asked Pete.

I think he already knew the answer, and that it didn't have anything to do with seeing the sights of Istanbul.

"Oh, I quite fancy seeing the Blue Mosque," I mumbled, glad that I had looked at the guidebook that Ruby lent me to read on the train yesterday; before that, I had never heard of the Blue Mosque.

"Of course you do," said Pete.

He looked at me directly and mouthed, "No chance".

And with that, they left us with plans to meet us at Camp Vatos in Corfu. Pete said he had a T-shirt of the

Canadian group Rush, which he would hang up outside his tent so we could find them in about ten days' time.

I couldn't believe it. What did this now mean? Gwen and Tigsy were a couple. Ruby and I were not, or rather I hoped we would be. I no longer had Pete in the way. My pursuit of Ruby would now go unchallenged. I had a full ten days to weave my magic. Ten days. Ten whole days. It was game on.

But first we had to sort out the practicality of where we would be sleeping tonight. It was already midnight, and sleeping at the station wasn't permitted. None of us fancied sleeping there, anyway. We headed out of Verona Station and decided to walk to the nearest campsite, which, according to Ruby's guidebook, was about a mile away. It had started to rain heavily now. It couldn't have been only a mile to the campsite, as after an hour of walking we had still not found the place. We were lost, wet and pissed off – not helped by being given some dubious instructions by some drunken Italian girls, who sent us off in the wrong direction. It was 1.15 a.m. when we finally got to the campsite. There was a sign pointing to some stone steps, which said we *thought* was the way to the campsite. The steps were quite steep, and the rain was now coming down hard. We must have walked up about a hundred steps when we finally came to a gate to the campsite. The gate was locked: we couldn't get into the campsite! Gwen completely lost it and started to cry with frustration.

"I don't believe it!" she screamed, shaking the gate in anger. I was struggling not to laugh, but contained myself as Gwen was clearly upset.

"Come on, Gwen, try and stay positive; it can't be that far now. I'll guarantee we'll be at the campsite soon.

After all, where there's a Will, there's a way …"

I was expecting a big laugh, but apart from Tigsy, who groaned, the girls didn't appear to find it funny. Everyone was tired, I suppose. We had to turn around and climb down the steps again and head back to the road. Luckily, we were able to flag down a passing taxi, which took us to the proper entrance to the campsite. We arrived at reception and rang the bell. It was now 1.45 a.m., and we were lucky to be greeted by a short, stout Italian woman who reluctantly checked us in. She looked annoyed at being disturbed but must have felt sorry for us in our dishevelled state. I half hoped I would be sharing a tent with Ruby, but it was almost as if Ruby and Gwen had discussed it beforehand, as they hastily began erecting Gwen's tent before disappearing inside, out of the rain. Tigsy and I quickly put up his tent, and by about 2.30 a.m. all four of us fell asleep – wet, exhausted and miserable.

The next morning we all got up at around 9.30 and had an ice cream for breakfast. We put our tents away and walked back to reception to pay for our short night at the campsite. We then headed off to see the sights of Verona, walking down the hundred or so steps with the gate, which was now unlocked, to get to the road.

We made our way to Juliet's famous balcony from *Romeo and Juliet*, on the Via Cappello. Apparently, the balcony isn't authentic and isn't linked to Shakespeare's literary couple. It is, however, still a popular tourist attraction as testified by the large crowds in front of the balcony, queuing to take a photograph.

Pete had told me that if we were going to Verona I had to "touch Juliet's tits".

I didn't know what he was talking about until I saw

large group of people taking photos of a bronze statue beneath the balcony. This is where people queued to touch the breast of the statue of Juliet. By doing so, it was thought to bring you luck in love.

As Pete, ever the wordsmith, had eloquently voiced, "Oi, Evans, if you touch Juliet's tit, you may get your wicked way with Ruby," before – you guessed it – laughing and throwing his head back in that annoying way.

I did manage to touch the aforementioned breast. I hoped it would not be my only mammary-gland contact of the holiday and that it would bring me luck in love.

If you're trying to impress somebody, you'd usually spend a lot of time getting ready: having a shower, a clean shave, putting on a nice new shirt or a splash of aftershave. No such luxuries on this trip. I was pursuing the woman of my dreams looking scruffy, slovenly and unkempt. My clothes were dirty; my skin was poor. I would have to rely on my conversational abilities, which relied heavily on an alcoholic lubrication. Gwen didn't drink and frowned upon any mention of buying alcohol for the train trips, citing expense as the main reason for not buying any wine. I still wasn't relaxed in Ruby's company and felt I wasn't being myself when it was just the two of us. This didn't bode well for the future.

# Chapter 19

## To Venice

I had another opportunity to cement our relationship on the train from Verona to Venice, the next destination of our trip. The journey was only an hour, and I found myself sitting next to Ruby in a packed railway carriage. Gwen and Tigsy were in the carriage next door.

I opened the conversation with, "What do you think of Gwen?"

"Oh, she's OK. I like her. She does moan a lot."

"Tigsy must be good."

I thought Ruby would laugh at my clumsy joke about Tigsy's sexual prowess, but she didn't laugh, or even smile, come to think of it. Note to self: no more sexual innuendo jokes. Maybe no jokes at all, as she didn't seem to be responding to them in the way I had hoped.

"I don't think she's enjoying herself much, to be honest. Did you see her ankles? They are really swollen. It's not good for you, sitting down for long periods on these trains. She should have bought some compression socks."

"I know we've done a lot of miles on the trains. What about you, Ruby? Are you enjoying yourself?"

"I suppose I am. I'm looking forward to getting to Istanbul. I've worked out the route. Here, I'll show you."

Ruby delved into her rucksack and pulled out her *Thomas Cook Timetable*. She leaned over me as she showed me the trips she had highlighted to get to Istanbul on the map, which she had unfolded over both our legs. To be honest, she could have been showing me the minutes of a local council meeting; I wasn't concentrating at all. All I could think about was that her thigh was touching mine, and we were sitting so close I could smell her. Given the circumstances, with our limited opportunities to wash, she smelled really good.

"You've been working hard on this, I see."

"I have. I suppose it passes the time on the train trips, though the trip from Thessaloniki to Istanbul will be a tough one – it's almost a day. That's going to be a long trip."

"Gwen's ankles will be in for a battering, then."

And this time Ruby did laugh, and I felt a surge of happiness at having made her smile. Finally.

The train to Venice was due to arrive at about 5 p.m. The plan was to catch the 9.15 p.m. train from Venice to Zagreb in Yugoslavia, so we only had a few hours to explore Venice. There was a left luggage facility at the station, which was quite cheap for a few hours, so we were all glad to dump our rucksacks.

It was amazing to actually be at a place that you had seen so often on television, usually with a smug presenter on those holiday programmes. We walked past the canals and through the streets of Venice, looking at the various glassware shops selling expensive Venetian glass. It was busy, though; there were tourists everywhere. I bought a set of small green glass snails, which were reasonably priced and took my eye. I tucked them away in my pocket. Ruby was looking at some expensive clothes shops with Gwen and hadn't seen me buy the snails. Maybe I could give her the green glass snails as a gift, should the moment arrive. Ruby came back with a necklace she had bought and was looking quite pleased with herself.

The four of us followed the crowds to St Mark's

Square, or Piazza San Marco as it is known in Italian, according to Ruby's guidebook. There was a crowd of people vying to get a good photo of St Mark's Campanile, the famous bell tower. There were pigeons everywhere. I didn't think tourists were encouraged to feed them, as they were becoming a bit of a problem for the city. Ruby had no such reservations and fed them some leftover pizza, which she had bought from a street vendor. We all took a lot of photos in the square, as we were all impressed with Venice. We wanted to get a drink at one of the many restaurants dotted around the perimeter of the square, but the prices of the beverages were ridiculously high, so we gave up on that idea.

We didn't have much time left, and Gwen was keen to see the St Mark's Basilica, the spectacular cathedral, and maybe take a quick ride on a Venetian gondola; after all, Venice was famous for its canals and waterways. This was quickly ruled out: we had limited time, plus it would blow our daily budgets, big style. We were shocked at how expensive it was to take a ride on the gondolas. It was a shame that we only had a few hours in Venice, as there was so much to see and do, but we had a train to catch to Zagreb in Yugoslavia. So far, we had been to France, Germany, Austria and Italy. Yugoslavia would be the fifth country of the trip. It was certainly a great way to see the world, even if it was a whistle-stop tour.

# Chapter 20

## On to Zagreb

The journey from Venice to Zagreb was another overnight train trip. According to the *Thomas Cook Timetable* it was about eleven hours in total, and we were lucky to get a carriage to ourselves again. Gwen and Ruby quickly settled down to get some sleep. I struggled to get any sleep. I always struggled to sleep on trains or planes, when you were sitting up in a vertical position. Your head flops about, giving you neckache. I decided to sleep on the floor between the seats. Tigsy seemed pleased with this arrangement as he now had the row of seats to sleep on to himself, opposite Gwen and Ruby.

I was able to sleep for a few hours before being woken by the ticket inspector who told me in broken English to get off the floor. This seemed to be a recurring theme of the holiday. He was a big bloke, so I quickly got up and sat back in my seat. About an hour later, two guards and what I assumed to be a ticket inspector asked to see our tickets again, and also demanded to see our passports. Or maybe they were checking to see if I was sleeping on the floor again. One guard wanted to look in all our rucksacks, and we all had to open them to display the contents. They left quickly after that, to return about half an hour later with another guard, who also wanted to see our interrail tickets and our passports. We didn't know what was going on. I was cold and felt a bit sick but managed to drop off again after they left, and it only seemed like a only few minutes before Tigsy's alarm clock was going off and we pulled into Zagreb station. We were all glad to be getting off the train.

By now we were all hungry and left the station to find somewhere to eat. Generally, we had to find a place – usually a bank – to cash our travellers' cheque first, and there was one at the station, so I was able to get some Yugoslav dinars. The exchange rate was good, according to Tigsy. I kept my traveller's cheques in a money belt along with my passport, and I had not taken off except for those rare occasions when I could take a shower.

Everything in Zagreb was really cheap and our dinars seemed to be stretching so much so that I was able to splurge on various food items. My eating around Ruby had stabilised after a few days, and today I stuffed and drank myself silly. Coffee and spaghetti bolognese for breakfast, followed by ice cream, a bag of cherry-flavoured sweets, cups of tea, sweetcorn from a street vendor, half a chicken, more spaghetti bolognese, more coffee. Everything was so cheap.

There were numerous trams in the city, which was bustling with life and vibrancy. I also noticed there were a number of hairdressers' shops, all empty. There were also many nuns walking down the streets, as well as large groups of men in army uniform. I was tempted to have a haircut in one of the empty shops as my hair was getting long, but I wasn't confident enough to wander in by myself.

To push on to Istanbul would involve leaving Yugoslavia for Greece, where we would get the train to Istanbul. So, after a few hours in Zagreb, we were all back on the train again – this time to Skopje, another epic train journey: about nine hours. Ruby had planned for us to get the overnight train to Skopje and spend the day there before taking another overnight train to Thessaloniki in Greece. However, this would mean we would be getting to Thessaloniki at 4.15 a.m., and there would be not much to do at that time, so Ruby said we could just stay on the train to a place called Bitola in Yugoslavia.

# Chapter 21

## To Ohrid

The trip from Zagreb to Bitola took about eighteen hours in total. The journey would involve buses and trains as there was no direct train. It had been a bit of a nightmare for me. When we finally got on a train to Bitola, it was so packed we were lucky to get a seat. Gwen and Tigsy managed to get seats together, but Ruby and I were forced to separate and had to sit in different carriages. It was eight to a carriage, and I was sandwiched between two overweight women, making sleep virtually impossible. The two women finally got off a few stations before Bitola, so I was finally able to get a bit of rest. I was really tired but still couldn't sleep.

By this stage we didn't relish trudging around another big city with our rucksacks. We wanted to be by the coast and swim in the sea. Ruby had heard about a place called Ohrid from a friend of hers, so we boarded a bus for a journey of about two hours. The bus was busy, like the train before it, but I got to sit by Ruby. She had bagged the window seat.

"How are feeling today?" I began.

"Not great. I think I've got a bit of a dicky tummy."

"Time of the month?"

"No, not that. I think I ate something that upset my stomach in Zagreb."

Ruby looked a bit annoyed. It was probably my clumsy 'time of the month' question. I really need to work on my conversational skills. I needed to come back from the stupid question. What was I thinking?

"Shall we play a game to pass the time?" I continued.

"What did you have in mind?"

"Rapid-fire questions so I can find out a bit more about you. I saw it in the paper once."

"OK, sounds like fun."

"Right, give me a minute to think of some questions and I'll start."

The bus was really hot, and I was starting to sweat. I really wanted a shower.

And a shave, a proper shave. My electric razor wasn't doing a great job on this trip.

"OK, I'll start, so I'll ask quick questions, and I want quick answers please."

"OK."

"Coffee or tea?"

"Coffee." I would have said tea.

"Dogs or cats?"

"Dogs." I would have said cats.

"Sunrise or sunset?"

"Sunset." I would have said sunrise.

"Staying in or going out?"

"Staying in." I would have said going out.

And so it continued. Everything I would have picked, Ruby was picking the opposite. She was salty to my sweet, night to my day, white wine to my red wine, bath to my shower (though I would have settled for any form of wash at that moment). The list went on. Eventually, I ran out of questions, and we sat in silence as the bus made its way through the beautiful countryside towards Ohrid. They do say opposites attract, but those questions I'd asked had left me feeling a bit down. What if we had nothing in common, no shared interests? But I knew that couldn't be true, or we wouldn't have been sitting next to each other on this shitty bus with no air conditioning, heading towards some place none of us had ever been to.

"Are you OK, Will? You look a bit down."

Ruby surprised me with her intuition.

"Yeah, I think I may be getting a bit of a dicky stomach too."

"Time of the month?" And Ruby laughed at her own question.

This time it was my turn to feel annoyed, but it was good to see Ruby laugh.

When we arrived in Ohrid, we made our way to the tourist information office to enquire about a place to stay. There wasn't much accommodation available, being the holiday season, we were told by the happy chap who worked in the tourist information office. But for a small fee with could stay at his house, which he shared with his wife. It was cheap – roughly the equivalent of £3 per person per night – so, not having many other options, we took him up on his kind offer.

"Are you sure we can trust him?" asked Gwen as we followed the man through the picturesque streets of Ohrid.

"Yeah, he looks respectable. I think we will be safe with him," said Ruby.

On arrival at the house, which was only a short walk from town, the man told us his name was Ilija, and we were introduced to his wife, Olga. Olga went into the kitchen to return a few minutes later with a pot of coffee and six glasses of plum brandy. We were then expected to knock back the plum brandy in one gulp, which our host, Ilija, was keen to demonstrate. The coffee itself was really strong, and I ended up with a mouthful of sludge from the bottom of the cup. The plum brandy was like paint stripper and Ilija laughed as I made a face after knocking it back in one. Gwen didn't want hers, so I ended up drinking that too. It was strong stuff and went straight to my head.

Eventually, we were shown to our rooms. I would be sharing with Tigsy, while Gwen would be sharing with Ruby again. Would I ever get a chance to share a room with Ruby? We arranged to meet in two hours' time and took turns to use the bathroom, where a warm shower was much appreciated.

Back in the room, Tigsy was sorting out the contents of his rucksack as Olga had kindly agreed to do some washing of our clothes. She must have felt sorry for us as we all did look a bit grubby. We had fallen on our feet finding this accommodation.

"How it's going with Ruby?" asked Tigsy.

"What do you mean?"

"Pete told me you're planning on making a move. You'd better do it soon as I think Pete is planning on having a go himself. He told me once she gets to Corfu the gloves are off."

"Great, I've got Pete having a go to look forward to," I replied.

"Don't worry, you've got a few more days to work your magic."

"Well, it's a bit difficult with you and Gwen getting in the way. Can't you give me a bit of space? You're cramping my style, mate. I mean, look at us now – you should be sharing a room with Gwen so I can be with Ruby."

"I wish I could but, to be honest, me and Gwen haven't been getting on great. She's not really enjoying the trip, and she's already asked if we could go home early."

"And I take it you don't want to?"

"No, I'm enjoying myself, seeing these amazing places. Let's face it, when we get back home it's back onto the treadmill, so I'm going to seize the day, as they say. Don't worry – I'll smooth things over with Gwen and try and give you some space."

"That would be good."

"But can I give you a bit of advice?"

"Knock yourself out."

"I think you're trying too hard with Ruby. You don't seem to be yourself when you're around her. It's almost like you're a different person when you're with her. For a start, what's with these constant questions? Give the girl a break. You don't need to be firing probing questions at her all the time. Some normal banal conversations would be good. Other conversational styles are available."

"I hadn't realised I was doing that."

"The way I see it is, you got to talk to girls like you talk to blokes. Just because someone has tits and a fanny doesn't mean you got to change who you are. Otherwise, she'll never get to know the real you. Just talk to her as if you're talking to a bloke. As if you were talking to me, for instance."

"But what if I do that and she doesn't like the real me?"

"I think you are over analysing things. For one, she's got to fancy you for you to stand a chance and, given that you're an ugly bastard, you'll have to rely on your personality. But at the moment you're hiding behind some personality that I don't recognise, and I've known – you a lot longer than Ruby has. Take that 'ugly bastard' comment I made did you take offence when I said that?"

"No, I thought it was funny, as it's obviously not true."

"Well, that's debatable – but that's what you need to do with Ruby. Stop putting her on a pedestal. Speak to her as if you were talking to me. Tease her, insult her even. Be a more honest version of yourself when you're with her. There's a big world out there. Literally millions of women, and you've pinned all your hopes on one girl."

"I suppose you're right. I can be that version of myself, my real self, but it just seems to come out with women when I'm drunk."

"Well, you'd better ask Ilija for more of his plum brandy," laughed Tigsy.

That evening we went back into Ohrid to find a bank where we could change some money. We ended up in a soup kitchen-type place where I was able to get a plate of Yugoslav sausage and some beans for next to nothing. They weren't the beans I normally ate at home in a sweet tomato sauce; these beans were much bigger, and white, in a spicy sauce. The jury was out on whether I liked them, but they did fill me up. We ended up getting lost on our way back to the house and walked much longer than necessary. I toyed with resurrecting the 'Where there's a Will, there's a way' joke but decided against it. The talk with Tigsy seemed to have made things even more awkward with Ruby, and I was boring myself with some of my conversations. I needed to act on Tigsy's advice.

"Hey, Ruby, you can borrow my electric razor for your legs if you want when we get back to the house," I bravely pronounced as we finally found the street where we were staying.

"I shaved my legs before I came out, you bastard, Will!" Ruby looked tearful as she made her way back to the room. I had never heard her swear before, so it was a bit of a shock.

Note to self: never listen to Tigsy's advice again.

Back in the room, Tigsy was laughing.

"What the hell was that, going on about Ruby shaving her legs? I mean, she hasn't even got hairy legs. Have you lost the plot?"

"You told me to be more of myself, to tease her and insult her," I replied angrily.

"Yeah, I didn't mean to insult her appearance, your stupid prick. Don't you have any idea how to talk to women?"

"Well, obviously not, though that's the last time I listen to any advice from you."

"You're welcome. Look, I'll go and try and smooth things over with Ruby."

"Do what you like – I'm going to sleep."

I knew sleep would not come easily. I had messed up big style and would have to apologise to Ruby in the morning.

Tigsy left the room and, surprisingly, I did manage to fall asleep before he came back. I had that dream again. I was on the platform of a station, and Beth was on the train about to depart. I was crying as the train started to pull away. I ran down the platform, trying to catch up with the train.

"Beth! Beth!" I was shouting at the top of my voice. Suddenly the train started to slow, and one of the doors of the train opened. Ruby, not Beth, stepped off. She was holding something in her hand. It was the green glass snails I had bought in Venice. Somebody else was getting off the train after her. It was my dad – he was clutching a form in his hand and waving it furiously.

"The council job, the deadline is tomorrow, the deadline is tomorrow!" And, in his haste to pass me the forms, he banged into Ruby and the glass snails were knocked out of her hand and smashed on the platform floor. I woke up at that moment, in a cold sweat. What was that all about?

Tigsy was sitting on the bed next to Gwen. Ruby seemed to be OK. She wasn't crying, at least.

"Look, I'm sorry about what Will said about your legs," began Tigsy.

"Why are *you* sorry? It's not *your* fault. You didn't say anything."

"Well, I think it may have been my fault. I may have encouraged him to speak to you like that; I told him to tease you, or insult you even."

"Why are you telling him to insult me?"

"Oh, eh, it's just I think he feels a bit awkward around you sometimes; he wasn't being himself. I was just giving him some advice. He's clueless when he talks to women sometimes."

"Advice on what?"

"Talking to women in general."

"Well, you didn't do a good job with him – he's useless."

"Yeah, I suppose he is, but don't be too hard on him."

"Why not?"

"Well, I shouldn't be telling you this, but he likes you. Didn't you realise?"

"He likes me?"

"Yes, he's got a crush on you or something."

"Oh, well, he's got a funny way of showing it. I'm sorry, Tigsy – if you don't mind, I'd like to go to sleep now. I'm not feeling too well."

"OK, yeah, sorry. I've probably said too much, anyway. You won't say anything to Will about what I've told you?"

"No, as long as you leave me alone now. I need to sleep."

"Yeah, on your way, Tigsy. We'll see you both in the morning," said Gwen.

# Chapter 22

## Salisbury to Birmingham

Tom Bellows had three days off and decided to go home for the weekend. He got the train from Salisbury to his hometown, Birmingham, straight from work. And it was good to be finally home. It had been a long day. His mum had done a cottage pie and peas, and it was nice to have a home-cooked meal again. He went to bed not long after tea as he was tired. He knew he should do some work for his upcoming actuary assignment but decided to tackle that sometime this weekend. Hopefully tomorrow.

Tom was up early in the morning as he was going to see his old school friend, Bazza, for a lunchtime pint. They were meeting up at The Pilot, which was where Tom had spent many a drunken evening with his friends growing up. It was his favourite pub.

"Do you mind dropping into the GP on your way home?" asked Tom's mum as she poured him a cup of tea to go with his toast.

"What for?"

"Oh, it's for your father – he's having some tests done and he needs to pick up some specimen bottles from the surgery."

"Why can't you or dad do it? And isn't the surgery closed on a Saturday?"

"Look, I wouldn't ask you if me or your father could get it. And the surgery is open one Saturday a month. Can you just pick them up, please?"

"OK, don't go on."

Tom had forgotten how irritating his mum could be sometimes.

It was good to catch up with Bazza. He hadn't gone to university but worked with his dad as a roofer. He seemed to be doing alright for himself. He had a nice car, though he was still living with his parents. Tom had drunk too much and was relishing the thought of having a nap when he got back.

Shit: he just remembered he had to pop into the GP surgery on his way home. The surgery was packed and there was a big queue of people waiting to be checked in by the receptionist. Some bloke was getting angry when he found out his prescription wasn't ready yet. Tom eventually got to the front of the queue and, after explaining to the receptionist why he was there, was handed a two-and-half-litre plastic sample collection bottle, with an instruction sheet on how to collect urine over a twenty-four-hour period. There was a small amount of acid in the bottle and a 'caution, acid' sticker was visible on the bottle.

Back home, Tom asked his mother what the tests were for.

"Oh. It's something to do with his blood pressure, and he's been having night sweats too. He's got to collect all his urine for twenty-four hours into the container and take it back to the surgery."

"OK, I'll have to remember not to drink it by mistake." Tom said crudely.

"Tom, don't be disgusting. Do you want a cup of coffee?"

"OK, go on then." It might sober him up a little. Four pints of lager was definitely not a good idea at lunchtime.

Tom sat at the dining room table and sipped his coffee. He should take it upstairs, really, for he knew his mum would start with the questions – and, sure enough, here they came.

"How's Bazza?"

"Yeah, good."

"I bumped into his mother in Marks & Spencer last week. She was telling me how well he's doing, though she does worry about them up on those roofs all day."

"Yeah, I wouldn't fancy it. I'm not great with heights. He did say roofing is the most inspiring thing in the world, though."

"What does he mean by that?"

"He said it was inspiring because everyone looks up to it."

Tom's mum groaned.

"Yeah, he also said he would do you a new roof on the house if you wanted one."

"Well, we don't need a new roof – and besides, how much would that cost us?"

"He said it wouldn't cost you anything he said it's on the house." Tom started to laugh. He and Bazza had spent almost an hour telling each other roofing jokes.

"Oh, I forgot to tell you, a postcard came for you a few days ago. It's from your old girlfriend, Ruby. Apparently, she's on her way to Istanbul on a train. Lovely girl. I don't know why you finished it with her."

"OK, Mum, don't go on – and you shouldn't be reading my mail."

"I only glanced at it."

Tom's mum handed the postcard over.

It had a picture of the Munich Olympic Stadium on the front.

Hi Tom,

Hope all is good with you. We are having a great time so far, though sleeping is hard on the trains and it's difficult to get a shower or even a wash sometimes!

We are hoping to get as far as Istanbul if we can. Should be fun.

Love, Ruby x

Tom took the postcard to his room and read it again. She had ended it with a kiss. He missed Ruby. He really did. It had been a big mistake breaking up with her. He had read somewhere that for a relationship to work it had to be the right person at the right time. He was starting to think Ruby was the right person, and maybe the time had been right too? If only he had realised it at the time.

# Chapter 23

## To Kiss or Not to Kiss

I woke up early the next morning and wanted to apologise to Ruby. What was I thinking with that comment about shaving her legs? Her legs were beautiful, to be fair, like her hair, her skin, her smile, those beautiful brown eyes. I decided to go for a walk. Tigsy was snoring loudly and didn't wake up as I got dressed quickly. It was only seven in the morning, so everything was quiet. I closed the door quietly so as not to wake anyone in the house.

As I walked towards the seafront I was shocked to see Ruby was sitting by herself on a bench. She looked so sad and alone, sitting there. She looked annoyed when she spotted me walking towards her.

"Hi, Ruby."

"Hi, Will, what are you doing here so early? Are you stalking me or something? Or did you bring your razor for me?"

"No, I didn't even know you would be here. I couldn't sleep so I came for a walk. I did want to see you, though. I wanted to say something."

"What's that, Will? Are you going to ask me if I've shaved my legs this morning and I could borrow your razor?"

"No. I wanted to say sorry about that comment. Tigsy told me to be more myself around you."

"And *that* is the real you?"

"Well, no, it's not really. I was trying to be funny. Look, I'm sorry, OK? I didn't mean to upset you. You haven't even got hairy legs. You've got lovely legs. It was just a bad joke."

"Well, you did, Will, and I was upset enough before that comment."

"Oh, I'm sorry to hear that. Is it the lack of sleep?"

"No, it was the anniversary of my mum's death yesterday."

"Oh, sorry again. I hadn't realised."

"Stop saying sorry, Will. You weren't to know. It's just, it's not getting any easier. I spoke to my dad yesterday – he had been to the spot where we scattered my mum's ashes. Maybe I shouldn't have come on this trip. Maybe I should have stayed with my dad, to go with him to that special place. I started to feel guilty".

"And where is that special place?"

"It's in the woods, not far from our house. We used to walk the dog there for years. She loved that place. I used to make fun of her, taking the dog – he was called Luna – to that place every day, but she loved it. It was so beautiful there, so tranquil."

"I thought your dog was called Bluebell?"

"How did you know about Bluebell?" asked a surprised Ruby.

"You told me when your dad was grieving, he used to cry while walking the dog. You told me on the beach in France, remember?"

"Oh, yeah, I did. We had Luna before we had Bluebell. Luna died. The sadness isn't going away, Will. If anything, it's getting worse. I think it's all the time you have to think on this trip. Sometimes, when we go to a place, oh, I don't know, like Juliet's balcony in Verona, I want to tell my mum all about it, and I think maybe I'll ring her later, and then I remember I can't."

We both sat in silence, and I racked my brains for

some words of comfort.

I didn't really know what else to say. Words would offer little solace. I decided action was needed here and boldly put my arm around Ruby's shoulder, pulling her closer to me. At least she wasn't wearing her red bikini. Ruby's head was nestling on my shoulder. It felt so good. We sat in silence for a few minutes, and all we could hear was the gentle breeze of the wind and the waves breaking onto the beach. It was quite warm, despite being early the morning, and I felt a feeling of total happiness. Here, in the moment with Ruby, it was possibly the happiest I had been on the trip so far. I didn't want this moment to end. I suppose I was being a bit selfish. Ruby was obviously hurting and struggling with her grief, and here was I trying to make some romantic moment out of it. It was pretty low of me, and I did feel a bit of shame, but it didn't last long. I was just enjoying the feeling of Ruby's head on my shoulders.

"We should go and meet the others, they'll be wondering where we are," said Ruby.

Ruby moved her head from where it had been resting on my shoulder and looked at me, and those big brown tear-stained eyes made me melt inside. It felt like she wanted to kiss me, or was I reading the situation wrongly? I really wanted to kiss her, though, there and then. On that bench, in Ohrid, by the sea, which, actually I'd read was a lake and not the sea.

But of course I didn't.

# Chapter 24

## Bonding

Tom and his dad were sat in the lounge. It was late on a Sunday evening and Tom was going back to Salisbury first thing in the morning. Unusually for a Sunday night, his dad was drinking a large tumbler of whisky.

"Pour yourself a whisky, son. It'll put hairs on your chest."

"OK, thanks, I will." Tom didn't really like whisky, but it would help him sleep.

It was nice to spend some time with Dad, thought Tom. They hadn't had an opportunity recently to talk, and sometimes, if the mood was right, they would have some interesting conversations. It was better that they had something to focus on, so they weren't looking at each other directly, and today it was the golf. Some British guy, who Tom didn't recognise, was doing quite well, and with four holes left to play in the final round of the competition he had a chance of winning. Though Tom had seen the script before, where the American, in second place, would inevitably win at the end. British golfers had a habit of falling by the wayside on the last few holes.

"I got those containers for you, Dad, from the surgery. What's that all about?"

"I was going to talk to you about that, Tom. I haven't been very well recently; I've had some tests done at the hospital. I'm sorry to tell you, but I've been diagnosed with something called a phaeochromocytoma."

Tom looked at his father, whose focus remained on the television.

"What is that?"

"It's a tumour of the adrenal gland."

"You mean cancer?"

"Yes, I suppose so. It's a tumour, but it may be benign."

Tom was racking his brains, trying to think of where the adrenal glands were, but his brain wasn't supplying him with the information.

"What are the adrenal glands?"

"Apparently, we all have two adrenal glands: one at the top of each kidney. They think I have a tumour on the left kidney adrenal gland. The tumour releases hormones that can cause various symptoms. In my case, it's the high blood pressure and night sweats."

"So what's the treatment?"

"Well, I've had imaging done, and they've suggested surgery to remove the tumour."

"Which will be when?"

"Hopefully on September the sixteenth, which is ironic as it's my birthday."

"Some birthday present."

"I know."

"Does Mum know?

"Of course she does. We don't have any secrets; she's been coming to the outpatient appointments with me."

"Why didn't you tell me earlier?"

"We didn't want you to worry. Tom. You had your exams, and then getting the job. You've done really well, Tom – at least we don't have to worry about you. Though I was a bit upset when you broke up with Ruby. She was a lovely girl."

"She still is, Dad. She still is. I've just got to nip to the loo a minute."

Tom knew he had to get out of the lounge; he didn't

want his Dad to see the tears that were forming. He couldn't believe what Dad had told him. He had been so wrapped up in his own little world that he hadn't been aware of what was going on around him. Tom wiped away his tears using a piece of toilet paper and went back into the living room where his dad was swearing at the television. It looked like the British guy had sent his drive into the woods. That's his chance gone of winning, Tom thought.

"It's always the same with watching sport," said Tom's dad.

"What do you mean?"

"A lot of time invested and disappointment at the end."

"That's just life, Dad."

"I suppose you're right there, Tom, though occasionally it would be nice to change the narrative – or maybe change my nationality to American."

Tom and his dad sat in silence as the British golfer sent his approach shot from the woods into the water surrounding the green, effectively ending any chance of him winning the tournament.

Back in his room, Tom thought about what his dad had said. It would be nice to change the narrative sometimes. Like with his dad's illness, or what he had done to Ruby. He really wanted to talk to Ruby. He wanted to talk to her about his dad. She was always a great listener. Not many people were, in Tom's experience. People liked to talk rather than listen. Ruby would listen and support him. It was such a shame she was so far away at the moment.

# Chapter 25

## Ilija and Olga's House

We were all gathered in the lounge at Ilija and Olga's house. Olga had kindly supplied us with more strong coffee, though this time there was no plum brandy on offer. We told our hosts we would be leaving in about an hour, and they left us to our packing. Ruby had the *Thomas Cook Timetable* out again and was working out the next train for us to catch. Ruby was speaking.

"Right, if we want to get to Istanbul, we'll have to get a train to Thessaloniki in Greece, from where there is a direct train to Istanbul. Everyone happy with that?"

I would have said yes if she had suggested a trip to the local sewage works if it meant going with Ruby, but I pretended I was looking forward to the trip.

"Yeah, I really want to get some photos of the Blue Mosque – it looks well nice," I offered.

Tigsy and Gwen nodded, though Gwen was looking a bit annoyed again.

"OK, we'll have to get the bus to Bitola, and from there we can get the train to Thessaloniki. Let's go."

We said goodbye to our hosts and, after an uneventful bus trip to Bitola, we boarded the train. The train was really busy, and we had to split into two groups – me, regretfully, with Tigsy. Ruby was at the other end of the train with Gwen, who wasn't happy and had a face that Tigsy said was like "a bag of spanners".

The train was full of flies, and it was so hot in the carriage it was like stepping into a sauna. We sat opposite two Germans, who proceeded to smoke even though there were clear signs for no smoking. I was a bit pissed off at this behaviour until one of the Germans pulled out a big bag of peaches and kindly offered one to me.

"What is with Gwen? She looked well miserable," I asked Tigsy, while simultaneously sucking all the juice from the peach.

"I know, I don't know what's wrong with her. To be honest, she's doing my head in. I'm thinking of breaking up with her."

"Why would you do that?"

"We just haven't been getting on lately. I think this holiday has shown how different we are. To be honest, I don't think she'll be too upset if we do break up, at the moment."

"Can't you wait until you get home? It might scupper my plans with Ruby. There'll be no chance of me sharing a room with Ruby if you break up."

"It's not all about you, Will – but I suppose I could leave it a few days, maybe until we get to Corfu."

"Yeah, do that, you selfish bastard."

Tigsy laughed, and the two Germans with the peaches smiled in unison and offered me another piece of fruit, which I greatly accepted.

"Is it all sorted with Ruby now, or is she still pissed off with you?"

"No, it's all good now. We had a good chat by the beach this morning. I started to feel we had a sort of moment."

"A moment?"

"Yeah, we were talking, and she was upset, and when she looked at me I got the impression she wanted me to kiss her."

"And I take it you didn't?"

"No, and I think it was a missed opportunity. I don't

think it would've been the right thing to do, though. It was the anniversary of her mother's death yesterday, and she was struggling with her grief. I don't think she would have appreciated me trying to muscle in on her grief, but then again, I did wonder if she may have wanted me to kiss her."

"Look, Will, I'm going to give you a piece of free advice."

"Oh, please don't, Tigsy – I'm still recovering from the last time you gave me some advice and I acted on it."

"That was your fault, Will. I still stand by the advice I gave you; it was just your clumsy way of interpreting it. I think you need to be more impulsive, Will; you seem to be overthinking every situation with Ruby. Listen, the next time you get a chance like that, just go for it, don't hesitate, just lean in and go for the kiss. What's the worst that can happen? If she pulls away, you'll know she's not interested, and you can stop behaving like a lovesick puppy for the rest of the holiday. If she does respond, then Bob's your uncle and Fanny's your aunt, and you will be one happy bunny."

"I suppose you're right. I just hope I get another chance this holiday."

# Chapter 26

## Birmingham Dinner Date

It was over a year now since his wife had died, and today was the first time that Alan had been out on a date. Probably his first date in about twenty-three years. He hoped it wasn't too soon, but he knew he couldn't spend the rest of his life alone. It was the companionship he missed the most. Having somebody to talk to at the end of the day. He had waited until Ruby had gone on her interrailing holiday before he took the plunge, and now here he was opposite Julie from his office, in an Italian restaurant not far from his workplace. Recently divorced, Julie was a quiet lady with a wicked sense of humour. She hadn't been in the office long, but Alan and she seemed to connect straightaway. It was hard to explain; certain people just seemed to be on the same wavelength. They had bonded over a shared love of strong coffee and a particular dislike for one of their colleagues during their breaks. It wasn't long before Alan told Julie about the circumstances around his wife's death and the effect it had on his and Ruby's life. The conversation moved on to children.

"Me and Rob never had children, as you know. We talked about it, obviously, but he was never that keen, and we just got used to the two of us – that is, until the two of us wasn't enough."

"Do you regret not having children?"

"I do now, but when I was with Rob during the good times we spent together, it wasn't really an issue. We seemed to be so busy just getting on with life."

"I know what you mean. We always planned to have

children, we wanted a big family, but after we had Ruby, we weren't able to have any more."

"Oh, that's a shame. Why was that?"

"We don't really know. Rachel had a difficult time giving birth to Ruby. She was in labour a long time, and because Ruby was facing the wrong way she ended up having an emergency caesarean."

"Sounds nasty."

"It was. They say it's supposed to be the happiest day of your life, but for me it was really stressful from start to finish. Also, I had to go out in the early hours of the morning to put more money in the car park machine, and then they wouldn't let me back into the delivery ward because the door was locked."

"Sounds a nightmare. Worth it, though, in the end."

"Yes, though the first few weeks after Ruby was born were a blur to be honest. I remember I wasn't feeling the love I was told you would feel with a new baby. And then, one day – I still remember this moment – I was lifting Ruby out of the bath and passed her to Rachel, who wrapped her in a big white towel. Ruby looked up at me, and it hit me like a thunderbolt – this feeling of complete and unadulterated love and joy for this little person who had come into our world. It was an incredible moment, it really was. It still gives me goosebumps just thinking about that moment."

Alan paused a minute, worried he had been talking too much and thought maybe he had drunk too much red wine. Though, to be fair, Julie seemed to be engrossed in his memories.

"That's lovely, Alan, that really is, and Ruby is lucky to have a dad like you."

"Well, to be honest, she was always closer to Rachel

than me. Those two were inseparable."

"And you were saying about not being able to have any more children?"

"Yes, we tried for years after Ruby was born. It would have been nice for her to have a brother or sister. We even went for tests. Secondary infertility, it was diagnosed as. It's quite common – there was no reason why we weren't conceiving, it just wasn't happening. After a while we stopped worrying about it and were just thankful we had Ruby. We could have gone down the IVF route, but we decided it was something we didn't want, and we couldn't really afford it either."

"I've never heard of that, secondary infertility."

"I know, it's a weird one. It's more common than you think, though. Couples have one child and then cannot conceive another child, often with no medical reason, like us. Though Rachel was convinced it had something to do with the emergency caesarean."

Julie took a sip of wine and looked at Alan.

"How is Ruby doing now, after Rachel and everything?"

Alan paused before he spoke. His eyes were tearing up slightly, and he didn't want Julie to see he was getting upset.

"I don't really know, to be honest. She stopped eating for a while, which was a terrible time. She did go back to finish her degree, and she had her heart broken by some boy she went out with for a while. A nice boy, Tom – he came to the house once. I liked him. But Ruby is strong, like Rachel was. I think. She's gone off travelling now, across Europe on the trains, with a group of friends. I think there are six of them that went. It'll be a great opportunity to see the world. I wish I could have done something like that when I was younger."

"Lucky thing. You've got to do these things while you're young. Good for her."

# Chapter 27

## Train to Thessaloniki

The train journey to Thessaloniki was long and boring. Tigsy and I tried to pass the time with stupid games like 'I Spy' and 'The Parson's Cat'. Tigsy showed his hand a bit when he was on the letter 'G', saying the Parson's cat was a grumpy cat called Gwen. I got to the letter 'R'.

"The parson's cat is a resplendent cat called Ruby."

"Oh, give it a rest with Ruby," laughed Tigsy.

We got to Thessaloniki quite late – about half past nine – and we had to get to the youth hostel that Gwen had booked by eleven, as that was when it locked its doors for the night. There seemed to be a bit of tension between Tigsy and Gwen again. As we tried to navigate the busy streets trying to find the youth hostel, Ruby and I hung back a bit as Gwen appeared to be shouting at Tigsy.

"What's up with those two?" I asked.

"Gwen isn't happy. She was crying on the way to Thessaloniki. She's had enough of travelling and, to be honest, I don't think she can stomach the trip to Istanbul."

"How long is it?"

"It's about ten hours from Thessaloniki."

"That's not too bad," I ventured.

"I don't think it's just the travelling. I think she and Tigsy are going to break up. She says this trip has revealed that they aren't compatible."

"I know, Tigsy has said the same thing. I suppose being in each other's company twenty-four hours a day would be enough to test anybody."

"Good job we're not a couple, Will. Let's hope things

look better in the morning."

Tigsy, luckily, had some Greek money so was able to pay for us all at the youth hostel. Tigsy and I had to share a room with two Germans who spoke no English, which was unusual, given the Germans we had met on the trip so far. Not only could they not speak English, but they also didn't hand out any free fruit. At least smoking wasn't allowed in the youth hostel. The water wasn't working in the toilets on our floor, so we had to walk to the bottom floor to wash. The bunk beds were squeaky, and the mattresses sank in the middle, but I was so tired and was soon asleep.

Plans went awry the next morning. The train to Istanbul was due to leave at 9.25 a.m., and we were down in the lobby with all our stuff by 7.30 a.m., as arranged. Gwen noticed that the reception wasn't manned until nine o'clock and they had our youth hostel cards, so this would leave less than thirty minutes to get from the youth hostel to the train station, which wasn't going to happen. So, it looked like we would have to stay another day in Thessaloniki. The youth hostel was fully booked for the night, so it looked like we would have to find a hotel.

Gwen wanted a word with Ruby. They looked like they were having a serious conversation.

"What's happening, Tigsy?"

"It looks like you've got your wish, Will."

"What do you mean?"

"Gwen wants to go home. She doesn't want to go to Istanbul. She hasn't been feeling too well, so she's planning to leave this morning."

"What about you?"

"Well, I'm going with her. I can't let her travel by herself."

"Are you sure, mate? She's a big girl, and I thought you were going to break up with her anyway?"

"I know, but we had a talk, and I think I want to go home too. To be honest, I've had enough of trains too. I don't think I could face the long trip to Istanbul."

"What about Ruby? Do you know what she plans to do?"

"That's up to you and her, Will. Go and speak to her."

We were all standing outside the youth hostel with our rucksacks. Gwen looked a bit pensive, and you could tell by her eyes that she had been crying. Ruby had gone over to talk to Gwen. I walked over too.

"I supposed you've heard now that me and Tigsy are going back home. To be honest, I haven't enjoyed myself much, it just seems to be rushing around from one country to the next, without really experiencing the culture or feel of a place."

"OK, why didn't you say anything earlier?" asked Ruby.

"Maybe I should have, but everyone else seemed to be enjoying themselves. I didn't want to be the party pooper."

"So you are going home today? "I asked tentatively, quickly stealing a glance at Ruby as I spoke.

"Yes, there's a train at 4.30 p.m., which we're planning to catch – so we have today together, at least. Look, I know it's a surprise. Me and Tigsy are going for a coffee at that cafe on the corner – we'll meet you there in thirty minutes so you can discuss what your plans are."

I couldn't believe my luck. I knew we would eventually be joining the others in Corfu, but to be given the opportunity to spend a few days with Ruby with no distractions was a no brainer. I just needed to play it cool.

Unless Ruby didn't want to travel with just me?

"Do you fancy going for a quick walk, Ruby, to discuss our plans?"

"OK, Will."

Thessaloniki was a crazy city: there were cars everywhere, beeping, revving their engines, and this was in addition to mopeds, bikes, police blowing whistles. It was a cacophony of sound. We found a bench and sat down to talk above the noise of the city.

"Do you think we should go home too, Ruby?"

"I suppose we should head back to see the others in Corfu. I don't want to go home yet. I'm enjoying myself."

"What about Istanbul? We're only about ten hours or so away."

"But it's just you and me, Will. We could drive each other mad."

I smiled, thinking she *would* drive me mad – but not in the way she was thinking. I decided to chance my arm.

"So, the way I look at it is this, Ruby. We probably won't get a chance to visit Istanbul again, and don't forget we can get to another continent from there. Imagine the bragging rights when we get home to say we got to Asia on the train."

"I suppose it would be a shame not to go, now we're so close. I could go there as a tribute to my mum. I remember her telling me about the Blue Mosque, so would like to go there in particular."

"So we carry on?"

My heart was racing. I looked at a pigeon that was feasting on a piece of discarded pizza as I waited for Ruby's reply.

"OK, let's carry on. Like you said, it would be a

shame to waste this opportunity."

Inside I was jumping for joy. *Play it cool. Play it cool, Will.*

"Right: Istanbul, here we come."

The day passed in a blur. To be honest, I couldn't wait for Gwen and Tigsy to leave. We arranged to split up for a few hours and to meet outside the railway station at 3.30 p.m. as Ruby and I had to find some accommodation for the night. It was so hot; I was sweating more than usual as we trudged along the busy streets. I was excited about the accommodation, though. Maybe we would be sharing a room …

We both knew that we were struggling with finances, so getting one room would make sense. A double bed would be good too, and I imagined all kinds of scenarios as to how the evening would pan out. We eventually came across a really cheap hotel which seemed to be a haven for backpackers. Annoyingly, there were only two single rooms left, so reluctantly – in my case, anyway – we booked the rooms. We were able to leave the rucksacks in the hotel and set off to buy some food for tomorrow.

At the supermarket I picked up some peanuts, luncheon meat, water, biscuits, crisps and a bottle of ouzo, the Greek aniseed liquor. I also bought a small tub of tzatziki, which I had tasted in Ohrid and enjoyed. It was a salted yogurt and cucumber dish, though I wasn't too sure how it would last until tomorrow. I would have to get some bread tomorrow for dipping purposes.

In the end I was sad to be saying goodbye to Tigsy as he was good company on the trip, and I even felt a bit emotional as I watched Gwen leave for the platform too.

Tigsy, making sure neither Ruby nor Gwen were

looking, made a circle with his thumb and index finger of his right hand and proceeded to push his index finger of his left hand back and forth through the hole he had made in his right hand. His face was grimacing in what I can only assume was his 'sex face'.

It made me laugh, and Ruby asked why I was laughing.

"Oh, it's nothing, just something Tigsy said."

And with that, Gwen and Tigsy were gone, and it was just the two of us. The next few days would define my relationship with Ruby. Would I get to second base, as Americans often talked about in films? Come to think about it, I probably should get to first base before I could be thinking about second base. Would Ruby allow me to get to first base?

Ruby said she was tired and wouldn't mind going to the hotel for a nap, so we headed back from the station to the hotel. Our rooms, it turned out, weren't even on the same floor, so we arranged to meet up at 7 p.m., later that evening. I was desperate for a shower, but we had been told that hot water was only available between 6 p.m. and 7 p.m., so it looked like a nap was on the cards for me too.

I don't know how long I had slept for, but when I woke up, I was drenched in sweat. The hotel didn't provide any air conditioning. I'd had another intense dream. My dad had been up for promotion in work. He was favourite for the position, which he said would change our lives if he got it. We could go on more exotic holidays and get the new three-piece suite that everyone wanted. The one where you pulled a lever at the side and a footrest came up. He had been with the company for over twenty years and was more than qualified for the job. He was shouting now. I had never heard my dad shout so loudly, but today it was all coming out,

"They have given the job to *her*. I can't believe it! She's only been at the company five minutes, and they've given her the job over me!"

Ruby was in our house and was trying to console my dad.

"Now, don't be bitter about me getting the job over you," Ruby was saying. "Don't forget, we've got to work together. Let's have a kiss to celebrate."

Ruby moved towards my dad, her lips puckering up as she moved closer.

My dad was shouting, "I don't care about the job anyway! I'm getting to second base."

I awoke from my dream, or should I say nightmare. I was sweating again, and my stomach was churning. I headed for the toilet. What the hell was that about?

# Chapter 28

## "I Love You"

Ruby couldn't sleep. Even though she was exhausted, she was unable to drop off. Probably the heat in the room. It was a cheap hotel, after all, which meant no air conditioning. She had about an hour before she was meeting up with Will, so she decided to look for a phone as she wanted to phone her dad. The lady on reception, in broken English, said there was a public phone box outside the bank and was able to change some Turkish money for some coins for the call. Ruby had her dad's work number as she figured he would still be in work as it would only be about 4 p.m. in the UK.

Entering the international code for UK, the call seemed to take a lifetime to connect, but eventually she was able to hear the dulcet tones of her dad on the other end of the phone.

"Hi, Dad, it's Ruby."

"Wow, Ruby! How nice to hear from you. How are you doing, Princess?"

Ruby squirmed a bit when she heard her dad use the word 'Princess'. He never used to call her that when Mum was alive.

"Good, thanks, we are having a great time. We're in Greece at the moment, heading for Istanbul soon, and then we're going to Corfu for a few days, staying at Camping Vatos."

Alan scribbled down the name of the campsite on his notepad on his desk. Just in case he needed to contact Ruby later.

"Are you all getting along?"

Ruby hesitated. She didn't want to tell her dad it was just her and Will going to Istanbul as he might start to worry or infer something about the situation.

"Yes, fine thanks, all good. How are things with you?"

"Yeah, not too bad. The weather has been awful here; you're lucky to be having some sunshine. I haven't been able to cut the grass for a couple of weeks."

Hearing her dad talk was making Ruby sad. Maybe it was the lack of sleep or the heat, but she was surprised that she had started to cry. Why was she so emotional?

"Look, Dad, I'm running out of money. I'll try and call you in the next few days. I love you, Dad." She had never said that to her dad before. She had surprised herself with the outburst of emotion, but it did feel good to say it. She really loved her dad, even more since her mum had died.

"I love you too, Princess."

Ruby headed back to the hotel. In a few minutes the hot water would be turned on, and she was desperate for a shower.

# Chapter 29

## The Phone Call

Tom was back in his flat in Salisbury. He was still reeling from the news of his dad's illness and wasn't looking forward to going back to work in the morning.

Although he had only just started at the company, he could really do with a few days off. He had exams coming up at Christmas, so he knew it would be full-on then, so if he was going to take any time off it would have to be soon.

He really wanted to see Ruby. He wanted her back. It had been a mistake to break up with her. He knew that now. What was he thinking when he broke up with her? He had to see her; he didn't want to wait until she was back from her holiday. There was only one thing to do: he needed to phone Ruby's dad and try to find out where she was. Then he would fly out to see her.

Picking up the phone, Tom dialled rapidly, his heart pounding hard.

"Hello."

"Oh, hello. It's Tom here. Tom Bellows."

"Oh, hello, Tom. This is a surprise. What can I do for you?"

Tom could sense some anger and hesitation in the reply.

"I was wondering when Ruby was coming home. I had a postcard from her last week."

"Well, she's on her way to Istanbul, and I think after that she's going to Corfu for a few days."

"Oh, I see. Do you know where, in Corfu?"

"I think she's staying at Camping Vagus or Vartoos,

something beginning with 'V', anyway."

"OK, no worries, thanks. Look, sorry to bother you. It was nice to speak to you. I've got to go. Thank you. Bye."

Tom put the phone down hastily. His hand was shaking. Tomorrow, after work, he would have to call into the travel agent on the high street. He had a return flight to Corfu to book.

# Chapter 30

## Thessaloniki

Ruby knocked on my door just after seven. She had showered, as had I, and was looking great. She had changed into a pair of black shorts, and she was wearing a white T-shirt with a picture of Mickey Mouse on the front. She had her hair pulled back and held in place with a red hair band. Her face had a shine to it, like when you've been out in the sun all day, and she had slight sunburn. I was wearing my white tennis shorts, which – despite being washed in the sink earlier – were looking grubby and were still slightly damp. At least my black T-shirt was hiding the dirt. I would give Ruby a solid nine out of ten in the looks department tonight, while I was feeling a solid four.

"Right, shall we go out and get something to eat? I'm starving," began Ruby.

"Yeah, me too. Let's go."

It was strange, just the two of us, with no other distractions. I wished it could have been like this from the beginning. I knew I had to make the most of the next few days. Time to bring my A game.

We managed to find a cheap place to eat and found a table in the corner to sit. After the waiter had taken our order – spaghetti bolognese for me again, and moussaka for Ruby – we sat in silence. *Come on, Will, it's time to step up.*

"Why do you think people go travelling?" A good opening gambit, I mused.

"What do you mean, Will?"

"Well, why are we rushing around from place to place,

with barely enough time to see anything? Most of the time we are just sat on a train. What's that about? Is it just about boasting rights?"

"I suppose it's a chance to experience a different culture, to experience something different to what you're used to, even if it is only a snapshot."

"And do you think you've done that? I mean, most places we've been so far haven't been that different to the UK, have they? Just hotter?"

"Well, I think you are being a bit cynical, Will – and besides, I think Istanbul *will* be different, when we get there."

"I suppose you're right."

We sat in silence again, and I was about to ask another probing question when the waiter arrived with two plates of food. The waiter, whose name was Spiros, spoke a little English and was keen to try out his linguistic powers.

"Spaghetti for you, sir, and for your lady we have the moussaka."

"Efharisto," replied Ruby, pleased she had learned the Greek word for thank you.

"Lovely jubbly," laughed Spiros, and he winked at me as he headed off to the kitchen.

"So I'm your lady now, I am?" laughed Ruby.

I could feel my face going red.

"Only in my dreams," I replied clumsily.

Ruby smiled at my reply. She ate a mouthful of moussaka and put down her knife and fork and looked at me directly. Her eyes glistened in the light of the small taverna.

"Do you like me, Will?"

"What do you mean? Of course I like you. I've liked

you since the moment I saw you, dancing like a maniac and when you fell into my arms at that disco in Swansea."

"Ha ha, that was embarrassing. Shall we buy some wine? It's quite cheap for a bottle of the house red?"

"Yes, that would be nice. I'll try and get Spiros over again."

Spiros came over quite quickly with the wine, which was decanted into a carafe. He poured a large glass for each for us.

"Wow that's well grim," laughed Ruby.

"I know, it's rough as a badger's arse."

"I've never heard that expression. Is that a Welsh thing?"

"No, it's a well-known saying. I'm surprised you haven't heard it before. Apparently, badgers fight to become top dog, or should I say top badger, and in doing so they often take bites of fur off the bottom of the other badger. Hence the term, rough as a badger's arse."

"I learned something tonight, anyway."

The wine was started to take effect, and I started to feel relaxed and not so tense as when we'd first sat down.

"Why did you ask me if I liked you?" I was keen to explore that further.

"Oh, I don't know – it's just sometimes you seem a little awkward around me, and it was something Tigsy said."

"What did Tigsy say?"

"That you liked me."

My heart was racing. I couldn't believe how quickly the conversation had escalated. One minute I was taking about badgers' arses and now Ruby was asking if I liked her. This was my chance. I had to take it.

"I do like you, Ruby. Very much. Why do you think I'm going to Istanbul with you?"

Ruby looked a bit shocked at my revelation. Though I don't know why. Tigsy had already given her the heads up, so it shouldn't have come as a surprise. Maybe she was surprised at me coming out with it so soon.

She looked about to speak when Spiros came back, asking us if we wanted desserts.

"Lovely jubbly. Baklava for you, sir, or lovely jubbly saragli for you, miss?"

Ruby shook her head at Spiros and rubbed her belly, miming she was too full. I too declined the offer of a Greek dessert. Spiros left us to attend to another group that had entered the taverna.

"I thought as much, Will. I do like you too, Will, but … "

I thought there would be a but.

"But what?" I prompted her.

"It's just I've just come out of a relationship with Tom. I was hoping the trip would help with that. It's just the timing isn't so great, Will. I don't really want a relationship at the moment."

"Yeah, no worries. No biggie. I didn't mean to get heavy or anything. Let's just forget I said anything."

"It was nice to hear, though, Will. Thank you."

"No worries. And I do want to see the Blue Mosque, so that was the other reason I wanted to go to Istanbul." Lies, all lies, I was thinking.

Back at the hotel, Ruby paused at the bottom of the stairs.

"I've still got that bottle of ouzo in my rucksack if you fancy a nightcap?" I was laughing as I knew what the answer would be.

100

"I'm a bit tired, sorry. Goodnight, Will. Don't forget we've got to get up early tomorrow to catch the train. Shall we meet in reception at 6.30? I think the train leaves at 7.30 a.m.".

"Yeah, great, see you then."

Ruby leaned towards me and kissed me gently on the cheek.

"Goodnight, Will."

"Goodnight, Ruby. Sleep well."

Back in my room, I started to pack for the early start in the morning, My mind was racing, as my heart had been earlier. Was it really all about timing? Why did she kiss me on the cheek? Had I said too much? I knew I wouldn't be able to sleep for a while but lay on the bed anyway. The room was so hot. How I wish it had air conditioning. I had done it, though. I had laid my cards on the table, metaphorically speaking, and they were all there for Ruby to see.

# Chapter 31

## Corfu

Pete and Mothball had slept outside of the tent on the campsite last night. It was so hot, and they were both drunk when they had got back to their tents. Sleeping outside seemed like a good idea at the time, but Mothball had woken up with bite marks all down his left arm. There were none on right arm, though, which was strange.

"Look at my arm, Pete. I think I've been attacked by mosquitoes in the night."

"Yeah, that does looks well messy, mate – almost as bad as that German piece I saw you kissing last night."

"She was alright, you are just jealous you never got to pull anyone. Anyway, I might be seeing her later at the bar."

"Great, what about me?"

"Oh, you can tag along if you want. I'll ask her to bring her friend, if she's feeling better. Apparently, she's got diarrhoea at the moment."

"I'll look forward to that – a German girl with diarrhoea. I'll bring some spare toilet paper, shall I?"

Mothball stood up and felt a bit woozy. It was that Retsina that he was drinking like beer last night that was making him feel ill. A strong Greek wine, made with pine resin. Never again.

"There's a bloke over there looks just like Tom Bellows from Swansea."

Pete stood up and looked to where Mothball was pointing. To be fair, he did look like Tom Bellows.

"He does a bit; I'll go and take a look. He's by the

toilet block, and I'm desperate for a tom tit anyway."

"A what?"

"A tom tit – a shit. Don't you know your Cockney slang?"

"Never heard of that one, mate."

Pete grabbed the toilet paper from his tent and walked over to the toilet block. The bloke that looked like Tom Bellows was walking in his direction.

Pete started to walk quickly, his desperation to evacuate his bowels growing by the minute.

"Oi, Pete – you better run, mate, there's a large group of Germans headed for the toilet block!" The bloke that looked like Tom Bellows had spoken.

"I can't believe it. Tom Bellows, what are you doing here?"

# Chapter 32

## Just as Friends

I had another weird dream again. I was at a wedding with the band, The Four Seasons. The lead singer, Frankie Valli, had been in a fight with Spiros from the taverna after he had tried to run out without paying. Spiros had punched Frankie Valli in the throat, and as a result he was unable to sing. I had been persuaded by the other members of the band to sing with the band as they had a wedding gig to perform. As I started to sing, I watched from the stage as Ruby and Tom took to the floor for the first dance as a married couple. Tears were streaming down my face as I sang along to the hit, 'My Eyes Adored You', its refrain about cherishing someone from afar echoing exactly how I felt.

The beeping of my alarm on my watch woke me up with a start, from a dream I was glad to escape. I quickly packed my stuff into my rucksack and went down the corridor to shave and brush my teeth. There was a queue for the toilet, but there was a sink free. I quickly shaved, though the electric razor ran out of power halfway through. It would need recharging. Luckily, though, now the toilet cubicle was free. The smell emanating was rank, and the last person to use the toilet had not only left a huge skid mark down the side but also a gigantic turd in the bowl. It was going to be a good day, I hoped, despite the start.

Ruby was waiting by reception and gave me one of her beautiful smiles when she saw me.

"OK, let's go, Will. Istanbul awaits."

There was a bit of confusion at the train station with

interpreting the timetable as the train we thought we were catching didn't appear to be running.

"I don't know what's going on. You have a look, Will." Ruby passed me the *Thomas Cook Timetable*.

"I don't understand what's going on myself. It's all Greek to me!" I laughed at what I thought was the joke of the trip so far, but Ruby either chose to ignore it or didn't understand the joke. Eventually, we boarded the 9.25 a.m. train, which would arrive at Istanbul at 6.50 the following morning. That was a long time. The train was really busy, and we struggled to find a seat initially, but eventually were able to find a carriage with five other people already seated. A Turkish man, who was playing with worry beads, kindly moved up towards the window so we were able to sit down. Ruby pulled out her book from her rucksack and I got out mine, which Ruby had already finished in Ohrid and had lent me to read. I was keen to read it so we could discuss the book. It was *Not a Penny More, Not a Penny Less* by Jeffrey Archer. The first few pages were a bit of a struggle, and I worried that I wouldn't be able to understand it, but as the book went on my concentration improved and soon I was engrossed in the story of a group of men who were trying to recoup money that had been stolen by a fraudster. I had already read over 200 pages when my watch showed we'd been on the train for almost eight and a half hours, and it was nearly 6 p.m. By 7.30 p.m. I had finished the book and was keen to discuss it with Ruby, but she was snoozing beside me. Only another twelve hours or so to go until Istanbul. At about 8.20 p.m. the train arrived at Pithion, on the Greek–Turkish border. Everyone had to get off the train and show our passports, and we were told we would all have to wait for another train, which apparently wasn't due for a couple of hours. We went to the far side of the platform, where there was a bench. We shared a couple of dry bread rolls with a tin of Spam, which I had been carrying at the bottom of my rucksack for a few days. It was still hot, and I was longing for a shower and a shave.

"How's your money lasting, Will?"

"Not great. I hope Istanbul will be cheap like Zagreb was."

"I'm the same. We may have to share a room in Istanbul to save money. What do you think?"

My heart immediately started racing. I couldn't believe what I was hearing.

"Yeah, we may have to. Hope you don't snore too loud."

"Just as friends, you understand, though, Will?"

"Of course, just as friends. I'm just glad we *are* still friends. This trip is enough to break any friendship."

"I know what you mean – it's not easy, all this travelling. I don't know what it is about travelling: most of the time you're just sitting there, but still it's exhausting."

"I know. And don't forget, we've got another overnighter – if this train ever arrives."

We sat in silence for a while, alone in our thoughts. Predictably, I was already thinking of the sharing of the room in Istanbul and what possibilities that could bring. There was a stirring in my loins, which I tried to repress: Ruby had clearly said, "Just as friends."

There was an announcement about the train over the tannoy. It was in Turkish, so we couldn't understand it – but, judging by the groans from the people on the platform, it wasn't good news.

"I think the train's going to be delayed by an hour," said Ruby.

"How do you know?"

"I think one in Turkish is *bir*."

"Great. Just what we need."

"I know."

We sat in silence again, and I looked in my rucksack for any food I'd forgotten about. My hand felt a small bag with something hard in it: the glass snails I had bought in Venice.

"I bought something for you in Venice. I meant to give them to you before."

I passed the small white bag to Ruby. It was one of those white paper bags that you used to get from the sweet shop. Ruby looked surprised at the impromptu gift and opened the bag, expecting to see sweets inside.

"Wow, that's unusual! Green glass snails – just what I always wanted ..."

Ruby was laughing now. She had a beautiful laugh. It was infectious, and I started to laugh too. I don't know what it was, whether it was just tiredness or the heat, but neither of us could stop laughing. On the border of Greece and Turkey, on that hot platform at Pithion, we both laughed about those tacky green glass snails I had bought for Ruby at that tourist shop in Venice.

"I'll treasure these, Will; nobody has ever given me green glass snails before."

"You're welcome."

People on the platform were gathering their possessions and moving to the far end of the platform.

"What's going on?"

"I think the train is coming, Will. Come on – we need to get a good seat."

"I thought it was going to be delayed?"

"Maybe my Turkish isn't all it's cracked up to be."

The train was really crowded, but we managed to get two seats together. The carriage was full. I had the seat by the window and Ruby sat next to me. We put our rucksacks in the overhead luggage compartment and settled down for the overnight journey. I was glad that we had both used the toilets on the platform as there only appeared to be one toilet on the train and already a queue was forming. I closed my eyes and hoped I could sleep. My hand accidently brushed against Ruby's hand, and instead of moving away Ruby put her hand in mine.

"I love the snails, Will. That was really sweet of you to give me those, thank you."

The train pulled away slowly, and, sitting there holding Ruby's hand, I fell asleep, a massive smile on my face.

# Chapter 33

## Strong Greek Wine

Tom was pissed, though he wasn't sure why. He'd only had two bottles of that disgusting Greek beer, and it seemed to have gone straight to his head. The beer must be strong over here.

He was sitting with Pete, Mothball, and Phil (who had been at the campsite for the summer but was leaving tomorrow).

"Oi, Bellows – you do know that's wine you're drinking and not beer?" shouted Pete, over the music of the disco.

Tom looked at the bottle of retsina. Why were they serving wine in a beer bottle? No wonder he was drunk. He thought the beer tasted funny.

"I've had *two pints* of wine! You could have warned me."

"Nice one, Bellows! You may be a Swansea postgraduate, but you're not the sharpest tool in the box," laughed Mothball.

A group of Dutch girls came over and asked if they could sit in the empty seats at the table. Almost immediately, one of the girls started talking to Tom. She introduced herself as Betje and told Tom she too was interrailing and was staying in Corfu for a few days.

"Looks like Bellows has pulled," said Mothball.

Unfortunately, Betje overheard what Mothball had said.

"What does he mean, 'pulled'?" Betje asked Tom.

"Oh. Nothing. He's just drunk. Ignore him."

The music stopped briefly and 'Money for Nothing'

by Dire Straits started up. The Dutch girls screamed in excitement and headed for the dance floor. Betje pulled Tom up too, and reluctantly Tom got up. Mothball and Pete quickly jumped to their feet and headed for the dance floor too.

'Shout to the Top' by The Style Council was the next track, and this seemed to be popular as Tom found there wasn't much room to dance, or for him to bring out his signature dance moves.

"Shout to the Top. Shout!" the crowd of people on the dance floor sang out in unison. Tom looked at Betje, she seemed to be totally absorbed in the music. She was a good mover. She was wearing shorts and a white vest which had 'Relax' written on it. To be fair, she was gorgeous, thought Tom – as all the Dutch girls he had ever meet seemed to be. They always seemed to be blonde. They always were beautifully tanned. Totally uninhibited.

'I Want to Know What Love Is' by Foreigner followed 'Shout to the Top', bringing the mood of the dance floor down a bit. Not for Betje, though: she threw her arms around Tom and pulled him closer to her. Tom wasn't sure what led to the next moment – maybe it was the weird wine–beer he'd consumed, or the fact that he was on holiday, or missing Ruby, or all of the above, but the next minute they were kissing. He had come to Corfu to win back Ruby, and now he was on the dance floor, under the stars, kissing a beautiful Dutch girl whose name he had momentarily forgotten.

# Chapter 34

## The Train to Istanbul

I don't know how long we held hands on the train to Istanbul, but eventually I had to let go as my hand was beginning to cramp up.

"What's the plan when we get to Istanbul?" I asked to deflect from the hand-holding situation.

"Well, we've got to get some hold of some Turkish money, so I suppose we'd better find somewhere to change some traveller's cheques and then find somewhere to stay."

"OK, so we have a few days before we meet the others in Corfu?"

"Yeah, I figure we've got a couple of days before we need to start the journey back. I should also try and find a phone and give my dad a ring with an update on our whereabouts."

"Yeah, good idea. I suppose I should phone home too at some stage. So, after this trip are you are going back to Birmingham to live with your dad for a bit?"

"Yes, initially. I start my new position in the last week of September."

"And that's as a trainee accountant?"

I pretended to yawn and coughed, as if to disguise the sound of me saying "boring" simultaneously.

"Ha ha, very funny – at least I have something lined up. What are you going to do with your sad life?" Ruby laughed.

"That's the thing: I haven't got a clue what I want to do. I hated my degree. I've got no interest at all in biochemistry."

"Has anybody?" Ruby laughed again.

The train stopped at a station and a lot of people were getting on board. We were lucky to have seats. I watched as an old Turkish woman berated who I can only assume was her husband as he struggled to get some suitcases on the train.

"To be honest, I had a miserable time in university – academically, I mean. The course was so boring, and every afternoon in my final year I had to go to the laboratory to work on my stupid research project. I remember feeling resentful when I came back late in the afternoon and all the students doing their Mickey Mouse degrees were just waking up from their afternoon naps."

"Hey, don't knock the Mickey Mouse degrees – it's got *me* a well-paid job, anyway. Why don't you apply for accountancy too?"

"I did think about it, but I only got a Desmond in my degree, and they only consider people with an upper second-class honours degree."

"What's a Desmond?"

"A Desmond Tutu: rhyming slang for a lower second-class honours degree. A Desmond Tutu – a two-two. That's what I got, and I was lucky to get that."

"Who is Desmond Tutu, anyway?"

"I think he is a famous anti-apartheid and human rights activist. He's a South African bishop."

"Well, I've learned something today, anyway. Badgers' arses, Desmond Tutu … you are a mine of information. To be honest, I didn't know what I wanted to do either until I went to those career fairs where you could get free food and drink."

"Oh, yeah, I remember those. Wasn't it called the milk round or something? I know Pete used to go there just for the free wine."

"Yeah, it was called the milk round. I don't know why, though. I had a few glasses of free white wine and must have impressed somebody, because a few days later I got an invite to an interview just before this trip."

"I think it is called the milk round because employers used to go around the same universities trying to recruit the best graduates, a bit like a milk delivery route. What was the interview like?"

"It was OK, to be fair – there were twelve of us going for two positions. I was quite nervous to start. They divided us into two groups and then we had to do some team-building exercises followed by a talk on a subject of our choice for ten minutes and then a formal interview."

"Sounds intense. What did you talk about?"

"That was the thing that clinched it for me, I think. Nearly everyone was talking about their achievements, like the Duke of Edinburgh award scheme or working at Camp America, whereas I talked about my mother's death and grief from a personal perspective. One of the interviewers told me afterwards that it had brought a tear to his eye, and he was impressed at how eloquently I'd spoken."

"That was a brave choice."

"Maybe. I found the whole process quite cathartic. It was a bit like when I wrote a eulogy for my mum's funeral. I spoke to my dad, who told me things I didn't know about my mum – her life when it was just the two of them before I came along. I wrote the eulogy, fully intending to talk about her life at the funeral. On the day of the funeral, I got up to read it and I couldn't. I broke down after the first line. Uncle David jumped up quickly and finished off the reading, but I felt disappointed in myself. Like I had let Mum down in some way."

"You did well even to attempt it. I know I wouldn't be able to do anything like that."

Ruby was quiet now. She had become a bit emotional recalling the events of the funeral. I needed to lighten the mood somehow and was glad when the door of the carriage opened and the guard asked to see our tickets.

We were both feeling tired, and Ruby had closed her eyes. I had half hoped she would hold my hand again, but I think that ship had sailed. I was still happy and optimistic, though; I closed my eyes and slept fitfully as the train edged its way ever close to Istanbul.

# Chapter 35

## Istanbul

The train eventually arrived at Istanbul at about 7 a.m. We'd forgotten that it was a Sunday and as a result the banks were closed so we wouldn't be able to get any money. Ruby had a little Turkish lira – about £5's worth – so we set off in search of a hotel. We bought a bus ticket as we were tired walking around with our rucksacks, but we were unable to find any buses that were running. They could have told us that when we bought the bus tickets. They probably assumed the tickets were for tomorrow. Eventually, we found and booked into a cheap hotel, the Hotel Gungor. I was excited to be sharing one room, though the room was large with two double beds, one at either end. It was, we discovered, a family room, but I didn't care – it was just nice to lie on the bed in a horizontal position and to be sharing a room with Ruby. We both wanted showers but there was a queue of people outside the hot water shower so we both had to have cold showers instead. Back in the room we both lay on the beds and, despite our intention to go out exploring, we were both soon asleep.

I awoke at around 2.30 p.m. I looked across to see Ruby was fast asleep, still. I was bored, so decided to leave Ruby a note and tell her I'd gone for a walk and would be back soon. I quietly closed the door of the room and set out to explore the city. I didn't know where I was going and was conscious not to get lost. My first impression of the city was that there was a lot of poverty and people seemed to be selling all kinds of stuff from improvised market stalls on the street. Men and young boys were selling water and what appeared to be old shoes. Another man stood by a weighing machine, where you could weigh yourself for a small fee. As in Zagreb, there were a number of men in army uniform walking along the streets. There were also several stray cats and the inevitable pigeons. There was a lot to take in. It reminded me of a travel programme I had once watched, when the presenter was in Delhi, India, and he had described it as an "assault on his senses". This was what Istanbul felt like to me. Everything was slightly different: the sights, the noise, the smells.

An old Turkish man with a limp was staring at me. He seemed to be taking a keen interest in me. I carried on walking towards a mosque, from which chanting had started. I knew that this was the call to the Muslims for prayer. Most of the mosques had loudspeakers on the towers, which were called minarets, to facilitate this. The old man was still shuffling along behind me. Surely, he couldn't be following me. I decided to take a left turn down a side street and was annoyed to see he was still in pursuit.

I started to think that this wasn't a good idea, walking by myself in a city I didn't know. I probably stuck out like a sore thumb. I should go back to the hotel. The old guy had increased his speed and was rapidly catching up to me. I decided not to risk anything any more and started to jog down the street. Amazingly, the old guy started to run too, albeit with a limp.

What the hell was going on? I had done a lot of running in my youth so decided to put on what I would call the afterburners, and started to sprint down the street. It must have been an unusual sight, and it made a strange race, but eventually I looked behind and there was no sign of the old Turkish guy with the limp. I was a bit unsettled now and ran all the way back to the hotel, which was probably not a wise thing to do in the heat. Ruby was still asleep, and I lay on my bed, exhausted. My heart was racing, and I was glad to be in the safety of the room and away from that limping Turkish maniac.

I fell asleep quickly after that and was awoken by the sound of Ruby rummaging through her rucksack.

"Oh, so you're finally awake, are you, Will? Come on, there's a whole city out there to see, and I'm starving."

"But we haven't got any money until we find a bank, and they're not open until 3 p.m. tomorrow."

"It's OK. I went down to reception while you were asleep and cashed a traveller's cheque. Not a great exchange rate, but at least we now have some money. I'll lend you some until tomorrow."

We decided to head out to try and find the Blue Mosque, which, according to Ruby, was a must-see attraction. We decided to find somewhere to eat first and soon found a cheap restaurant. I wasn't sure what I had ordered – I had thought it was pizza, but when it arrived it appeared to be some kind of sausage in a spicy pizza base. Ruby had gone for a kebab-type dish, which looked nicer than my weird sausage–pizza combination.

"You can't drink the water here, Will. Make sure you buy bottled water."

"Shit, you should have told me that earlier – I cleaned my teeth before I came out, and I'm sure I swallowed some water."

"Oh well, just don't drink any more."

The meal was incredibly cheap but too spicy for me, and I was unable to finish it. Judging by her empty plate, Ruby had enjoyed her kebab.

Ruby had spread a map on the table. She'd picked it up from the hotel reception and it showed the Blue Mosque was about a mile away.

"There's a lighting show which starts at eight I think we should try and make that."

"Lead the way."

I had been impressed when I first saw the Eiffel Tower that day in Paris (which seemed a lifetime ago), but I was blown away when I first saw the Blue Mosque. Ruby had filled me in on some of the history of the place on our walk. It was built sometime in the seventeenth century as a show of imperial strength, and is distinctive for having six minarets. Most mosques only have two or four minarets, Ruby went on to tell me.

"OK, smart-arse – anyone can read a guidebook."

"Well, you didn't. Do you even know what a minaret is?" laughed Ruby.

I was about to answer when a local guide stood in our way,

"You English?"

"Well, Welsh, actually," I replied.

"You need a guide?"

"Oh, er, no thanks."

"Come on, is cheap, is very cheap." He carried on in broken English.

"How much?" asked Ruby.

"Only 500 Turkish lira. Very cheap."

He was very persistent, so reluctantly we agreed, and he took us inside the mosque. His name, he told us, was Demir, and he went on to say he had been doing this job for over ten years. He handed Ruby a scarf as all women who enter the mosque have to have their hair covered. We had to remove our shoes too, as this was mandatory for everyone entering the mosque.

The inside of the mosque was more spectacular than the outside. The central dome was encased in myriad blue tiles, giving rise to the name, I assumed. I would have liked more time to walk around and appreciate the architecture, but Demir was like a man possessed, rushing us round, probably anxious to finish the tour so he could extract another 500 lira from more unsuspecting souls.

"These are the carpets on the floor," he rambled on, pointing to the carpets on the floor of the mosque.

"Yes, carpets on the floor." Ruby was trying not to laugh.

"These are the very big pillars," Demir went on, pointing to the very big pillars.

"Yes, very big pillars," I said, also trying to suppress a laugh.

"Elephant feet," Demir went on.

"Yes, elephant feet. I read about those in the guidebook – the dome of the Blue Mosque is supported by four elephant-feet pillars. Is that right, Demir?" Ruby asked.

"Elephant feet," Demir added.

After about ten minutes, Demir's tour was finished. He made a big show of shaking hands with me, and he kissed Ruby on the back of her hand before taking his leave.

"Good luck." He waved his hand, walking away.

We had about half an hour before the lighting show was due to start so we made our way outside the mosque and found a couple of free wooden chairs to sit on. The mosque looked resplendent when the light began to fade and the lighting show began. A large crowd had gathered. It was another warm night and, amazingly, the commentary was in English. Every night the commentary was in a different language. We were lucky that tonight's was English, though it was hard to understand what was being said as the crowd was quite noisy and the dialogue barely audible. Still, the show was good and, as an added bonus, was free to watch.

A young couple to the side of me were holding hands. The girl was laughing at something the boy had said and leaned over to kiss him. They looked so happy together. I was envious; here I was, sitting next to the girl of my dreams, in the most auspicious of surroundings, with nobody to distract me, longing to be holding Ruby's hand, like when she had held mine on the train before. I knew I wouldn't get many better opportunities than this. What was that expression I'd learned in my Latin class at school? *Carpe diem*, "seize the day". I moved my hand so it was close as it could get without actually touching, hoping Ruby would notice and put her hand in mine. My heart was racing as I edged my hand closer, and the side of my hand finally made contact with Ruby's. Just at that moment, a firework exploded into the night sky, causing Ruby and me to jump. And with that, the moment had passed. But, to my surprise Ruby, grabbed my hand and pulled me up from the chair.

"Come on, Will, let's see what else we can do around here."

She dropped my hand as soon as I stood up, which was disappointing, but surprised me again by linking her arm in mine as we walked. It felt nice. We decided to make our way back to the hotel and began the walk back through an area of shops selling rugs and carpets. A young Turkish man, who was standing outside a shop, approached us.

"Hello, English?"

"Oh, no, Welsh," I replied, again trying to walk away.

"Wales, yes. Wales. Neville Southall! Neville Southall!" he shouted.

Neville Southall, I knew was the goalkeeper for Everton. And Wales. That much I knew.

Ruby joined in with the conversation.

"Neville Southall," she shouted.

"You come in my shop and look at my carpets?"

"Oh, eh, no thanks. We've got to go home," I answered.

"You come. Come. I make you apple tea."

With that, the man put his arm around my shoulder and ushered us both into the shop.

"Sit, sit, I'll bring apple tea." We sat, apprehensively, on a bench in the small room when the man disappeared out the back.

"What do we do now?" said Ruby.

"It looks like we're buying a rug," I replied.

The man returned, carrying a silver tray on which there was a silver teapot and three small glasses. He poured three glasses of the amber liquid from a theatrical height and passed us a glass each.

"Good health!"

"Good health," we relied in unison.

"My name is Mert. I am to be pleased to meet."

"Hello, Mert. I'm Will."

"And I'm Ruby."

"Your girlfriend?" asked Mert, smiling at me and exposing a set of beautiful teeth.

I wish, I thought.

"No, just my friend."

Mert looked at Ruby and patted her on the shoulder.

"Your friend." He started to laugh.

I took a sip of the apple tea. Usually, I drank my tea with milk and sugar, often with a custard cream, so I wasn't expecting to like the apple tea, but it was surprisingly good.

"You like tea?" asked Mert, looking at me.

"Yes, it's good."

Mert picked up the teapot and replenished my glass, again from a theatrical height. I was impressed by his dexterity with the teapot. He did the same for Ruby.

"My father, he buy the shop. I work with my father and my mother, and my family make the rugs. My son, when he is older, he will work in shop."

Alright, Mert, I didn't ask for your life story, I thought – but obviously didn't say out loud.

"Let me show you rugs," he continued.

Mert disappeared again and returned almost immediately, carrying two small rugs on his shoulder. He stood one of the rugs up and unrolled the other rug in front of us.

"You like?"

To be fair, it was a beautiful rug; even I could appreciate the quality and vibrancy of the colours, and, if I'd had the resources and somewhere to put said rug, then I may well have purchased it.

"We can't buy it, sorry. We won't be able to carry that home," said Ruby.

"You do not carry home. I post. I post rug to you."

We hadn't expected that answer.

"How much is the rug?" I asked. Ruby was looking worried.

"My friend, to you, 2,000 lira."

I did a quick calculation, and I think that worked out at

way more than our daily budget. We needed to get out of the shop as a purchase was unlikely. There was no way we could afford that.

"We have a friend who needs a rug," began Ruby.

"We will bring them to shop tomorrow," I added.

"Wait! Wait! Let me show you the other rug!" Mert quickly rolled up the first rug and replaced it with the second one. Again, it was beautiful; it wasn't hard to recognise the quality.

"You like, you like? Only 2,500 lira."

"We are sorry, Mert – we can't afford that."

The rugs were getting more expensive. Mert jumped up and smiled.

"No worries, my friends." He started to shake our hands vigorously, almost as if he had made a sale.

"You like to see more carpets?"

"Oh, eh, no thanks, Mert. We have to go," Ruby said as she got to our feet.

"We will tell our friends to come to the shop." I added to the fictional friend story.

Mert seemed happy with this and patted us both on the back.

"You go, my friends. Happy friends. Happy girlfriend!" He was laughing now as he showed us out of the door.

Waving us goodbye, he watched us as we walked away from the shop. Ruby was laughing now.

"I was a bit nervous there," she said.

"Me too, but it turned out OK in the end. He was a nice bloke. Great teeth too."

"That apple tea was well nice, as well. I didn't expect to like that."

"I know – I might buy some to take home."

It was still really warm as we walked back to the hotel. I loved Istanbul; it had really made an impression on me. I didn't even think it was because I was here with Ruby. They say travelling broadens the mind, and I was started to see why.

I was thirsty now; it was a warm evening. Ruby said she was thirsty too, so we decided to go for a quick drink before returning to the hotel. We sat outside a cafe and the waiter took our order for two Cokes. There was something to be said about drinking an ice-cold Coke from a bottle, outside, when thirsty. An elderly Turkish man, who was sitting at an adjacent table, appeared to be watching us as we drank our beverages. He stood up and came to sit at our table. He smiled at us both but didn't speak. He seemed to be taking an avid interest in Ruby and was smiling at her.

"Shall we go, Will? This man is starting to make me feel uncomfortable."

"Yeah, we should go."

As we went to stand up the man put his hand on my shoulder and pushed me back down gently.

"Sorry, sir – you stay. I like to talk, please. I buy you and your wife Coke?"

Ruby winked at me. I didn't think she was feeling threatened any more by the strange Turkish gentleman.

"Thank you. OK, yes please – buy a Coke for me and my wife, Ruby," I said.

"My name is Ali. Your name, please?" Ali was looking at me now.

"I'm Will, and this is my wife, Ruby."

"Hello, Will and wife Ruby. Wait, I'll bring Coke."

Ali disappeared into the cafe.

"Shall we go?" I asked Ruby.

"No, I think that would be rude. And besides, Ali has gone to get us a drink. We can stay for a bit. I don't think we're in any danger."

Ali returned with the drinks. They were not Cokes, though. They were a clear colourless liquid. He pulled out a tin in which were several cigarettes and offered us one.

"No thank you, Ali – we don't smoke," I said.

"You, drink, please. Drink. Raki. I bring Raki."

Raki, I knew, was a Turkish aniseed-flavoured drink, the Turkish national drink and similar to ouzo. It tasted OK, but it was strong. I knew that if you added water to Raki then the drink would turn from clear to a milky colour. Aniseed oil dissolves in the alcohol but not in the water, resulting in the milky appearance. I think it was called 'louche' when this happened. I should have mentioned this to Ruby. She may have been impressed by my alcohol-related knowledge, but I think I was a bit intimidated by Ali, so said nothing.

"If you like, I can take to shop to buy carpet?"

"Oh no, thanks, we haven't got any money," replied Ruby.

"I can take you for carpet. Very cheap. Then I go with you to your hotel?"

"Oh, that's very kind – but it's a long way from here."

"I come now. We buy carpet on way. I come to your hotel. We put carpet in room. I come to your room. I'll sleep in your room and then in the morning I'll go."

"Oh, that's very kind of you, but we can't afford to buy a carpet."

"You want Turkish bath? Come, I take you."

"Oh no, thanks – I already had one this morning." Ruby burst out laughing when I said this.

Ali started to laugh too, showing a set of yellow teeth.

"I get more drinks." Ali disappeared again, this time returning quickly, with three small glasses of a brown liquid. It looked like some form of spirit.

"Drink? I bring Metaxa." I had seen signs advertising Metaxa everywhere. I think it was a strong alcoholic spirit, like brandy, but it was a Greek drink, not Turkish.

"I teach you how to count, yes?" Ali continued, after downing his Metaxa in one gulp.

"To count?" Ruby said.

"Yes, to count in Turkish." continued Ali.

"Oh, OK. Yes, please," I replied nervously.

"Bir," said Ali, and he looked at me and Ruby, waiting for our response.

"Bir," said Ruby and I in unison.

"İki," said Ali.

"İki," said Ruby and I in unison again.

Ali started to laugh and was slapping me on the back. He then stood up and kissed Ruby on the cheek. He then asked us both to stand up – and slapped us both on our backsides, quite hard! He then started to do a strange dance around the table, with his hands in the air. He was chanting something indecipherable. He then danced his way into the cafe and disappeared. We took this as our opportunity to leave and hastily made our way back to the hotel, nervously looking over our shoulders to see if Ali was following. It was only when we thought we were safe that we relaxed a bit.

"Well, that was a strange evening," Ruby said.

"Tell me about it. What was that with the counting? I mean, he gave up after two – and that slap on my backside was really hard."

"Makes for another good anecdote, though."

"It certainly does, wife."

"It certainly does, husband." And we both burst out laughing at what, indeed, was a strange night.

# Chapter 36

## Toilet Trouble

Back at the hotel, Ruby went down to the bathroom to change, and I quickly changed for bed while she was out of the room. I was surprisingly tired and got into bed and fell asleep before Ruby had returned from the bathroom. It must have been the combination of heat, raki, Metaxa and having my backside slapped that made sleep easier.

I woke up a few hours later, sweating and feeling sick. My stomach was aching; sporadic cramps came and went. I looked across to Ruby, and, although she was facing the wall, I could tell she was asleep from the gentle breathing coming from her. I propped my pillow up against the wall and sat up, hoping the nausea would pass. It didn't. If anything, I felt worse. I knew that as soon as I stood up I would be sick.

I put it off as long as I could before I made a sprint down the corridor. The nausea had passed momentarily, but my bowels were ready to explode. Luckily, there was nobody in the bathroom, and I ran into the cubicle and only just managed to pull down my trousers before a torrent of diarrhoea evacuated from my nether regions. The smell was horrendous; in fact, it was so bad it was making me want to throw up. There was a small sink within reach of the toilet, and I was able to rest my neck on the edge of the sink while still sitting on the toilet. I immediately projectile vomited into the sink. I was literally defecating and vomiting simultaneously. It was almost as if my body was determined to rid itself of whatever bug was causing my discomfort as quickly as possible, by whatever means necessary. My bowels continued to expel diarrhoea into the bowl. I pulled the flush to alleviate the smell of the faeces and turned on the taps in the sink to clean away the vomit. Alarmingly, the flush didn't work, so I pulled the chain, this time with more force. The ancient plumbing system sprang into life and, thankfully, took away the offending mixture. I had a brief respite before the vomiting returned, and with a final flourish of diarrhoea my ordeal was over – for a minute.

I wondered if Ali had poisoned us, but if that was the case, Ruby would have been ill too. I sat on the toilet and felt slightly better, although now I was really thirsty. I needed some water. I had a bottle back in the room. It was then I realised I had some 'paperwork' to finish, and I'd forgotten to bring any toilet paper with me … I glanced down at my leg to see a suspicious brown mark on my left calf.

There was no choice but to jump into the shower. It was one of those showers inside a dirty bath, where the shower attachments were on the bath taps. I quickly took off my clothes and got into the shower. As I pulled the shower curtain the whole shower rail, which must have been balancing precariously, came off and clattered to the ground with a loud bang. I picked up the rail and shower curtain and tried to fix it back on, but to no avail. I would just have to shower without the curtain. There was no lock on the door but it was the middle of the night so I figured I would be safe. There would be no hot water, though, as it was only turned on for a few hours every day. The water was freezing, but I had to get clean. I took off the shower head from its fixing and angled it down my leg and between my buttocks. I was surprised at the amount of faecal material that was still present on and in my body. Just as I aimed the jet of water again between my battered buttocks, I heard the door of the bathroom opening, and there was Ruby – looking at me with an expression of abject horror on her face.

"Oh, sorry, Will, I didn't realise you were in here– the door was unlocked." And she quickly ran out.

*Well, that's a nightmare. Ruby has seen me naked and showering down faecal matter from my anus. It doesn't get worse than that.* I then realised I didn't have a towel either, so had to dry myself with my clothes. Surreptitiously, I made my way back to the room. Ruby was back in her bed and, I think, pretending to sleep. I quickly got into bed and grabbed my water bottle, taking a big gulp of water before I fell asleep again.

I woke up again a couple of hours later. I looked at my watch. It was five in the morning. I'd had another weird dream: I was running down a platform, trying to catch the last train. I was wearing only a shower curtain and carrying a glass of apple tea. As the train started to pull away, I started to run faster and faster trying desperately to catch the train. In the process of running faster, the apple tea shot out of the glass and went down my legs. The shower curtain flew off me, and I was running, naked, screaming in agony as the apple tea burned my legs. A ticket inspector stopped me and told me it was too late as the train had left the platform. He also issued me with a fine for trying to board a train naked and with apple tea marks on my legs. Apparently, no hot beverages were allowed on the train.

I was starting to think there must have been some mushrooms or something in that apple tea, contributing to my weird dream. I slept fitfully on and off again, with one more trip to the toilet where another bout of diarrhoea ensued. This time I pulled the flush almost immediately to stop any offending smell from reaching my nostrils. Back in the room I slept again, until I heard Ruby moving about in the room.

"Sorry about last night," I said sheepishly.

"Oh, don't worry – although it was a shock to see you in that position in the middle of the night. I must admit, it wasn't what I was expecting to see."

I could feel myself blushing but, because of the distance between us, don't think Ruby noticed.

I started to tell Ruby about the events that led up to me being found in that compromising position. As I regaled Ruby with my story, I could see she was trying not to laugh. Eventually, it was too much for her to contain, and she started giggling and then made a deep guttural noise that was almost animalistic. Finally, she was laughing hysterically. Tears were forming in her eyes as the laughter continued.

"Oh, Will, you have made my day. At least you have another good anecdote to tell at parties."

"I don't think I'll be telling that one. What happens in Istanbul stays in Istanbul," was all I could offer in response.

Ruby had some diarrhoea tablets which she threw over to me, and I took a couple. I had no water left, so swallowing them was difficult, but I managed to get them down.

"Bananas are good for diarrhoea. I think it's something to do with all the starch they contain. It absorbs water in your stomach or something like that. Also, they're rich in potassium, and you need to replace your electrolytes," Ruby stated.

"Thanks, Doctor. You are right, though. I've heard

that it's important to replace your electrolytes. I need to go out and get some bananas and more water."

I was still feeling a bit rough, to be fair. My stomach, although now empty of its contents, was making a lot of strange noises. In the quiet of the room it was becoming more and more noticeable. I pressed my hand hard against my stomach, hoping to stop the embarrassing noises, but to no avail. I needed to get out into the noise and hustle and bustle of the streets of Istanbul before Ruby could hear my stomach complaining. Though, after last night, I didn't think I could embarrass myself any further. Too late, though, for Ruby had heard the loud noises coming from my stomach.

"Blimey, Will, you sound like you're laying an egg. Are you OK?"

"Sorry. I think I need some fresh air."

"OK, Will. We'd better start making our way back to Corfu to meet up with the others, anyway. I've looked at the timetable and there's a train that leaves for Thessaloniki at 7 p.m."

"Yeah, that sounds good," I unenthusiastically replied.

It *didn't* sound good: soon we'd be reunited with the others, and my time alone with Ruby would be at an end. *Time to step up, Will.* What was the expression? "Faint heart never won fair maiden"?

# Chapter 37

## Cheryl

I remember the first time I tried to win the heart of a fair maiden. Her name was Cheryl Wilson, and it was back in school in my A-level biology class. Most of my friends in school hadn't chosen to do biology at A-level, so I nervously sat at a bench near the front of the class, on my own, waiting for the first lesson to begin. Amazingly, Cheryl Wilson entered the classroom, dropped her bag on the bench, and casually announced she would be sitting by me. Wow. Cheryl Wilson: she was up there in the higher echelons of the coolest girls in the year. Cheryl Wilson was the girl who hit puberty early and had many a boy drooling over her chest – me included.

Everyone knew Cheryl Wilson was going out with Jim Pepperman – or 'Pepps' as he was known to his year group. They made up the golden couple of the year group. Pepps was annoyingly handsome, captain of the rugby team and the joker in the pack. He seemed to have it all. He had the whole class in stiches of laughter once, during a famous PE lesson. There we were, in the school hall, in our shorts and vests, with Mr Manley barking instructions at us.

"That end!" he shouted, pointing to the far wall of the gym, and the class diligently ran to the aforementioned wall. No sooner as we had all run to the wall then Mr Manley would point to the other wall at the opposite end of the hall.

"That end!" he barked again, and we would all set off for the far wall. This went on for about five minutes, after which he told us to lie on the floor. We were all struggling to get our breath back.

"Right, you're now going to pretend to be riding a bike. Everyone put your hands on your hips and legs in the air. We're coming to a big steep hill, so everyone start to pedal slowly."

All the class lay on their backs and simulated riding a bike by spinning their legs slowly, as if we were going uphill.

"Right, good work, class – we're coming to the top of the hill now, so get ready for the descent. Faster, faster! Right, we've reached the top, so it's downhill now – pedal as fast as you can," continued Mr Manley.

The whole class were spinning their legs as fast as they could manage myself included. All, that is, except Pepps: he was just lying on his back, hands on his hips, supporting his stationary legs.

"Pepperman, what are you doing? You should be going down the hill now! Why aren't you pedalling fast?" asked Mr Manley angrily.

"It's because I'm freewheeling, sir," replied Pepps, to raucous laughter from the rest of the class. To be fair even Mr Manley was struggling to keep a straight face after that and the whole lesson seemed to descend into laughter.

Cheryl Wilson, although beautiful, had her faults, one of which she wasn't good at biology, and I seemed to end up helping her most lessons. I remember once we were dissecting a rat – a yellow rat, I recall, as they were preserved in formaldehyde, with a pungent odour. We had to display the thoracic cavity and Cheryl inadvertently cut through the top of the leg of the rat. I should have been annoyed as it was part of our assessment and, to be fair, the leg was nowhere near the thoracic cavity. But it was hard to be annoyed with Cheryl, when she was sitting there with that school blouse struggling to contain her ample bosom. It was very distracting for a seventeen-year-old boy in the midst of puberty. And so, an inevitable crush ensued, which got stronger and stronger every time she sat next to me in biology. It was well known in the school that Pepps and Cheryl had split up. Pepps had moved on and was dating Ann Harbottle, and Cheryl was now single. The school disco was on Friday to signify the end of term, and during another biology lesson I found myself attempting to win the heart of this fair maiden.

"Are you going to the disco on Saturday?" I nervously began.

"Yeah, I suppose I'll show my face."

"Eh, do you want to go with me?" I blurted it out quickly. But I'd done it. It was out there.

Cheryl hesitated.

"Oh, that's sweet, Will, but I'm having a break from dating. Thanks for asking, though."

I wasn't too upset as it was the answer I'd been expecting. I mean, Cheryl Wilson was hardly going to go out with me after Jim Pepperman. Still, I was proud of myself for asking a girl out for the first time, even if it had ended with the inevitable rejection.

But then a strange thing happened. A few days later I was at the school disco, milling around the dance floor again. I could see Cheryl dancing. She was a great dancer. The music had slowed down, and I remember the song clearly: it was 'Make It with You' by Bread – a slow one. I remember David Gates singing, his voice carrying a gentle invitation, wondering aloud if it was possible to reach for something just out of grasp – even if it felt as unrealistic as chasing rainbows. And in that moment, with her moving in time to the music, it all felt possible.

Suddenly, Cheryl walked across the dance floor and grabbed my hand, and the next minute she was kissing me. What was going on? It was my first ever kiss and would be forever etched into my memory. I didn't really know what I was doing. A happy memory, I hoped, until the next minute I felt a sharp tug on my shoulder followed by a punch in the stomach. Pepps was standing there, glaring at me as I fell to the floor.

"I'm sorry, Will," said Cheryl. I was expecting her to help me up or even admonish Pepps. Instead, the pair of them walked off to the side of the dance floor, leaving me to get up quickly and trying desperately to maintain my dignity. I think Cheryl had just kissed me to make Jim Pepperman jealous, and it had worked. I mean, why else would he punch me in the stomach? The following term, I remember the next biology lesson came and Cheryl smiled and walked past me to sit at another table. A faint heart had tried and failed to win fair maiden. But still, I had finally kissed a girl, so not all bad – and Cheryl Wilson was a good start.

Where did that seventeen-year-old Will get his courage from? I knew I had to bring that fortitude to my current situation, even if it ended in rejection again. It was just a matter of timing, though my time was running out. I knew I'd already told Ruby I liked her in the restaurant in Thessaloniki, but I had to try again. Maybe she had changed her mind, or was warming to me? I needed to tell her once more, just to get closure – even if it ended badly. I just wished my stomach would behave itself.

# Chapter 38

## Another Day, Another Continent

We had to check out of the hotel that day, so that meant we'd be carrying around our rucksacks again. Ruby had planned a full day, as she was keen to tick off a few sights in Istanbul: the Topkapi Palace, the Grand Bazaar, and a boat trip on the Bosphorus, the strait connecting Europe and Asia.

Ruby was looking particularly good this morning. But then again, she always looked good. She had tied back her hair, and her face had a glow to it again. It was only a short walk until we reached the Grand Bazaar, but it was already really hot. We passed a post office, and there was a phone outside where you were able to make international calls.

"I'm just going to make a quick call to my dad. Will, can you look after my rucksack?"

"No worries. Have you got enough coins?" I replied, simultaneously rooting around in my pockets for some currency.

"Yeah, I should have enough – I just want to catch my dad before he goes to work."

"Yeah, don't forget Turkey is three hours ahead of the UK."

"I know; he should be still in the house."

Ruby went off to make the call. I amused myself watching the sights and sounds of the busy city. A chicken was loose and pecking at some discarded food on the pavement. Was it a chicken or a hen? I wasn't sure. Come to think of it, what was the difference between a chicken and a hen?

About ten minutes later Ruby was back.

"You're never going to believe this."

"What?"

"Tom rang my dad and asked when I'd be back from interrailing."

"Oh, why do you think he wants to know that?"

"No idea. Strange, though, don't you think?"

"Yeah, weird."

I didn't know what else to say. It wasn't the news I wanted to hear. He was obviously intent on seeing her again; no doubt he wanted to win her back. I needed to say something to put doubt in her mind again about Tom. But again, my brain was struggling to provide me with any insight.

"Do you know what the difference is between a chicken and a hen?" was all I could miserably come up with.

"Your mind works in a strange way, Will – are you sure you're not autistic? But, to answer your question, I think a hen refers to an adult female chicken that can lay eggs and the term chicken is the general term for the species."

"Oh, OK, good to know," I replied, impressed with Ruby's domestic fowl knowledge.

The Grand Bazaar was huge and, according to Ruby's guidebook, the largest covered market in the world. There was no way we'd be able to see it all in the time we had allowed. A myriad of stalls competed to sell spices, rugs, jewellery, handbags, clothes – the list was endless. It was really busy, and not easy walking with our rucksacks. Ruby saw a pair of earrings she liked and tried to haggle with the proprietor of the stall. It soon became apparent that most of the items were way out of our budget, so we left the Grand Bazaar and carried on walking to find the Topkapi Palace. Listed as one of the top attractions in Istanbul, again I was impressed when I first saw the magnificent building. We didn't have much time there if we were going to make the boat trip, so we didn't get to go into the Topkapi Palace Museum. Instead, we both took some photos outside, and I asked a Turkish man to take a photo of the both of us, which he happily did. I was still not feeling too good, and my stomach was making gurgling noises again. We passed a chemist and, despite the language difference, I managed to buy a Turkish diarrhoea medicine called Superlokit.

"How are you feeling, Will?"

"Yeah, not great – hopefully these bad boys will do the trick," I said, as I popped two Superlokit into my mouth. It was strange, because I was feeling sick and hungry at the same time. I wasn't sure whether to eat a kebab or throw up into the Bosphorus. We had reached the famous Bosphorus Bridge, which connects the European and Asian sides of Istanbul. It reminded me of the Severn Bridge, connecting Wales and England – though I think the Bosphorus Bridge is slightly bigger.

A boat was selling freshly caught fish from the Bosphorus, served between hunks of fresh bread. It was surreal: the fishermen were casting their nets on the far side of the boat and bringing in the fish, which was then grilled on the boat and sold on the other side. It was a slick operation and, judging from the queue of people waiting to be served, must taste good. We joined the queue, and soon we were eating hot fish in fresh bread. Apart from a few bones, it was some of the nicest fish I had ever tasted, and the mixture of bread, fish and Superkolit tablets seemed to finally settle my stomach.

We finished our meal and walked further along the harbour to where the boat trips were operating from. They were being marketed as a trip on the Bosphorus to Asia, and were quite reasonably priced.

"Ready for a trip to another continent, Ruby?"

"I am indeed."

As we boarded the boat, I decided that on the trip I would tell Ruby how I felt. I knew it had been briefly mentioned earlier, but I felt it had to be said again, and this time I would ask her out. Although, technically, I was already out with her. I would ask her to be my girlfriend. Yes, that's what I would do. As Tigsy had said, what was the worst that could happen? And besides, there wouldn't be a better opportunity than this, and my time was running out. Although she had already said she wasn't ready for another relationship, I could still ask. There were a few backpackers on the boat, and we were able to stash our rucksacks in a small room at the front of the boat, or the bow, as I think it's called. Was it bow and stern or something? Though I do recall something about port and starboard too. Who knows? Our guide announced over the tannoy that the trip to the small island called Büyükada would take about one and a half to two hours. Büyükada was one of the Princes' Islands in the Sea of Marmara. What I hadn't anticipated was how rough the trip would be. Bobbing up and down on the Bosphorus with a stomach full of fish and diarrhoea tablets wasn't a good mix, and within thirty minutes I was embarrassingly vomiting over the side. Everyone else on the boat seemed to be handling the waves with ease, and a number of them were looking over in my direction. I couldn't believe that after the embarrassment of the 'shower head' incident I had further embarrassed myself. Ruby, though, was struggling not to laugh as she watched me retching into the water below. As well as the seasickness, my stomach was still not feeling right, and I had to find a toilet on the boat, where I was sorry to see my diarrhoea had returned. I was feeling sick; my stomach was churning like a washing machine. It was incredibly hot, despite the sea breeze. I didn't think I'd felt worse at any stage of the holiday. Ruby seemed to be unaware of my predicament and had struck up a conversation with an English girl who was holidaying in Turkey with her parents. We eventually arrived at Büyükada and were told to return to the boat after two hours on the island. Any thoughts of me telling Ruby about how I felt towards her had disappeared as I was now feeling so ill and just needed to concentrate on feeling better.

"Are you OK, Will? You're looking a bit green around the gills."

"No – to be honest, I'm feeling really rough. Do you mind if I stay here by the harbourside for a bit?" I hadn't heard that expression before: "green around the gills" – what was she on about?

I'd noticed there was a toilet near where the boat had docked and felt it was wise to stay close by.

"No worries, Will. I'll go and check out the island. I'll come back in an hour to see how you're doing."

Ruby set off to explore the island, leaving me sitting on a small wall at the harbourside. Most people had left their rucksacks on the boat, and I realised the diarrhoea tablets were on the boat too. I walked back and managed to get my rucksack after explaining my predicament to the captain – or whatever you call the person who drives the boat. Do you even drive a boat?

I started to feel homesick. It wasn't nice feeling, being ill, at the best of times – and all I wanted to do was sleep in a comfy bed, preferably with an en-suite toilet. After about half an hour – and another trip to the toilet – I started to feel a bit better and decided to go and find Ruby. It didn't take long as she was coming out of a shop holding a pair of earrings, which she'd obviously just purchased. She smiled as she saw me.

"Feeling better? What do you reckon, Will?" She held up the pair of green tear-shaped earrings to show me.

"They're really nice; did you get a good price for them?"

"I did! I haggled for the first time, and he knocked quite a bit off. Hold on a minute – I want to put them on. Do you know why I bought these, Will?"

"Eh … because you like them? Or you wanted to try out your newly acquired haggling skills?"

"Well, yes, Will, it's because I liked them – and also, they're the same colour as the glass snails you gave me."

I'd forgotten about the glass snails. That had been a good idea, to buy those snails in Venice.

Cars were banned on the island of Büyükada, and the main form of transport was the horse-drawn carriage. The island was stunning, with beautiful villas nestling among the pine trees. It was probably one of the most beautiful places I'd been to. We had about an hour before the boat was leaving to go back to Istanbul, and Ruby had the idea to go on a trip around the island in a horse-drawn carriage. Apparently, it would only take about thirty minutes and was within our meagre budget.

"Come, come!" shouted a diminutive local as he opened the door of the carriage.

It was quite a squeeze in the carriage, and our legs

were pressed up against each other. The trip would take us along the narrow streets to the top of the island and back. The scenery was really impressive, and we both took a number of photos along the way. This was my opportunity to talk to Ruby again. *OK, Will. You're up. Again.*

"Ruby, do you remember in the restaurant in Thessaloniki, when I told you I liked you?"

"Yes, Will, I do. It wasn't that long ago."

"Well, the thing is, I still do – and, to be honest, I can't stop thinking about you."

Ruby didn't speak for a while. My heart rate had increased rapidly, and I could feel it beating in my chest. It felt like an eternity before Ruby replied.

"I think I'm starting to like you too, Will."

I couldn't believe what I was hearing. Ruby liked me too … Ruby liked me too. There had to be a but … there had to be a but. I was waiting for the but. It had to come, surely.

But there was no but. Instead, Ruby took my hand in hers and we both sat in silence as the horse let out an enormous fart and then defecated on the road.

The diminutive Turk brought the carriage to a stop and jumped out. He deftly scooped up the offending equine waste into a silver bucket, which he then hung from a hook on the back of the carriage. It was quite a pungent smell and deflected from what should have been a beautiful moment.

"Talk about timing," I said.

"I know," laughed Ruby.

We had reached the top of the island, and we could see the sea again and the magnificent coastline. I couldn't think of anything to say. I wished Ruby would say something. Was she saying she liked me as a friend, or was she saying she liked me in a romantic way? She was holding my hand, after all, so surely it must be the latter? But I still had doubts. Best not to say too much more. She said she liked me. We were holding hands. We were in a beautiful setting, and we still had a few days left with just the two of us. The horse farted again as the carriage began its descent to the bottom of the island.

After being dropped off ,we still had about twenty minutes or so before the boat was due to leave. We were keen to get rid of our remaining Turkish lira as this would be our last day in Turkey, so we ducked into a few shops near the harbour, emerging with a nutcracker shaped as a crocodile and some bread. The bread we bought, from a man wheeling a trolley full of bread sticks, looked like the French baguette, except they were a darker brown colour. The trip on the boat back was a bit better than the trip *to* the island. My stomach was much better, and the sea seemed to be much calmer. As the early evening sunlight bounced off the Bosphorus, I wondered if life could get any better.

# Chapter 39

## Jim Pepperman

Ruby had been studying the *Thomas Cook Timetable* again as we were cutting it a bit fine to get off the boat and then make it to the station for the train to Thessaloniki. There was a later train that we could catch that went to Thessaloniki, from where we could travel on to Athens. Though this would mean a three-hour wait at Thessaloniki Station. We decided to go for this option and set off for the walk to the station. We were getting tired by this stage and, with the few Turkish lira we had left, we were able to get on a tram to the main railway station. According to the guidebook, we would have to book reservations to travel to Athens – even with an interrail ticket – so we joined the queue of people waiting at the ticket office. It was quite a lengthy queue so I suggested to Ruby that she should go and sit down and wait with the rucksacks, while I queued for the reservations. It was hot in the station, and noisy. Somebody was shouting in the distance. The shouting was getting louder; it sounded like somebody was shouting my surname.

"Evans! Evans!"

Somebody was shouting my name. I turned around to see where the shouting was coming from. I couldn't believe it. It couldn't be. Surely not.

"Evans! Will Evans, what are the chances? I can't believe it's you."

"Pepps! Jim Pepperman – what are you doing at Istanbul Station?"

"I could say the same thing to you! What are *you*

doing at Istanbul Station?"

I'd forgotten what a good-looking bloke Jim Pepperman was. He was wearing white chinos and a blue shirt with the three top buttons opened to reveal his muscular, tanned torso. He was tall, good-looking in every respect, with long luscious black hair that could be utilised in a shampoo commercial.

"I'm interrailing around Europe with my friend, Ruby."

I pointed to Ruby, who was engrossed in the *Thomas Cook Timetable* and was yet to notice me talking to Pepps.

"She's a good-looking girl; you're punching a bit above your weight there, aren't you?"

Pepps playfully punched my shoulder to indicate he was joking.

"She isn't my girlfriend; she's just a friend. I still remember the last time you punched me at the school disco."

"Oh, yeah, over that girl – Cheryl, Cheryl Wilson. I'm sorry about that – it was a long time ago. She got under my skin, that one, made me act irrationally."

"What happened to her, anyway?"

"Cheryl? Oh, we knocked around for a while and then just sort of drifted apart. The last I heard, she was training to be a nurse in Cardiff. She had to resit one of her exams, as I remember. She looked upset when we collected our A-level results."

"Probably biology," I offered.

"Anyway, where are you headed, Will?"

"I'm queuing up for seat reservations. We're going to Corfu to meet some of our friends there, via Athens."

"That surreal, I'm off to Athens tonight myself.

Maybe I could join you? I could do with a bit of company."

Great, just what I needed: a good-looking, smooth-talking bastard, hanging around like a bad smell. This could scupper all my efforts with Ruby.

As the queue went down slowly, I found out what Jim Pepperman had done for the last few years and why he was standing here talking to me now at Istanbul railway station.

# Chapter 40

## Cardiff

Cheryl Wilson sat in the break room on the side of the ward and switched on the kettle. She didn't really want a cup of tea, but she wanted to keep herself busy to avoid reflecting on what had just happened. Her hand was shaking as she dropped the teabag into the cup. The milk in the fridge had gone off yesterday, but a quick sniff confirmed to Cheryl it was OK to drink. Predictably, she couldn't find a teaspoon. What was it with teaspoons that they always went missing? She remembered a boring story her manager had told her during her induction, about how he went out in his lunch hour to buy six teaspoons for the break room and the next day there was only one left. She found a dirty fork and used the handle end to remove the teabag from the mug. Picking up the mug of tea she sat down in her favourite seat. It was only then that Cheryl started to think about what she had done. Cheryl had helped to save somebody's life. Well, she had played a small part in saving his life. An elderly male patient, who had been on the ward for a number of days with a respiratory infection, had gone into cardiac arrest. It was fortunate at the time that Cheryl had been on the other side of the ward and was at the bedside almost immediately. She had pulled the emergency cord, which sounded the alarm for an emergency, and assessed that the patient wasn't breathing. Her three years of training had led this moment, and she began to perform chest compressions. She was conscious that she didn't want to break any ribs as the patient was quite frail, but she knew that a few broken ribs would be a small price to pay for a person's life. Despite the alarm sounding, she was still the only staff member on the ward. Some of the other patients on the ward had been woken up by the alarm and were now watching the unfolding drama. Rashid, one of the junior doctors on call that night, had entered the ward and was now racing towards the bed.

"What's going on, Cheryl?"

"Patient has gone into cardiac arrest, I think. I've started chest compressions."

Cheryl estimated she must have performed the procedure for about two minutes, and just as Rashid approached the bed the patient let out a loud cough.

"OK, Cheryl, good work. You can stop for a second while I assess the patient."

The patient was now breathing on his own now as Rashid continued his examination.

"Well, Chery,l it looks like you've helped to save a life. The patient has stabilised and appears to have survived the ordeal. I'll need a blood gas, and a set of bloods sent to the lab, after which you should take a well-deserved break. Well done." Rashid gave Cheryl a congratulatory pat on the back.

Cheryl was still shaking, though not as much. She had saved a life. She had actually saved a life and was feeling proud as punch. She remembered the struggle it had been to become a nurse. How she had to resit her biology A-level. She suddenly thought of that boy she used to sit next to. Will Evans. *I wonder what happened to him.* She still felt guilty about that night at the school disco when Jim had punched him to the ground. She should have asked how he was. She knew she had hurt him when she no longer sat next to him during biology, but she had felt embarrassed by the incident. Maybe if she had continued to sit next to him she wouldn't have had to resit biology. He had helped her a lot, and it had all worked out in the end. At least, for her it had. Cheryl wondered if it had all worked out in the end for Will Evans.

# Chapter 41

## On to Athens

I was surprised to hear Jim Pepperman had gone to Cambridge University. I hadn't realised he was that bright. But then again, I didn't know him very well in school. Apparently, his mother and father had both been to Cambridge University – in fact, that was where they had met. They were anxious for Jim to follow in their footsteps, after his older sister Lucinda had failed to get a place and ended up at Durham University. They had hired a tutor for him in the run up to his A-levels, and the tutor must have been good as Jim had achieved three straight As. A place at Cambridge soon followed, to study Law and Politics.

During his time at university he became a Cambridge Blue for his rugby prowess. He was one of those annoying people who seemed to have it all, though he had suffered some tragedy in his life: his mother was knocked off her bike and killed by a hit-and-run driver while he was away in his second year of university. His father, stricken with grief, could no longer stay in their family home and had sold up and moved to London.

Jim had a job lined up with a big American bank in London, starting in the second week of September. He too was interrailing, with his friend, Toby. Toby had met a girl at the beginning of the holiday in Biarritz in France and was so smitten with her he decided he wanted to stay with her for as long as he could. Jim, it seemed, wasn't fazed or upset by this and had set off to explore Europe by himself. He too had been keen to visit Istanbul, and after a few days there was now making his way back to the UK. I was a bit annoyed, to be honest, as I felt my relationship with Ruby had reached a new level, and now I had Jim tagging along as a third wheel. Hopefully, he would leave us at Athens – he did say he was on his way home, and we were on our way to Corfu. We had reached the front of the queue, and I made three reservations for the train, which was now direct to Athens from Istanbul via Thessaloniki.

We walked over to where Ruby was sitting. She was still engrossed in the *Thomas Cook Timetable*.

"Hi, Ruby. You're not going to believe this, but I've bumped into an old school friend in the queue. This is Jim. Jim Pepperman."

Ruby stood up and offered her hand, which Jim shook enthusiastically.

"Hi Jim, nice to meet you. Talk about serendipity."

"Hi, Ruby, nice to meet you too."

Note to self: try and look up what "serendipity" means. And "green around the gills".

I wasn't sure if it was my imagination, but I think Jim was checking Ruby out. And, come to think of it, was Ruby blushing slightly? I think I must have been tired, but even so, I knew of his reputation in school and how devilishly handsome he was.

"Is it OK if I tag along with you and Will to Athens? It would be nice to have some company."

"Yes, that would be great," replied Ruby – somewhat quickly, in my opinion.

We had a few hours before the train was due. I was starving and asked if anybody fancied getting some food.

"I've got some bread and chicken I've just bought that we could share," said Jim, and he pulled out the aforementioned food from his rucksack, plus a bottle of red wine and some plastic cups.

The next few hours passed quickly. The bread and chicken were delicious, and the red wine was going to my head. Jim was regaling us with his stories of his trip so far. Ruby seemed to be hanging on his every word and was laughing a lot more than usual. And, to be fair, he was a good storyteller – to add to all his other talents and good looks.

When we finally boarded the train, we were able to get a carriage to ourselves. I don't know whether it was the red wine or the heat, but I soon fell asleep, and when I awoke we were only a few hours from Thessaloniki. There was no sign of Jim. Ruby was sitting opposite me.

"You were out for the count there, Will. You must have slept for about four hours."

"I think it's my dodgy stomach and all these tablets I've been taking. They're making me really sleepy. Where has Jim gone?"

"I think he met somebody that he knew on the way to the toilet. He said most people use the same routes while interrailing, so you often bump into people you've met earlier on the trip."

"What do you think of him?" I asked pensively.

"Oh, he's great. He's so funny. Some of the stories he has been telling ... And he told me a bit about himself. We had a long discussion on grief after he told me about his mother and the hit-and-run. That was so sad. I felt I could relate to the shock of losing a parent so young."

How intimate had their conversation been? I wish I hadn't gone to sleep now. How had he managed to tell her his mum had died already? I wish he would leave us in peace. Hopefully, once we got to Athens, we could ditch him.

The door of the carriage opened, and Jim was standing there grinning.

"Back in the land of the living, are we, Will?"

"Oh, eh, yeah. I must have been tired."

"You must have been, Will – you were dribbling."

Ruby and Jim both started to laugh.

"Good news," said Ruby.

"What's that?" I asked.

"Jim is coming with us to Corfu. He's never been and asked if he could join us."

"You don't mind, do you, Will?" asked Jim, looking at me with what appeared to be false anticipation.

"No, that would be fine," I answered quickly. I knew it wasn't fine, though. It was a nightmare. My time with Ruby on my own was officially over, and although I thought we had shared a moment on that horse-and-carriage ride, I felt as if the moment had passed. Stupid Jim Pepperman.

# Chapter 42

## Hotel Joy

The train finally arrived at Athens late in the afternoon, after another relentless train trip, and we knew we had to find somewhere to stay the night. With the new dynamic, now there were three of us, I wasn't sure how this was going to work. A lot of the hostels were fully booked, but eventually we came across a cheap hotel called, rather optimistically, 'Hotel Joy'. For 250 Greek drachma we could sleep outside, on the roof of the hotel. This attractive offer included use of a cold shower and nowhere to safely leave our rucksacks. It was getting late, so – reluctantly – we booked in and made our way to the roof. The roof was full of backpackers, and, we struggled to find a space. Annoyingly, Jim had managed to set his rucksack down near a wall in the corner, in such a way that he would be sleeping in the middle. Clever thinking by Jim – or was I just overthinking things? It was still too early to settle down for the night, so Ruby suggested we go and find the Acropolis. The guidebook that Jim had told us the Acropolis itself refers to the hill, which is the site of several temples and ancient buildings, the most famous of which is the Parthenon. I remembered the Parthenon from watching *Summer Holiday* – the film from the 1960s, which seemed to be on every year – where a group of four London bus mechanics travel across Europe on a double-decker bus, picking up a group of stranded girls and a stowaway on the way. As you do.

We weren't keen to take our rucksacks with us and noticed there was a big pile of them by the side of the stairs. A group of Dutch girls saw us discussing whether it was safe to leave them unattended and shouted over to say they had been here all week, and it *would* be safe to leave them there. I wished we could have left stupid Jim Pepperman by the pile of rucksacks.

And so, the three of us set off for the Acropolis. When we eventually arrived it was too late to be admitted so we decided we would return the following morning. Jim suggested we climb the top of the hill opposite the Acropolis, which a lot of people were already doing. From the top there was a spectacular view of the Parthenon, and Athens itself. I think it was the same spot that they used in *Summer Holiday*, where Cliff Richard played the sad Don singing 'The Next Time'. He was reflecting on his failed relationship with the stowaway, initially disguised as a boy. Who thinks these stories up? A bit like me and Ruby, in a way – apart from the stowaway and dressing up as a boy bit, and travelling on a London double-decker bus.

A number of people were already on top on the hill with cameras and tripods, waiting to film the Parthenon, which apparently is lit up every forty-five minutes. I made the mistake of talking to a really boring American bloke, who started to tell me in great depth about how good his camera was. It was one of those fancy ones with a long lens, and he had it on a tripod, pointing towards the Parthenon. He then started telling me how rich he was and how he made more money than the president of the international federation. I had no idea what he was talking about, or what the international federation was, so I quickly made my excuses and left.

It was a beautiful summer's night, and the view from the hill, to be fair, was unbelievable. I got my camera out and took a few photos. It would have been nice to have one of me and Ruby, in this most romantic of settings, to add to my collection, and I handed Jim the camera, asking him to take a photo of the two of us. But Jim had other ideas: he passed the camera to a tourist and asked if he would take a photo of the three of us instead. Eventually, the light started to fade so we headed back to the hotel. I was still tired and was soon asleep, after staring at the stars for a while. Sleeping on the roof of the hotel had its compensations, not to mention a gentle breeze. Apart from a few trips to the toilet (the diarrhoea had returned), I slept well and enjoyed the experience of sleeping in the open air. When I awoke, I was squashed up against the outer wall of the hotel. Jim was still sleeping, as was Ruby, and I was annoyed to see he had slept quite close to Ruby. It was almost as if he had moved his sleeping bag in the night to move closer to her. Or was it my imagination again? They did look quite cosy, sleeping next to each other.

I was starting to hate Jim Pepperman, with his perfect acne-free skin and his stupid hair. Why did he have to appear just as things were getting better with Ruby? I looked at my watch, and it was still early. I made another quick trip to the toilet, stepping over Jim. There was barely enough room for me to put my foot down in the space between him and Ruby. He had definitely moved during the night – or, worse still, Ruby had moved closer to Jim.

I walked down to the toilets where both available cubicles were occupied. I didn't trust my bowels enough to wait, so had to duck into the women's toilet, which, luckily, was now unoccupied. The smell I left behind was animalistic again. I would have to sort my stomach out when I got home. As I was coming out of the toilet, a pretty Danish girl was waiting to enter. She gave me a filthy look, as if to say, *What are you doing in the ladies' toilet?* and *What was that terrible smell?* – and then proceeded to hold her nose in an exaggerated manner as she entered. All very embarrassing.

I decided to venture out for a walk around Athens for a bit, but even at this early hour, the heat was exhausting, and I was feeling a bit sick. I returned to the hotel to find both Jim and Ruby were awake, and she was laughing at something he had said.

"Hi, Will. Where have you been? We were worried when we woke up to find you gone."

"Oh, I just went for a quick walk, but it was too hot."

"Yeah, it was pretty hot last night."

Was it my rampant imagination again, or did Jim wink at Ruby as he said that?

"OK, shall we grab some breakfast and head back to the Acropolis?" said Jim.

When did he start making all the decisions?

We weren't staying another night at Hotel Joy as we were catching a ferry tonight from Patras. We were able, though, for a small fee, to leave our rucksacks for the day in a safe room, just off to the side of the hotel reception. The three of us set off for the Acropolis. It was so hot, probably the hottest day of the trip so far, and I could feel my face burning. Jim passed me some sun cream. He was good for some stuff, I suppose. We passed a pharmacy, and I told Ruby and Jim I wanted to pop in and buy some more stuff for my stomach. I was surprised when Ruby said they would go on, and to meet them at the Acropolis. There was nobody in the pharmacy except a Turkish lady behind the counter. Luckily, she had a grasp of English as I stuttered through my predicament and showed her the box of tablets I had been taking.

"No, no – you need antibiotics, you must have antibiotics, you have stomach disease."

"Oh," I replied anxiously. "Can I buy some?"

"No buy antibiotics. You need medical team."

I think she meant *doctor*, as opposed to a whole medical team.

"I'm not able to see a doctor – we are leaving tonight."

"You must see medical team. First, I give strong tablets. They will – how you say? – put a cork in it."

"OK, thank you. I'll go to the doctor when I get home."

The pharmacist disappeared into a room behind and returned a few minutes later, holding a box of tablets. She also was carrying a small glass of water.

"Take now, please." She passed me two brown tablets, which I gratefully swallowed. "Take two in morning and two at night. With food. Will stop the shit."

"Oh, OK, thank you." I could feel myself blushing. I quickly paid for the tablets and left the shop. Hopefully, the tablets would start to work their magic and would "stop the shit" – not only from my bottom, but what was coming from Jim Pepperman's mouth too.

# Chapter 43

## Alone in Athens

You would have thought it would be easy to find the Acropolis and the Parthenon, given the size of the hill and the ancient ruins, but I must have been walking for about thirty minutes until I spotted a sign saying it was another fifteen minutes away. In the distance, I could see a couple holding hands. They looked a bit like Ruby and Jim, but I quickly dismissed the thought as the couple disappeared around a corner. When I finally climbed the hill and reached the Parthenon, I was disappointed to find a lot of the structure was covered in scaffolding. It was quite cheap to get in, and you could get student discount. Although, technically, I was no longer a student – but my student card had not yet expired and was still good for price reductions. I looked around for Ruby and Jim, but there was no sign of them. I thought it was a bit selfish of them to leave me at the pharmacy. What if I couldn't find them? I would have to try and get to Corfu by myself, but that would leave Jim alone with Ruby, and who knew what would happen then?

I started to feel a bit panicky as I had never travelled by myself, and, to be honest, so far I had relied on the others on the trip to navigate around. I wished I'd paid more attention to all that planning with the *Thomas Cook Timetable* . Come to think about it, I didn't even have my own copy, so what was I going to do? My heart was starting to race. It felt like when you turned over an exam paper and couldn't understand any of the questions. *Keep calm, Will. Keep calm.* I had to tell myself this over and over again. To be honest, it wasn't much fun, walking around tourist sites by yourself, and the relentless sun wasn't helping. I needed to find some shade and try and calm down a little. I hoped I could find me way back to Hotel Joy. I started to feel homesick, and, at that moment, the holiday had lost its appeal. It's funny how, in the space of a few days, things had changed so badly. I blamed it all on Jim Pepperman – but, if Ruby really liked me, it wouldn't have mattered if Jim Pepperman or anybody tagged along. I would never have left Ruby, though, if it had been her in the pharmacy looking to buy diarrhoea tablets. I found a shaded place to rest, and listened to an English tour guide talking to a group of Japanese tourists. They were looking hot and bored.

"Two fifths of the height of each pillar of the Acropolis is convex in shape," droned the English tour guide. With comments like that, I was glad I hadn't paid for an escorted tour. If I were on that tour I would have been tempted to put my hand up to ask what fraction of each pillar of the Acropolis wasn't convex in shape? What even is a convex shape? I was fed up now and tried once more to find Ruby and Jim, but there was still no sign. I knew they would have to go back to the hotel to pick up their rucksacks, so decided it would be better to wait there. If I could find the hotel again, that is. I walked down the hill and soon was among the busy streets of Athens. It was more by luck than judgement that I managed to find the pharmacy where I'd got the brown pills, and from there I could find my way to the hotel. I went to get my rucksack; if I collected my bag, I could at least see if Jim and Ruby's rucksacks were still there. They *were* still there, and I felt a bit happier. I went to put down my rucksack again but was told I had to collect my bag or pay again to leave it. I reluctantly chose the former option and left the hotel and sat on the wall opposite to wait for Ruby and Jim. I was starting to get hungry, as I realised we hadn't got to have any breakfast this morning. There was a cafe a bit further down the road, so I went into there and ordered myself a spaghetti bolognese and a Coke. The café had air conditioning, and it was lovely to sit and not sweat for a change. When the food came it was lukewarm, as was the Coke, as there was no ice on offer. I didn't have the confidence to complain so ate as much as I could stomach and returned to Hotel Joy to wait for Ruby and Jim. Finally, after about two hours, I could see the pair of them walking towards the hotel.

"Will, finally! We've been looking everywhere for you. Where have you been?" enquired a red-faced Ruby.

"I could say the same thing about you two. Thanks for waiting, by the way.'"

I was feeling angry at the pair of them, mainly Pepperman and that stupid smug face of his.

"Yeah, we're sorry, Will," he began. "We should have waited for you, but no harm done – we're all here now."

I would have loved to have punched him to the ground at that moment.

"Yeah, I'm sorry, Will." Ruby came over and hugged me, and kissed me on the cheek.

I could feel myself blushing again, and tried to hide my embarrassment. It was hard to stay angry with Ruby after she had done that.

"No worries. It was too hot, anyway, to stay too long up there. Plus, it was a shame a lot of it was covered in scaffolding."

"I know – what was that about?" interjected Jim. "Look, I feel bad you spent most of the morning by yourself. I'll tell you what: after we collect our bags, why don't you and Ruby go for a coffee, and I'll go and buy the ferry tickets for tonight? We passed a place on the way back down."

"Oh, OK. Thanks, Jim," I mumbled. Hopefully, he would get lost – or, better still, die of heatstroke. On second thoughts, the latter option was a bit harsh ...

About half an hour later Ruby and I were back in the same cafe where I had eaten the lukewarm spaghetti. We both ordered coffees and sat at a small table outside. I would have preferred to sit inside with the air conditioning. Since Jim had joined us, we hadn't spent any time together, and now the opportunity had arisen, it felt awkward between us, when it hadn't been before. I was struggling to think of anything to say, even though I felt I had a lot to say. Luckily for me Ruby, started a conversation.

"So, Corfu tomorrow. Are you looking forward to it?"

"Yes, it'll be good to see Pete and Mothball again and nice to go swimming in the sea again. What do you think of Jim, now you've spent more time with him?"

Ruby hesitated slightly.

"He's nice – very confident, mind you. He can be a bit overbearing at times."

"Yeah, he was like that at school. All the girls loved him. He broke a few hearts in his time."

"Yeah, I suppose he is good-looking, if you like that sort of thing."

I was hoping Ruby didn't like that sort of thing, not really knowing what that sort of thing was. I don't think I had ever had that sort of thing.

I wanted to bring the conversation back to when it was just the two of us and Ruby had said she liked me. I wouldn't have many more opportunities, what with

Pepperman hanging around like a bad smell.

"I think Jim likes me," said Ruby.

My heart rate started to increase.

"No surprise there. He always had an eye for a pretty face. Do you like him?" I nervously asked. If she said yes, I might as well jump on the next train home.

"Oh, I don't know. He is overbearing, as I said, but he's funny and handsome. But I thought you and I were getting closer, and then there's Tom. I'm so confused. Will."

So I was still in the mix. Not a good mix, with Pepperman and Bellows, but I was still in with a chance. I think. Albeit an outside bet.

Pepperman was walking towards us, waving three tickets in the air.

"Three tickets on the 7.30 ferry tonight, from Patras to Brindisi."

We had to get the train from Athens to Patras, for the ferry to Brindisi, and I think we had to get another ferry from Brindisi to Corfu. Brindisi was in Italy, so I started to count the countries we had been to so far on this trip. France, Germany, Austria, Yugoslavia, Greece, Turkey, and now Italy – so, seven so far. Not bad for a few weeks. If things didn't work out with Ruby, at least I could bore people with stories about all the countries I had visited.

The thing with Ruby was starting to get me down. I felt like I was in a horse race, unexpectedly in the lead, coming towards the finishing post, but when I looked over my shoulder I could see two big horses rapidly making ground, and my horse was tiring. I mean, what did I expect to happen? That Ruby would miraculously choose me over Tom, and now Jim, and agree to be my girlfriend? We would break away from everyone and enjoy the last few days travelling across Europe, very much in love? Then we would return to the UK, and I would move to Birmingham into a small flat with Ruby? I would find a job and knuckle down for a few years? We would both get promotion and move from the flat into a small house? Ruby then becomes pregnant, even though it wasn't planned? We had a new kitten to contend with too? Ruby gives birth to a little girl, and we settle down as a small unit: me, Ruby and baby Nina and our cat, Crunchie? And we would live happily ever after? The end.

I know that the formula for a relationship is the right person at the right time. Ruby, to me, was the right person, but was it the right time? I mean, realistically, once this holiday was over, I would have to move back home for a while and try and find a job. I would try to keep in touch with Ruby, but these things eventually had a way of fizzling out. Eventually, Ruby would meet somebody else, and I would be a distant memory of just somebody she had gone travelling with in the past. It was no good me trying to get Ruby alone all the time and keep telling her I like her. She knew I liked her. She must have been sick of me telling her I like her. I decided there and then to change my approach. I would try and be more fun, make her laugh, keep things light. Make her see what I was really like. Give her the 'full Will treatment'. Put all my cards on the table again, although I had already done that, and hope my hand was strong enough to win. I didn't want to be just a memory of a boy she once went travelling with. I wanted to be the boy she spends the rest of her life with. I wanted to be the right person at the right time.

"Thanks, Jim, for getting those," began Ruby. "We had better set off for the station."

# Chapter 44

## Ferry to Brindisi

It was a short walk to the station, and soon the three of us were on the train to Patras. The train was really busy, and for the first hour we had to stand. We did manage to get a seat for the last two hours of the trip, and we wearily got off the train and headed for the ferry terminal. It would be a long ferry crossing to Brindisi – about sixteen hours – and the plan was to find a quiet place on the ferry and sleep. I took some more of the brown stomach pills and was relieved my stomach had calmed down. Nobody had expected a rough crossing, though. After about an hour the ferry seemed to be lurching from side to side and up and down. Ruby was feeling sick, as was I. Jim seemed to be fine, though, and said he had found his sea legs after a summer sailing in the south of France. Trust him: Mr Perfect. Ruby was now vomiting over the side of the ferry, and I too had succumbed to sickness, but was vomiting more discreetly into a toilet bowl in the men's toilet. It seemed like about half of the passengers on the boat were being sick. It was like something out of a horror film. There was vomit all over the deck, and one of the workers – obviously used to this sort of thing – was hosing the vomit into the sea.

After a few hours the sea got a bit calmer, and we were able to lie down on the floor of the second deck and sleep. When we woke a few hours later we were all covered in a thick film of black soot, which appeared to be coming from one of the funnels from the front of the ferry. Jim explained it was due to poor quality of fuel that they used to power the ferry and something to do with incomplete combustion. *Oh, shut up, Jim. Do you have to know everything?* But we were covered in soot, and my red rucksack now had a dirty black covering.

It was a miserable crossing, and I was glad to see dry land. Because of the seasickness, Ruby and I had not eaten anything, though Jim had been tucking into a chicken sandwich on the ferry, the smell of which had made me feel worse. After cleaning ourselves up in the toilets at the ferry terminal, we discovered we had a few hours to kill before the next ferry to Corfu, which, to my dismay, meant about twelve hours more of sea travel. I was hoping it would be a smooth crossing – though it is strange that, with seasickness, you recover really quickly once you get off the boat, so I was now starving.

# Chapter 45

## History Speak

We decided to get something to eat and set off to explore Brindisi. We only had a few hours so would not be able to go too far, so we ended up at a small taverna, where I once again ordered spaghetti bolognese. Ruby was still feeling a bit queasy, so she shared a Margherita pizza with Jim. I wanted to share a pizza with Ruby, but, to be fair, I preferred pasta. Maybe we could share a plate of spaghetti at one stage, and we would both suck on a piece of spaghetti like in that film 'Lady and the Tramp', where two dogs eat from the same strand of spaghetti, pulling them closer together and ending in a kiss. *Yeah, Will. As if that is likely to happen.*

"So how are you both enjoying interrailing?" asked Jim, waking me up from my spaghetti-induced daydream.

"I'm really enjoying it, though it's hard work with all the travelling and having to carry your rucksack everywhere. But it's worth it for the experience," replied Ruby.

"Yeah, it is hard work, as Ruby said, but it's a great way to see a lot of Europe. To be fair, we're lucky to be able to do it."

"True," said Jim, and the three of us sat in silence for a while. It was true, though: we were so lucky to be able to be doing this trip. A few weeks ago I hadn't even thought about travelling anywhere and now I was sitting in a small taverna in Brindisi with the girl of my dreams and some annoying bloke I wasn't even friendly with in school.

"So it's off to the big smoke after this, is it, Jim?" I asked.

"The what?" he replied.

"The big smoke. London."

"Oh, yeah. I've never heard somebody describe London as the big smoke. What's that about?"

I loved history in school, and wished I'd pursed it further instead of going down the science route. Time to impress Ruby and Jim.

"I think it comes from all the smoke that used to be produced in London, as most people used coal fires then to heat their homes. As a result, London started to be known as the big smoke. I think it dates back to the nineteenth century. I remember being fascinated at school when they told us about the Great Smog of London in 1952."

"What was that, Will?" asked Ruby.

"Well, for five days in December 1952, London was engulfed in a thick smog. It was a combination of fog and industrial pollutants, not to mention all the smoke coming from the coal fires in the homes, making it worse."

Jim was pretending to yawn, and did one of those coughs when you try to mask a word.

"Boring," coughed Jim again.

"Don't listen to him, Will. I find it fascinating. Carry on, Will." Ruby to the rescue.

"You can't really call it boring, Jim – thousands of people died as the result of the smog. People were literally struggling to breathe. It must have been horrendous. It led to the Clean Air Act of 1956, which was a turning point in public health and improvements in air quality."

To be honest, I wasn't even sure why I was going on about the smog of 1952, but Ruby seemed to be enjoying my monologue, even if Jim wasn't.

In fact, Ruby seemed to be looking at me with a renewed interest. Note to self: try to include more historical dialogue in conversation with Ruby. Will Evans: 1; Jim Pepperman: 0.

"Anway, back to me, before we get another history lesson from Professor Boring here."

I think I had Jim rattled.

"Yes, I'm starting a job in London in a few weeks' time," continued Jim. "I'm working for a big American bank in the city as an intern."

This time I coughed the word *boring*, and Ruby laughed.

"Yeah, you're probably right – it will be boring, but apparently you make shit loads of money too."

"Don't most people drop out, though? Something called burnout?" asked Ruby.

"Well, yeah, I suppose they do. I'll probably only do it for a few years. What's that expression – 'make hay while the sun shines'?"

I spotted another opportunity to jump in with some historical facts.

"Did you know the expression 'make hay while the sun shines' dates back to medieval times, when English farmers recognised the importance of haymaking while the weather was good, as rain could easily ruin the harvest?"

"Oh, shut up, Professor! You *are* boring us now," said Jim, and both he and Ruby laughed, until Jim started to choke on his pizza and Ruby had to slap him on the back. I suppose I may have been overplaying my historical facts just a tad.

# Chapter 46

## Ferry to Corfu

We had a quick walk around the historic port of Brindisi, and then it was time to catch the ferry to Corfu. Corfu must be popular, as there was a large number of backpackers getting onto the ferry. I couldn't believe we faced another overnight ferry, and were not due to get into Corfu until about eight in the morning. We found a space on the floor, set up a makeshift camp with our rucksacks and settled in for the night. We had chosen our spot well, as it was quite close to the toilets and not far from the restaurant, though we probably wouldn't eat there as it was expensive, and the queue was really long. I don't know why I was feeling so tired. I was sleeping OK, albeit in fits and starts, but tonight I was exhausted. I didn't realise how tired I was until I was woken up by Ruby the following morning.

"Wake up, Will! You've slept right through! We're only thirty minutes away from Corfu. You've been asleep for ten hours."

"Oops, sorry – I think it's these tablets I'm taking. They must be making me sleepy. Did you get any sleep?"

"I didn't sleep much – it was a really rough crossing. I was a bit seasick. I've had enough of ferries this trip. You were lucky to have slept through it."

I was feeling a little bit groggy, even though I had slept through the night. I started to recall another intense dream. I had been climbing a mountain and nearing the top. For some reason, I was holding my sleeping bag in one hand, and it was making the climb more difficult, but I persevered with it, as I planned to put it in my rucksack once I reached the summit. The last little climb to the summit was a struggle, but soon I had reached the top and was staggered at the beauty of the view from the summit. Amid an abundance of purple moss, black rocks resembled Pontefract cakes, the small coin-shaped liquorice sweets I had eaten as a boy. They were arranged in a symmetrical pile, and the black rocks and purple moss were encased in the greenest grass I had ever seen. I needed a psychoanalyst to unpick these dreams. I reasoned maybe the climb to the top of the mountain was representative of my pursuit of Ruby. Who knew? What I *did* know was that Jim was flirting with Ruby again: he was playfully holding her rucksack down as she attempted to put it over her shoulders, and she seemed to be enjoying it.

I was starting to feel overwhelmed and despondent with this Ruby and Jim business, and decided there and then that I was done with the whole thing with Ruby. I saw it as a game of poker. My hand was there on the table. After all, I had made my feelings known – and it was now up to Ruby to respond. I was done, finished, end of. Though Tom and Jim were yet to play their hands. I would just see out the last few days of the holiday and then return to my life in Cardiff and see what opportunities came my way. All that was left for me was to try and enjoy the rest of the trip and get as much out of it as I could.

# Chapter 47

## Corfu Reunion

The three of us walked off the ferry into the Kerkyra port of Corfu. Almost immediately, we saw a number of minibuses lined up by the harbour, ready to provide transport to the campsites for backpackers. They were waiting there, hoping for the business from the many backpackers now leaving the ferry. We looked and soon found the Camping Vatos transport, which turned out to be a bright orange VW camper van, driven by a beautiful Greek girl with long brown hair. She was wearing cut-off denim shorts, like the ones Beth was wearing in Paris, revealing long brown legs – which seemed to go on for miles – and a T-shirt with 'Smile, you're on holiday' written on it. The three of us got on the camper van, which was pretty full already and within ten minutes or so we had set off for the campsite. After about thirty minutes of a bumpy, sweaty ride we pulled up in front of the reception of camping Vatos and booked in for a few nights. We then set off to try and find Pete and Mothball's tent. We had been told to look out for a T-shirt, on a makeshift washing line, with the Canadian rock group Rush on it. We had been walking for about ten minutes or so, and there was no sign of the T-shirt on any of the washing lines dotted among the pine trees. Eventually, we came to the toilet block and the three of us made use of the facilities. As I came out of the toilet block, I almost bumped into somebody coming in, and, to my great surprise, it was Tigsy.

"Tigsy! What are you doing here? I thought you'd gone home?"

"Alright, Will – finally made it, then?"

"That was always the plan. But why are you here?"

"Sorry, Will – I'm desperate for a shit here. Go and set up camp, and I'll explain everything in a minute. We're over to your right, by that big Polish flag."

About ten minutes later, the original group of travellers, who had set off a few weeks ago, reunited among the pine trees. I introduced everyone to Jim, and it was only then that I noticed another person sitting by Tigsy's tent.

"Oh, yeah," said Tigsy. "I forgot – we've got another guest staying with us, Mr Tom Bellows."

Tom Bellows. *Tom Bellows!* Why was he here? Well, it was pretty obvious why he was here: he was here to get Ruby back. I looked at Ruby for her reaction and was annoyed to see her face break out into an enormous smile when she saw that Tom was here in Corfu.

"Who's he?" Jim whispered in my ear.

"Oh, that's Tom, Tom Bellows. The boy who broke Ruby's heart."

Ruby walked over to Tom and gave him a big hug. Gwen was hugging Ruby too.

"Nice to see you, Ruby. I need some more female company – there's too much testosterone here," said Gwen.

Everyone was hugging each other, and we quickly set up camp. Pete explained it had been so hot that everyone had taken to sleeping outside, and they just used their tents to store their stuff. It was decided that a trip to the beach was on the cards. It was about a twenty-minute walk to the beach and the path was quite narrow, so only two people could walk side by side.

To my dismay, Ruby was walking alongside Tom, and

the two of them were talking animatedly at the front of the group.

I was with Tigsy, and we were at the back of everyone. We dropped slightly off the pace, so we were out of earshot of everyone else.

"So I thought you were going home, Tigsy?" I asked again.

"Well, we were, initially when we left you. Then we decided there was no point in rushing back, so we went straight to Corfu and have been here ever since. To be honest, it's been nice, not rushing from place to place, and sleeping under the stars."

"But I thought you and Gwen were splitting up?"

Tigsy looked a bit sheepish.

"Turns out we were, but now we're not. It's a long story, but we're getting on much better now, and I started to remember why I first liked her in the first place. But enough about me – what happened with you and Ruby?"

This time it was my turn to be a bit sheepish.

"Nothing much. I thought I was wearing her down with my charm, and we had a few moments when I thought she was starting to like me …"

"And?"

"And nothing. It was all simmering to the boil nicely, and then we bumped into an old school friend of mine, Jim, and he got in the way – and I think *he* likes Ruby too, and now Tom Bellows is here. Why is Tom Bellows here, anyway? And how did he even find us?"

"You know the answer to that one, Will. I think he phoned Ruby's dad, who told him we were at a campsite in Corfu, beginning with a 'V'. He's been wandering around all the campsites in Corfu beginning with a 'V'. There are more than you'd expect. Anyway, eventually he found us. It was really funny – he got really drunk on the first night, declaring his love for Ruby in a drunken rant. He was on the Greek wine, retsina, and then he got off with some Dutch girl. We've been sworn to secrecy not to mention that bit to Ruby, so don't say I told you."

We carried on walking in silence for a while, until a gap in the pine trees led to a sandy beach and the sea.

It was a beautiful beach, and I should have been enjoying myself, but my mind was reeling with everything Tigsy had said.

Ruby was looking stunning in her red bikini again, and she and Tom were running to the sea, where they were playfully splashing each other with water. Jim was looking a bit lost, and I thought of trying to ingratiate him with the others, but he was a big boy and would have to look after himself. And besides, I had bigger things to worry about.

"Come on, Will!" shouted Pete. "Let's get that skinny body into the water."

"You coming, Tigsy?" I shouted.

"Oh, no, thanks. The waves are pretty fierce, and I don't like water enveloping my body."

"You don't like the water enveloping your body? What are you on about, Tigsy?" I was laughing as I said it.

"It's the waves. I'm OK in a swimming pool – I just don't like swimming in the sea. I'm going to stay here. I can mind the stuff for you all."

Pete and I headed for the sea. In the distance, I could see Tom still splashing water over Ruby. She was laughing and splashing water back. They looked like a couple in love. *Get a room, you two.*

"Bet that makes you sick. I told you that you have no

chance with Ruby," began Pete. "I mean, you had your chance and didn't take it."

"Well, at least I tried, unlike you and Mothball. I bet you haven't even talked to any girls."

"Well, surprisingly, that's where you're wrong. We've hooked up with a couple of Dutch girls."

"As if."

"I'll introduce you tonight – there's a disco later on this evening, on the campsite. The Dutch girls are coming. They've gone out today, to explore the island on mopeds."

"Will Tom's Dutch friend be there too?"

"How did you know about that? Tigsy, I suppose?"

"Yeah, he did mention it."

"Well, don't say anything. Anyway, Betje is with Mothball now. After that first night, Tom wasn't interested. He said he was really drunk, and it was all one big, fat mistake."

"And Betje didn't mind that it was only a one-night thing?"

"No, Betje is a cool, chilled Dutch girl. She introduced me to her friend, Adrie. We've got quite close. Though I think they go home in a few days."

"You seem to have been quite productive in Corfu, then?"

"We have, to be fair – it's been brilliant. You should have some fun while you're here. Stop moping over Ruby – it's obvious she only has eyes for Tom."

He was right. It was plain for anybody to see. They were walking back to the beach. I could see that their beach towels were overlapping. Could they be any closer? Why did their beach towels have to overlap? Stupid, overlapping beach towels. There was plenty of room on the beach. There was no need for those two towels to be touching.

Tom was telling Ruby about his dad. They had gone back into the sea.

"It's strange, Ruby, but when my dad told me about the tests he was having, I got really emotional, and the only person I wanted to talk to was you. I phoned your dad, which was awkward, but I managed to find out where you were going and got a flight over."

"It is nice to see you, Tom."

"The thing is, Ruby, I think I made a mistake when I finished with you. I've been doing a lot of thinking lately, and a lot of growing up, and I've realised I made a big mistake the way I treated you."

"You've said mistake twice now, Tom."

"Oh, yeah, sorry. Mistake, mistake, mistake. I've said it five times now."

"The thing is, Tom, you really hurt me when we broke up. It's taken me a long time to get over you. That's why this trip was important to me. It was a chance to get my life back, and, to be honest, I've started to. Will has been really nice, and I've enjoyed his company the last few days. He told me he likes me too."

"What, Will? You don't like him, surely – that lanky string of piss?"

Ruby didn't want to, but laughed at the description.

"I've enjoyed his company – and his friend Jim's, too."

"Well, yes, it's obvious why you like *him*, good-looking bastard, but Will … I mean, come on."

"Let's leave it for now, Tom. Let's just enjoy the sun and the sea. I do like Will, though, Tom – he's funny and has been good company this holiday. You should get to know him."

# Chapter 48

## Retsina

We all stayed on the beach for a few hours before we set off back to the campsite. A few hours later, we had all showered and headed off to the restaurant on the campsite, where the disco was being held later.

We all sat around a long table with those picnic-style benches, and after a while the Dutch girls that Pete had been telling us about arrived: Betje, Adrie, Sophie and Olivia. To be fair, they were all gorgeous, especially Betje. I could see why Tom fell for her charms. I found myself sitting next to Olivia. Jim was sitting next to Sophie, and quite quickly you could tell there was a spark between them. Ruby was with Tom. I had barely spoken to her since we got to Corfu, and she was so far down the other end of the table it was unlikely I would get much chance to speak to her tonight. Everyone was drinking the retsina again, and it was already going straight to my head. I was really drunk. I needed some food to soak up the alcohol. I didn't know if it was the sun, the tablets I'd been taking for my stomach or just the retsina. What I did know was that I was really pissed. Down at the other end of the table I could see Tom and Ruby having a very intense conversation. Jim was kissing Sophie. That didn't take him long. I turned my attention to Olivia. She was eating the Greek dish, souvlaki – pieces of pork and vegetables grilled on a skewer. Time for the old Will charm. I put on an exaggerated Cardiff accent, hoping it would make Olivia laugh.

"I'm not going to lie to you that *souvlaaaaaki* looks well nice." I purposely lengthened the word 'souvlaki' in my best 'Ceeeehdiff' accent.

Olivia looked at me blankly.

"Are you trying to speak Dutch?"

"No. I'm just doing a Cardiff accent. I'm from Cardiff."

"Oh, that is nice. I've been to London, but I am yet to find Wales."

"Oh, it's just down the M4 from London." I laughed at my own joke.

Olivia looked at me blankly again.

"Have you been to the Netherlands, Will?"

"No, I haven't, though I'm hoping to go to Amsterdam on the way back. Thought I would find myself a nice girl in the red-light district."

I was hoping Olivia would laugh, at what was obviously a joke, but she didn't. She looked quite shocked. She had taken what I'd said literally. My two attempts at humour had failed to hit the back of the net, to use a footballing metaphor. I had almost kicked the ball off the pitch.

"There is more to Amsterdam than the red-light district. It is a shame that is where you want to go."

"I was only joking. I mean, I don't *just* want to see that, obviously. I mean I want to see the, eh … " *Come on, Will, think of something else you would want to see in Amsterdam.* I remembered the song and quickly said, "The tulips. Yes, the tulips. I would like to see the tulips."

I was so drunk I started to sing 'Tulips from Amsterdam'. I never sang, normally. My voice was terrible, but I was drunk and thought it would lighten the mood.

The table had suddenly gone quiet as I started to sing,

and everyone was watching and listening to me sing. I croaked about spring returning and the tulips blooming in Amsterdam.

"Ha ha, looks like the pub singer is in the house. Don't give up your day job, Will!" shouted Tom, from the top of the table. Everyone started to laugh. I was angry now. Angry at the situation, and angry that Tom had made a joke at my expense, in front of Ruby.

"Yeah, and you don't give up *your* day job, Bellows – seducing Dutch girls."

I was slurring badly. I couldn't believe I'd said that out loud. Maybe I was so incoherent that nobody had understood what I'd said, but one look at Tigsy – who was shaking his head – confirmed my fears, that everyone had heard and understood what I'd said. I quickly got up from the table and went to the toilet. It wasn't turning into a good night. Tigsy followed me into the toilets and stood behind me as I urinated. Some urine had gone down my leg, splashback from the urinal wall. Maybe cream trousers weren't a good idea. But I think that was the least of my problems.

"I can't believe you said that, Will. I thought I told you not to say anything. I wish I hadn't told you that now."

"I'm sorry, Tigsy. I think it's the retsina. Do you think Ruby heard?"

"Yeah, I think she did. They both got up from the table and were talking quite heatedly."

"Oh, well, he shouldn't have done it in the first place, if he came here to try and get back with Ruby."

"Well, if I were you, I'd keep a low profile for a while, and keep out of Tom's way."

I had thought about going back to try and sleep it off,

but as I walked back to the table I noticed virtually everyone was now on the dance floor. Everyone was in a big circle with their arms on the shoulder of the person next to them. I'd heard the song before: it was 'Zorba the Greek'. The music starts slowly, with the circle of people slowly rotating, with leg-kicking and much laughter. The music was infectious. I pushed my way into the circle of people. I could see Mothball with his Dutch friend, Betje, opposite me. Everyone started to move faster as the tempo of the music increased. I felt somebody behind me trying to push in to enter the circle too, and moved aside to let them in. It was Tom. Great, he was the last person I wanted to see. The tempo increased again, and the circle moved faster and faster. As the song came to its climax, I felt a sharp shove in my back. I fell forward into the centre of the circle of dancers and tried to stay upright. I was too drunk, though, and staggered forward as the circle of revellers broke in front of me. I lost my footing and careered forward, banging my head into the wooden bench at the side of the dance floor. I had hurt myself, not just my pride, and I could see that I was bleeding. The music had stopped. I knew that it was Tom who had pushed me, but I had no proof, and, to be fair, he was looking concerned, as was Mothball, who had come over to see if I was OK. There was no sign of Ruby. Mothball helped me up to my feet. He was struggling not to laugh but could see that I had hurt myself.

"I'm glad you think it's funny, Mothball," I slurred.

"Oh, lighten up, Will – it's only a small cut. Though probably best if you call it a night, Will. You've caused enough damage tonight, and not just to your head."

"Don't worry, I'm going."

# Chapter 49

## Sore Head

I staggered back to our part of the campsite, grabbed my rucksack and sleeping bag, and found a secluded spot by a large pine tree. I needed to get away from everyone.

Feeling sorry for myself, I got into the sleeping bag and pulled it right over my head, and within a few minutes I was asleep and having yet another strange dream. This time I was on a merry-go-round, the ones that you used to see at the local park, that you pushed yourself. I was the only one on the merry-go-round and, for some reason, I was naked. Why was I always naked in these dreams? I was holding the glass snails I'd given to Ruby in one hand, and so could only hold on with one hand. Tom Bellows and my dad were pushing the merry-go-round faster and faster, and I was telling them to stop. They wouldn't listen, though, and the more I protested the faster they pushed. Eventually, I released my hand, and the next minute I was flying through the air, still desperately holding onto the snails, though now I was no longer naked. I was wearing the same T-shirt that the girl who had picked us up at the ferry terminal in the camper van had on, with 'Smile, you're on holiday' on it. I landed with a bump, and the snails had broken in my hand. My hand was a mixture of blood and glass. I tried to smile, but every time I tried to, Tom Bellows poured retsina into my mouth, laughing all the time.

I woke up sweating. My head was thumping, and there was blood all over my sleeping bag. I had only been asleep for about fifteen minutes, and my mind was racing with not just the dream but the events of the night. I needed to sleep, and started thinking of Smiths lyrics again to help – one of my favourite Smiths songs, 'Please, Please, Let Me Get What I Want'.

I didn't think I would get what I wanted this time, or any other time, but reciting the lyrics helped me fall asleep, as when I opened my eyes again it was light. I headed over the toilet block and tried to go to toilet as my stomach was hurting, but I was unable to go. Those brown tablets were doing their job too well. Maybe I should just go home – the thought of watching Ruby and Tom getting closer wasn't something I wanted to witness. Maybe it was time to cut my losses and head back to the UK. After all, I had given it my best shot and had failed in my endeavours to win Ruby. I wandered back to join the others. Only Gwen seemed to be awake.

"Oh, hi, Will. Where did you get to last night?"

"Oh, I passed out by some pine tree. I think I've had enough Greek wine to last me a lifetime."

"It was a fun night. Though, to be honest, I wouldn't mind going somewhere else now. Every day is morphing into one. It feels like I've done Corfu now."

"You've changed your tune. A few days ago, you just wanted to go home."

"I know, but me and Tigsy seemed to have got over our rough patch, and I'm even contemplating getting back on the trains again. I think my batteries have been recharged."

"What's happened to Ruby? Is she annoyed at me?"

"No, not really, Will. I think she's more annoyed at Tom. Though you probably shouldn't have said what you said. He has left, though – his flight back is this afternoon, so Ruby went to the airport with him."

"What, she's going home too?" My heart was racing.

"No, she's just seeing him off. She's left all her stuff here."

I breathed a sigh of relief. For some reason, I felt like crying, I don't know why. Maybe things were getting to me. Gwen was looking at me, with an expression of concern on her face.

"Are you OK, Will?"

"What do you mean?" I replied.

"I mean, after last night. You made a bit of a fool of yourself with that comment, and then falling over into the bench."

"I didn't fall, I was pushed – but yeah, I'm fine. My head is a bit sore, though."

"Do you fancy grabbing a coffee at the restaurant? Tigsy won't be awake for a few hours. When I left him last night, he and Pete had started on the ouzo."

"They'll be suffering when they wake up. Oh, yeah, thanks, Gwen. That would be nice. A coffee would go down well."

A few minutes later I was sitting again at the wooden benches, nurturing a cappuccino. It tasted like I was feeling: bitter.

"I think you should forget about Ruby now, Will," Gwen began.

I could feel my face redden.

"I have. I mean, I'm not stupid. You can see she still has feelings for Tom."

"That's good, then, Will. I'm glad you've started to see it. You've got a lot going for you, Will. Do you know, when I first met you, I thought you were a bit blah."

"Blah – what do you mean by that?"

"Oh, I don't know – I thought there wasn't much to

**185**

you. What's the expression, 'all fur coat but no knickers'? But Tigsy speaks highly of you, and I've realised there is more to you, Will. You've got layers. And I like that."

"Thanks, Gwen. To be honest, I thought you were a bit of a moaner."

"Tigsy been going on about our sex life again?"

I laughed.

"You were the one who mentioned fur coats and no knickers. No, it's just you were moaning a lot at the beginning of the trip, but I think I've misjudged you too. You've got layers as well, and talking to you has cheered me up this morning – and I needed cheering up."

"I suppose I was a bit moany at times – but, in my defence, it is tough on the trains, and I've had a bad stomach at times."

"Tell me about it. Well, here's to a couple of onions, with lots of layers," I said, and we clinked our coffee cups together in the early morning sun.

It was nice sitting with Gwen in the Greek sun, and we must have been talking a while because when we got back everyone was up. We all decided another beach day was on the cards as it was so hot and a dip in the sea was beckoning. And, to be honest, there wasn't much else to do. The day passed effortlessly, and my skin, which had previously been an angry red, was turning brown. At about 4 p.m. we all decided we'd had too much sun and returned to the campsite. I was pleased to see that Ruby was back, but she appeared to be packing up her stuff. She didn't acknowledge me.

"Not leaving us Ruby, are you?" said Gwen, a look of concern on her face.

"Well, I would like to do a bit more travelling. I was

hoping I would have some company. Any takers?"

Ruby appeared to be looking directly at me as she asked the question.

"Oh, eh, yeah – I would like to see a few more countries," I muttered, somewhat incoherently.

"Thought you would," said Pete, winking at me as he said it.

# Chapter 50

## Seasick and Lovesick

Pete and Mothball wanted to stay in Corfu, but, surprisingly, Gwen and Tigsy wanted to come with Ruby and me. That just left Jim. I wasn't really bothered what happened to Jim but was a bit relieved when he said he wanted to stay in Corfu with Pete and Mothball. He seemed to be quite smitten with his new Dutch friend. There was a ferry leaving tonight to Brindisi, and Ruby said the last bus to the ferry terminal was leaving just outside the campsite in an hour. We said our goodbyes and about an hour and a half later I was sitting next to Ruby on the bus to the Corfu ferry terminal.

"I'm sorry if I upset you last night. I had too much retsina. It's powerful stuff, but I shouldn't have said that about Tom, though. It was none of my business."

"That's OK, Will. I'm glad I found out, to be truthful."

"So what's happening with you and Tom?" I asked bravely.

"It's complicated, Will. We've had a good chat this morning. He was mortified when you mentioned that Dutch girl, but he explained it was just a drunken mistake, and he was going to tell me about her."

"I bet he was."

"I believe him, Will. He's going through a hard time at the moment. His dad's got cancer. Did you know that?"

"Well, no, obviously. He doesn't really speak to me."

"He has asked me to be his girlfriend again."

"Oh, and what have you told him?"

"I think, when we get back home, we may pick up where we left off. Do you think that's a good idea, Will?"

I wanted to say, "No, it's a terrible idea. He has already broken your heart once, so what's to stop him doing it again?" I mean, it was only a few days ago that he was kissing a Dutch girl. I wanted to tell her I was in love with her. I wouldn't go kissing Dutch girls behind her back. I wanted to tell her to pick me. Pick me. Pick me, please. Let me be your boyfriend. But, of course, I didn't. I didn't say any of these things. Not now the retsina had left my system.

"Whatever makes you happy, Ruby. Whatever makes you happy."

"He was sorry, though, for pushing you over on the dance floor. He isn't like that normally. He was mortified when he saw the blood."

"It looked worse than it was. I didn't notice you coming over to check on me, though."

Maybe I shouldn't have said that, but it was true. Ruby hadn't come over to check on me. She was more interested in finding out why Tom had kissed the Dutch girl.

"Yeah, I'm sorry about that, Will. I should have checked on you – though in my defence, Mothball was already there to see if you were OK."

It seemed like a recurring theme in my life, being pushed over at discos: first Cheryl, and now Ruby not checking on me.

We sat in silence for a while, and the music playing on the bus seemed to perfectly echo my feelings at that precise moment: 'Smile' by Nat King Cole. As Nat sang one of the lines from the song, I wondered if light would ever break through fo me. Probably not this trip. Still, I knew I'd have to keep a brave face – even if my heart felt like it was splintering, as in the song – if I was going to get through the next few days.

The ferry crossing from Corfu to Brindisi was worse than on the way over. Within about an hour of setting off, I reckon over half of the ferry were vomiting, anywhere they could find a suitable place, although suitable places weren't always an option.

"We should have stayed in Corfu," said Tigsy, before he too was vomiting over the side.

"I know. I'm starting to think that too," said Gwen.

The shop on the ferry sold some seasickness pills, and we all chipped in for some and quickly took them. We found some floor space and lay down, hoping the boat would calm down soon and we could get some sleep. Ruby was in a bad way. As well as the seasickness, she had picked up a stomach bug and spent the crossing rushing back and forth to the toilets, which were taking a battering. I wasn't envious of the cleaner who would have to deal with that in the morning. Following the longest night ever, we were all relieved to see the sunrise and dry land. Again, as soon as we were off the boat everyone felt a lot better and headed for some food.

# Chapter 51

## Train to Rome

A few hours later we arrived at Brindisi's train station and were on a train headed for Rome. We had chosen a slower overnight train again, and the journey would take about eleven hours, getting into Rome at around seven in the morning. We had brought some supplies at a Brindisi supermarket, and Tigsy and I had bought a bottle of wine between us, to help us sleep. We found a carriage with only one person in it, so we settled in for the night. Ruby wasn't herself, and immediately fell asleep. Gwen was quiet too, and soon fell asleep. Tigsy opened up another bottle of wine, which was disgusting, so we called it a night. I was desperate to be lying horizontally again. I'd had enough of vertical sleeping, so I climbed up on the luggage rack and was able to stretch out fully, until a guard came into the carriage and told me to get down. This seemed to be a recurring pattern this holiday too.

Outside, it was raining, and as the train sped towards Rome I was still feeling melancholy. Again, I searched my lyric bank from songs I liked to help me match my circumstances. 'This Boy', one of my favourite songs by The Beatles, seemed a perfect fit for my current circumstances. It told of heartbreak, and a desire for a love interest to return after going off with another boy.

I needed to stop feeling sorry for myself. I mean, at the end of the day, it is just unrequited love, a story that has been playing out for generations. I should count myself lucky: I'm on a trip of a lifetime, visiting amazing countries. I should count my blessings. I remembered, once, listening to a sermon one Sunday morning, a few years ago, when my mother used to drag us along to our local Methodist church. The minister was preaching from the pulpit, the crux of which was to "count your blessings". He quoted a hymn by an American, Johnson Oatman, written in 1897, which for some reason I've always remembered.

When upon life's billows you are tempest-tossed,
When you are discouraged, thinking all is lost,
Count your many blessings every doubt will fly,
And you will be singing as the days go by.

I wondered when I, again, would be singing as the days go by. It wouldn't be 'Tulips from Amsterdam', that was for sure.

Tigsy was now asleep too, as my mind raced away, trying to remember the rest of the lyrics. I slept fitfully, on and off, until eventually we pulled into Rome's railway station. I was excited to see Rome, but we only had one day here before we took another overnight train again, to save money on accommodation.

We headed for the toilets, where we could get a good wash. Much better than trying to use the tiny basin on the train.

# Chapter 52

## To Stay with Ruby?

We were all waiting for Ruby now, and when she finally emerged from the toilets, she wasn't looking good.

"I'm sorry, but I don't feel up to walking around Rome. My stomach is well dodgy. I think I've got to stay near a toilet. I'll meet you here later – don't worry about me".

"Are you sure, Ruby? One of us could stay and keep you company," asked Gwen.

*Let it be me. Let it be me.*

"No, we've only got a few hours in Rome. Besides, I've been to Rome before. I'll be fine by myself."

Reluctantly, we agreed to Ruby's request, and, putting our rucksacks in storage again at the station, we set off to explore. We had a lot to pack in, having only a few hours, and made first for the Colosseum. Impressive on the outside, I found it a bit uninspiring on the inside and was more taken by the numerous cats wandering around the ruins. It was also quite expensive to get in, which was annoying.

"Did you know around 400,000 people were killed during the Gladiatorial games in what is the world's largest amphitheatre?" said Tigsy, reading from his guidebook.

I didn't know that, though I did remember watching that film, *Ben Hur*, one Christmas. I think that was set in Rome – maybe in the Colosseum? It was really hot in the Colosseum, and, to be honest, I was desperate to leave and find some shade. Luckily for me, Tigsy and Gwen were struggling with the heat too, and so we all set off for

Vatican City. As the smallest country in the world, it would be another country to add to the list. We had to go on the underground to get to Vatican City, though it was nice not to walk for a bit. When we got to St Peter's Square, we were fortunate to see the Pope, who was holding his weekly audience. We would have liked to have seen the Sistine Chapel, but the queues and the cost put us off, and we had limited time. We saw two more famous Rome landmarks that day, including the Trevi Fountain, where we all threw a coin over our shoulders into the water. Tradition ensures that by doing this you would return to the city one day. Finally, we went to visit the Spanish Steps. Gwen had found a public phone box and went off to phone home. I sat with Tigsy on the famous steps and watched as various portrait artists who had set up camp on the steps looked for someone to paint.

"Don't you think you should go back and check on Ruby?" asked Tigsy.

"Do *you* think I should?"

"Well, I would, in your situation."

"What do you mean in my situation?"

"A lovesick puppy," laughed Tigsy.

"I *was* a lovesick puppy, but I've realised I'm wasting my time with Ruby, so my lovesick puppy days are behind me."

"Thank the Lord. Well, you gave it your best shot, though I still think it would be nice to check up on her … as a friend."

I suppose he was right, at the end of the day. If it were me who wasn't feeling too good, I probably would appreciate somebody looking out for me – even though she hadn't checked on me after Tom had pushed me over. We were catching the 9.30 p.m. train to Basel in

Switzerland tonight, so I told Tigsy I would go back to the station and wait with Ruby. On the way to the station I passed a supermarket and picked up two ham rolls and two bottles of water. I also bought two huge nectarines – the kind of nectarines that you could only find in hotter climates and tasted so much better than those you could buy in the UK. In the UK, the nectarines were always rock hard when you bought them, so you had to leave them for about five days to ripen. You'd forget about them, and they'd go bad and end up in the bin. I mean, sometimes, buying nectarines in the UK, you'd probably be better off putting them in the bin on the way out of the supermarket, to save time. Ruby was sitting in the waiting room at the station. She was looking at the *Thomas Cook Timetable* again.

"Planning your escape from us, are you, Ruby?" Ruby jumped. I think I must have surprised her.

"Oh, hi, Will. What are you doing here?"

"I've come to check if you're OK. Are you feeling any better?"

"I am, thanks. Though I was sick in the toilets after you left. I'm starving now, though."

"That's good, then – I've bought you a ham roll and some water. Also some mega nectarines."

"Thanks, Will – that's really sweet of you. You must have read my mind. I'll tell you what, let's eat it at the Piazza della Repubblica. It's a square not far from here. I read about in my guidebook. I need to get away from this station."

# Chapter 53

## Nectarines for Two

The circular piazza featured some spectacular architecture. Near the edge of the square were some benches, and we sat down to enjoy the picnic. The ham rolls were unlike anything I had tasted. The bread had a chewy texture, and the freshness of the bread coupled with the saltiness of the ham, was a combination made in heaven. I passed Ruby a nectarine and when she bit into the luscious fruit the juice shot out and down her white T-shirt. I passed her a tissue, and we both laughed. In the Italian sun, sitting here with Ruby I was so happy. I wanted this moment to never end. Again. A beautiful girl, a beautiful place, the sun, the architecture. It was perfect. Expect she was in love with Tom Bellows and not me. At least Jim Pepperman was out of the picture.

"How do people think up jokes?" I asked.

"What do you mean?" Ruby replied, her face breaking out into a smile.

"Exactly that – how do people think up jokes? I mean, have you ever wondered?"

"Well, no, not really."

"I have. I've given it a lot of thought. I think they must start at the punchline and work backwards."

"OK," said Ruby nervously, not sure where the conversation was going.

"I remember laughing in school, at a joke the comedian Bob Monkhouse told."

"What was that?"

"They all laughed when I said I wanted to be a comedian. Well, they're not laughing now."

"Ha ha, that's a good one. Your mind is so abstract, Will. Why would you even think about stuff like that?"

"I think it must be all the time we had on the trains. It gets your mind thinking all sorts of strange thoughts."

"I suppose it does."

"Shall we try and think of a joke now? Me and you? Let's put our minds together and come up with a joke."

"OK, how do we start?"

"With the punchline, or a route to the punchline. Think of a well-known saying and we can use that or work back from there."

"OK, I've got one – a leopard can't change its spots."

"Right, I'll give it a go." I thought for a moment and then replied. "A leopard goes into a department store and heads for the kitchen department. 'Excuse me,' the leopard says to the lady behind the counter. 'I'm after some new pots for my kitchen. Can you recommend any?

'I'm sorry,' the lady behind the counter replies. 'I can't serve you.'

'Oh. that's a shame,' replies the leopard. 'Is it because you don't serve jungle animals?'

'No, sorry, it's not that. It's because a leopard can't change its pots.'

Ruby groaned when I delivered the punchline.

"Will, that's terrible. I think even I could come up with a better joke than that. Give me a well-known saying and I'll try."

"OK, I will. What about an apple a day keeps the doctor away?"

"Right, give me a minute". Ruby was smiling now, and started giggling. It was infectious. I started to giggle too.

"Come on let's hear it," I managed to say through the

giggling.

"OK, OK. I've got one."

"The doctor has been trying to check on gran every day this week. She's been ill in bed, but he still hasn't managed to see her. Oh, why is that? I've been throwing apples at him from the bedroom window." Ruby burst out laughing and that started me laughing too. Ruby was laughing so much, tears had formed in her eyes.

"That is way worse than mine."

"I beg to differ."

"Shall we get an ice cream? I hear they're something special out here. Yeah, come on – a gelato is beckoning."

"One more made-up joke first, though. I think my apple joke is winning so far. Here is your saying, Will – don't put all your eggs in one basket."

Ruby was still giggling. This game had obviously amused her.

"OK, OK, give me a minute." We sat in silence for a while, as I racked my brains for another joke.

"Right, I think I've got one," I continued.

"A man goes into a farm shop and wants to buy some eggs. 'Have you any fresh eggs?' the man says to the girl behind the counter.

'Yes, we have, they were freshly laid this morning,' the girl replied.

'Great, I'll take a dozen'.

'No worries. The only problem is we've run out of egg boxes.'

'That's OK. I have a basket in the car,' the man said.

'A basket,' said the girl. 'Haven't you heard the expression, don't put all your eggs in one basket?'

I started to laugh. I couldn't think of an end to the joke.

"And?" said Ruby.

"I have no end. Not yet, anyway. It just goes to prove my point, how difficult it is to write a joke – or maybe I just need more time. I'll come back to the joke at a later date."

"Come on, let's get that gelato."

# Chapter 54

## Train to Basel

Now that I knew where I stood with Ruby, we seemed to be getting on better than at any stage of the holiday. It was like I didn't have to try so hard, and this made things more relaxed, more natural. We were laughing together, gently insulting each other. It was like we had been going out for years. The few hours in the square seemed to pass in a flash, and soon it was time to return to the station and get the train to Basel, Switzerland – another country to tick off the list. Tigsy and Gwen were already on the platform. They had bought supplies for another overnight train journey. I was getting fed up of sleeping on trains – you never slept well. I was craving a nice sleep in a big, cool bed. Although it saved us money, it was sometimes frustrating because we never got to see much of the spectacular scenery, as it was usually dark outside the window. The train to Basel was annoyingly busy, and we were unable to find seats together. At one stage it looked as if we may have to stand, but eventually we all found seats. Unfortunately – although Tigsy, Ruby and Gwen managed to find seats in the same carriage – there was no room for me, and I had to find a seat in another carriage, further down the train. It was going to be a long night, and Tigsy and Gwen had all the food too. I was already hungry, and the train had only just departed. I sat down and tried to sleep, and I must have been really tired because I fell asleep almost immediately. I think we had about another three hours until the train got to Basel. The door of the carriage opened, and there stood Tigsy.

"Come on, Will – there's a space in our carriage now."

I quickly grabbed my stuff and went with Tigsy, and, to my delight, found the spare seat was next to Ruby.

"I thought you would be pleased," whispered Tigsy.

"Hi, Will – thought of an end to that joke yet?" asked Ruby.

"I'm still working on it."

"What's that about?" asked Gwen.

"Oh, nothing – just a game me and Will were playing in Rome," said Ruby, and she started to giggle again.

I think it was raining outside, but it was nice and warm in the carriage, and it felt cocooned from the outside world. The soothing sound of the rain on the window and the familiar sound of the train were making me sleepy. It wasn't long before I fell asleep. I don't know how long I slept, but when I awoke my hand was tingling. My hand felt a bit strange. My face was itching, and I used my tingling hand to scratch it. There had been something on my hand, and now it was on my face. Shaving foam!

Ruby, Gwen and Tigsy simultaneously burst out laughing.

"We thought you would never wake up. Ruby squirted that shaving foam in your hand about twenty minutes ago," laughed Tigsy.

Ruby was laughing uncontrollably.

"That has made my day, that has. Your face, Will! I wish I'd taken a photo."

I must admit it was quite funny, and it was nice to see Ruby so happy.

# Chapter 55

## The Old Town

The train eventually arrived in Basel, and after leaving our rucksacks in luggage lockers at the station, we headed off to explore the city. Situated on the Rhine River, not far from the borders of both France and Germany, the guidebooks informed us that the city was famous for its town hall and its twelfth-century Gothic cathedral. We stopped off for some food and walked around the shops for a bit. After we had visited the cathedral, Gwen said she was tired of walking and wanted to sit down for a bit. We discussed further plans, which involved another train tonight, to Copenhagen via Hamburg.

Ruby was keen to visit the Old Town in Grossbasel, the older part of Basel.

"I think I'm going to chill here and enjoy the sun. You and Will, go – we can meet you at the train station later," said Gwen.

"Yeah, good idea. Will was keen to see the Old Town," said Tigsy, winking at me for the second time that day.

And so it was just Ruby and me again, and we set off for the Old Town. I was starting to like this Old Town place already. We only had a few days left of the holiday, and I was running out of time with Ruby. I decided to quiz her about Tom again. Maybe I could put doubts in her mind. Time to play dirty.

"So, that day when you went with Tom to the airport – what happened again?"

"Why are you bringing this up again, Will? I thought I'd already told you?"

"Oh, sorry – I was just curious. Forget it. It has nothing to do with me, anyway."

"We did talk about you."

"And?"

"I told Tom you liked me, and I was starting to like you back."

My heart started racing again.

"And what did Tom say?"

"Well, that was the funny thing. He didn't say anything. He started to cry."

"Cry?"

"Yes, he broke down. He said he regretted the way he'd treated me. He had made a mistake. He wasn't happy with his life. He was worried about his dad, and he wanted me back. He must have felt threatened by you, because he called you a lanky string of piss."

"That's not nice to hear, though it's an accurate description of me, I suppose. And do you want him back too?"

"I do, Will. Sorry. Yes, I do."

I didn't say anything else. There was nothing more to say, really. I had to just try and enjoy the rest of the holiday and appreciate the time I had left with Ruby. Tom Bellows was one lucky boy. Ruby couldn't have spelled it out any more clearly.

We carried on walking to the Old Town. We hadn't even got there, but it had lost its charm. The Old Town itself was what guidebooks would describe as charming, with architectural diversity. Ruby seemed to be more interested in the various touristy shops, and we spent a few hours pottering around those. Ruby bought a red beret and some bubble mixture. I spent a number of minutes debating whether I should buy a beautiful cuckoo clock, which I could give to my mum and dad. Switzerland was expensive, though, and I soon realised that the clock was way out of my price range. Ruby was now wearing the red beret she had just bought. It matched the red shorts she was wearing. She was looking even more alluring.

"I think we should get back to the station. Any idea which direction?" I asked.

"Why are you asking me? I thought you always said, 'Where there's a Will, there's a way.' I think it's this way, though – I remember that unusual building we passed," Ruby said, pointing down the street we had not long walked up.

# Chapter 56

## Train to Hamburg

It took us a while to get back to the station. We took a number of wrong turns and had to ask directions from a young couple. They were keen to help and also told us to pop into a cake shop on our way to the station. The smell of the cake shop hit us before we came across it. There was a big queue outside, and we had to wait about ten minutes before we could get served. Again, the prices were a bit steep, but we ended up buying four pieces of apple strudel, which we planned to eat on the train later. We had another overnight journey on the train to look forward to.

We met up with Tigsy and Gwen and boarded the train. The train, surprisingly, was quiet, and we had a whole carriage to ourselves.

"Do you know, we've got to get a train that goes onto a ferry soon?" began Tigsy.

"Yeah, good one, Tigsy. I don't think that is the case," I replied.

"I'm telling you, it is. I've been reading about it in my guidebook. We have to change in Hamburg for the train."

It was just over seven hours to Hamburg, and the four of us had the carriage to ourselves the entire journey, which was unheard of. The door to the carriage was opened twice, though: once by the ticket inspector, and then by an old woman who didn't seem that keen to enter and gave us all a dirty look before quickly closing the door and moving on. Ruby was still wearing her red beret and began blowing bubbles into the air. I pulled out the apple strudel from my rucksack, and Gwen pulled out another cake she had bought: a Tirolercake – a beautiful cake stuffed with chocolate and nuts. Everyone was in good spirits, and the seven hours seemed to fly by. Four friends enjoying each other's company.

# Chapter 57

## Train on a Ferry

We had to change in Hamburg for the train to Copenhagen, Denmark – another country to tick off. Tigsy had read that there were three departures every day from Hamburg Hauptbahnhof to Copenhagen Central Station. We were scheduled to catch the last departure, on the train that would board a ferry.

As the train embarked onto the ferry there was an announcement by the conductor in three languages: Danish, German and English. We were told that once the train boarded the ferry we had to leave the train and enter the boat. We were not permitted to remain on the train. The train would be locked for the crossing, which would only take about an hour in total. We were crossing the Baltic Sea, and the sea air could only be described as bracing. My geography was improving as a result of this holiday. If I included Vatican City as one of my countries, I calculated I was up to ten countries so far: France, Germany, Austria, Italy, Greece, Yugoslavia, Turkey, Switzerland, and soon Denmark.

The one-hour crossing passed quickly, and soon they had unlocked the train, and it felt no sooner had we got back and settled down we had arrived at Copenhagen's train station.

# Chapter 58

## Copenhagen

It was coming up to midday, and we headed, first, for the interrail information centre. This was the only one of its kind in the world at the time, where you could get tourist information, free maps of the city, and – best of all – free use of the toilets and showers. The showers were a godsend, as, to be honest, none of us were smelling too good. The water pressure was really powerful too, and it was nice to have water that was actually hot for a change. We left the station fully refreshed. Leaving our rucksacks at the station, we set off to explore Copenhagen. Again, we only had a day here as we were taking another train to Amsterdam tonight. This was another overnight trip of about ten hours, and so another uncomfortable night ahead.

We had two things we all wanted to see in Copenhagen: the Little Mermaid statue and the Tivoli Gardens. The Little Mermaid statue, according to our recently acquired free map, was about a fifty-minute walk away. The weather was so nice that we decided to walk there. The walk took us through the city centre and along the waterfront. Gwen and Ruby walked on ahead. Tigsy and I walked behind.

"Wow, Danish women are beautiful," began Tigsy.

"I know, tell me about it. Nearly everyone is tall and blonde, and they all look so healthy."

"And they have a confidence about them. Everywhere you look there is a beautiful woman. Maybe you should move here, Will. Hook up with a Danish bird and stop moping over Ruby."

"I'm not moping over Ruby. That ship has sailed."

"Tell that to your face, then," laughed Tigsy.

"We're just friends. I've realised that now."

"Still, it must be hard, mate, spending so much time with her."

"I suppose it is."

Tigsy was singing another Smiths song, this one about the frustration of unrequited love and how it can drive someone to the point of insanity. I think it was called 'I Want the One I Can't Have'.

"OK, OK, Tigsy – can we change the subject now?"

"Sorry, mate. I was just teasing. But seriously, though, when you come to a place like this you can see how many beautiful women there are in the world. There'll be one for you soon, Will. It's a world full of Rubys."

"I'm not that desperate, Tigsy. I'm still only twenty-one, and it's only a matter of time before they come a-running."

"Yeah, in your dreams, son."

The famous Hans Christian Andersen fairy tale inspired the Little Mermaid statue: a mermaid gives up everything to join a handsome prince on land. It is one of Copenhagen's most iconic landmarks. When we got there, it was a lot smaller than I'd imagined. There was a small crowd waiting for a photograph of the statue. We were able take a few photos, including one where Ruby put her red beret on the the statue's head.

"Right, that's ticked off. Let's get some food and head to Tivoli Gardens," said Gwen.

Tivoli Gardens were about three miles away, so we decided to get a bus and underground, once we worked out where the bus departed. Luckily, most Danes could speak perfect English and were more than helpful, directing us to the bus stop when asked. Tivoli Gardens is the world-famous amusement park found right in the centre of Copenhagen. With beautiful scenery and gardens, there were also a number of rides, from high-adrenaline to more child-friendly attractions. Unfortunately for the four of us, on a limited budget, most of the rides and attractions were too expensive. As a result, we just wandered around the park looking at the rides we would have liked to go on. We managed to stretch to an ice cream each and tried the famous Danish Brunsviger dessert, which was a coffee cake, rich in flavour, with a crunchy caramel topping. But, because of our lack of finances and limited time, we soon set off back to the station.

# Chapter 59

## Train to Amsterdam

Another long train journey lay ahead of us. As the train for Amsterdam pulled in, Tigsy left his rucksack with us and ran onto the train to secure us a carriage. The train was due to get to Amsterdam in just over eleven hours, getting there at around eight in the morning. We shared some food and settled in for the night. An elderly couple joined us in the carriage and were speaking in a language I didn't recognise. The others must have been tired, as they had all closed their eyes and were attempting to sleep. I looked at Ruby. She was sitting directly opposite me. We both had window seats, but there wasn't much to see outside in the darkness. Her head was tilted slightly to the right. One of those positions that mean you wake up with a slight neck ache. Her hair nestled on her shoulders, and she had her legs tucked up so they were off the floor. I needed to stop looking at her. I could see that she wasn't in a deep sleep and could open her eyes at any moment. It wouldn't be good if she caught me staring at her. But it was almost as if I was hypnotised; I couldn't look away. *Stop it, Will. Stop it.* I finally stopped looking and thought of Smiths lyrics again, but kept coming back to the same song: 'I Want the One I Can't Have'.

The lyrics of the song – about the all-consuming angst of loving someone who doesn't love you back – were on a loop in my brain. These were the lyrics Tigsy had sung earlier, now stuck in my mind.

I thought I was getting over Ruby, but I still couldn't stop thinking about her. There were only a few days left of the holiday, and I think I would only start getting over her when I was no longer in her company. I needed to think about something else. This wasn't healthy. I tried to think of the end of my egg joke, but still couldn't think of an ending. My mind returned to lyrics. How did someone like Morrissey, from The Smiths, think of those beautiful words to the songs? I mean, 'This Charming Man' opened with a vivid image of a damaged bicycle on a lonely hillside – where did that come from? I had a notebook and pen in my rucksack and decided I would have a go at writing some lyrics. How hard could it be? A lot harder than you would expect, as after half an hour of thoughts and scribbling later I hadn't written anything. I looked at Ruby again for inspiration, and began to write my first ever lyrics – or was it a poem?

On the train that night, I stare at your beauty,
Guiltily staring at your fragile form,
As you sleep, you do not know what you do to me,
As you sleep, you do not know of my plight,
I just hope for that time when you look at me,
And love me with all of your might.

Well, not good – but, to be fair, it was my first attempt. I wasn't sure about the plight and might bit, though. I wondered how Morrissey had written the first line from 'This Charming Man' when he wrote about a bicycle with a flat tyre abandoned on a lonely hill. I mean, he could have written "Stray bike at the side of the road", initially – who knows? Mine was a work in progress. I'll come back to lyric–poem writing another time. I put my notebook back in my rucksack and finally fell asleep.

When I awoke, I had slept for quite a few hours. My stomach was hurting again. I hoped that the diarrhoea wasn't making a reoccurrence. I still had a few of the brown pills left and decided a trip to the toilet was necessary. The queue was long: there were four people in front of me, and, as I joined the queue, two people quickly joined behind me. Deep joy. I hoped my bowels would behave at least until I was off the train. The queue was moving slowly, and finally it was my turn. The smell in the toilet was horrendous, and I looked into the toilet bowl to see an enormous turd was blocking the toilet. This seemed to be another recurring theme of the holiday. I pressed the button to activate the flush but there was no resistance to my pressure. Great. The flush wasn't working. I quickly peed on the giant turd and returned to the carriage. I needed a 'number two' but wouldn't be able to use that toilet. When I got back to the carriage my rucksack was open, and Tigsy had my notebook in his hand and was reading out aloud.

"'Guiltily staring at your fragile form …' What's this about, Will?"

I snatched the book back from him.

"Get off my stuff! What do you think you're doing?"

"Sorry, Will – I was just looking for some food, and I found the notebook."

"Well, it's private! You shouldn't be looking at my stuff – and I haven't got any food. Buy your own!"

I was shaking now. A mixture of anger and embarrassment.

"Sorry, Will. Calm down, it was only a bit of fun."

Ruby was staring out of the window, like she didn't want to be involved in any drama. I hoped she hadn't realised the poem was about her. I hadn't mentioned her name, after all. But I suppose it was obvious it was about her.

"I told you, Tigsy, to leave the notebook alone," said Gwen.

"OK, OK. I'm sorry, Will. I won't mention it again."

"We did manage to find some food. Though. Will, do you want an apple?" said Gwen.

"I'm OK, thanks." I looked out of the window as the sunrise bathed the carriage in light.

# Chapter 60

## Amsterdam

The train pulled into Amsterdam station. I was also able to use the station's toilet facilities, which, thankfully were a lot cleaner than the train, and the flush was working. Ruby was quiet as we made our way out of the station. Amsterdam's station building was quite impressive, and we took a number of photos outside before we hopped on a tram for the city centre. I got on the tram first and thought Ruby would sit next to me, but she walked past me and sat a bit further down the tram. She must have been annoyed, or even embarrassed, by my poem too.

The day was spent going around shops, feeding pigeons, walking, more walking, and eating and drinking. I bought some tulips – tulips from Amsterdam – and some Dutch cheese. We then went on a boat trip, taking in sights such as the Skinny Bridge and the Cat Boat, a sanctuary for stray cats. I was glad Pete wasn't there to see the Skinny Bridge, as no doubt he would have fired off some joke aimed at me. Finally, we went to a pancake house where I splashed out on a banana pancake.

As darkness descended on the city, we were keen to see the other side of Amsterdam, described in the guidebook as fast food, fast sex and fast drugs. I was approached a number of times by some dodgy-looking characters, asking if I wanted to buy some hash, which I politely declined. Besides, I had spent most of my money on the tulips and cheese, and the only hash I had any interest in was my mum's corned beef hash. We walked through the red-light district, where the sex workers sat in the windows of big posh houses by the river, plying their trade.

Soon we went back to the station, as we were catching another overnight train, this time to Paris. Ruby had barely spoken a word to me all day, and, as we walked towards the station, I decided to see what the matter was.

"You're quiet today, Ruby," I began.

"Am I?"

"Yes, you are. Is anything the matter?"

"That poem you wrote – was it about me?"

"That was private. It wasn't meant to read out aloud."

"But was it about me?" Ruby looked at me quizzically.

"Well, maybe … I'm sorry, I was just messing around. I couldn't sleep. Everyone was asleep. I was bored. I was trying to write a poem or a song lyric. I'm sorry if I upset or embarrassed you."

"You didn't, Will – I liked it. Obviously, it needs a bit of work, but I liked it. Nobody has ever written anything for me like that before."

"Not even the great Tom Bellows?"

"No, he would never do a thing like that. First the glass snails, and now a crap poem. It's enough to make a girl blush."

# Chapter 61

## Luxembourg

That made me happy, and I was keen to explore this further, but we had arrived at the station. The train to Paris would only take about four hours, but we planned to change in Paris for another train to Luxembourg and, finally, another train to Brussels. This would add another couple of countries to our trip: Belgium and Luxembourg. I think that made twelve in all. The train was busy again, and we had to split up. This time Tigsy and Gwen got a place in one carriage, and Ruby and I squashed in next to each other in another carriage further down the train.

As the train pulled out of the station, I wasn't looking forward to another sleepless night. The last time I had slept in a bed had been in Istanbul, many days ago.

"Well, Will, the holiday is over – back to reality soon. What will you miss most about the holiday?"

"That's an easy one – you," I replied quickly.

Ruby blushed slightly.

"I'll miss you too, Will. We've had some fun this trip. I'm looking forward to seeing the photographs when we get them developed."

"Me too. Are you looking forward to going home? Don't you start your new job soon?"

"Yes, at the end of September. I'm a bit nervous, and there are more exams to do, but they are spaced out over a few years, and once I qualify I'll be earning good money."

"You should be able to buy some hash next time you go to Amsterdam, then?"

"Yeah, good one, Will. What about you? Do you think you'll find a job soon?"

"Who knows? I've applied for loads already. Hopefully, something will come along soon – a job, and a beautiful girl who will fall in love with me."

"Yeah, I really hope that happens for you, Will."

We were both tired, and Ruby had shut her eyes. She linked arms with me and rested her head on my shoulder, and it was heaven. *Enjoy the moment, Will, there won't be many more moments like this.* It was a shame that the journey to Paris wasn't longer because the time flew by, and soon we were pulling into Paris Gare du Nord station. Gwen approached us as soon as we got off the train.

"Me and Tigsy have been talking, and we're going to give Luxembourg a miss. We're going to go straight home."

Ruby looked confused.

"I don't understand. We've only a day left – you might as well see the trip out."

"I know, but it my dad's birthday tomorrow. It's a big one, his fiftieth, and I'd like to surprise him."

"That's a shame," I said, looking at Tigsy, who was looking a bit guilty.

"But it's been great, it really has," said Gwen, and she gave both Ruby and me a big hug.

Tigsy hugged Ruby and gave me a playful punch on the arm.

"Take it easy, Will. Keep in touch, and good luck with the job-hunting."

"Thanks, Tigsy. Oh, and Tigsy, if you're ever passing Cardiff ..." I paused for dramatic effect. "Keep going." I started to laugh at my own joke.

"Good one, Will, though I may come and stay sometime."

"Yeah, I was only joking, mate – you're always welcome. Just give me a call in advance so I can make sure I'm not in." I winked at Tigsy.

And with that, they walked off down the platform, and it was just Ruby and me again. I was elated, to tell the truth. I wasn't sure what Ruby was thinking. I never was.

"Do you want to go home too, Ruby?"

"No, we may as well tick off another two countries before it's back to real life."

"I know, it's scary, isn't it?"

"It sure is."

"Shall we get something to eat? I think we've got about an hour until the train to Luxembourg."

"Yeah, I'm starving. Let's go."

We both bought the same thing: a cappuccino and a croissant. The croissant was sweet and buttery, and the coffee was bitter and strong. The caffeine hit, and I felt alive and energised as we walked down the platform for the next train. We had picked a train especially so there would be no changes, and the journey would take about three hours. The train was quieter than what we had been used to of late. Ruby chose to sit opposite me, by the window. I helped her put her rucksack on the luggage rack and settled down for the journey. This was our last day of the holiday. My last day with Ruby. We were comfortable in each other's company now, and we sat in silence as the train left the station, and we were soon out of the city and into the French countryside.

"So, Will, what's your favourite album?"

I loved these kinds of questions and loved the random conversations we'd had on this holiday. I thought for a moment and then answered.

"I suppose it was the first album by The Smiths."

"What was it called?"

"*The Smiths*."

"Oh, original. I never really got The Smiths. I mean, all that wailing, and Morrissey swinging gladioli around. What was that about?"

"Yeah, I suppose he is a bit weird. I think it was more about the lyrics for me, and Johnny Marr's guitar playing."

The ticket inspector came round and asked to see our tickets. We both took out our little brown book, which was the interrail ticket, and showed him the ticket. Satisfied, he carried on down the train.

"What about you, what's your favourite album?" I asked.

"I like *Tapestry* by Carole King."

"Never heard of her."

Ruby looked at me, surprise on her face.

"I can't believe that, Will – she's sold millions of records and written hundreds of songs. That's the thing, Will – you're too closed off with your musical genres."

"Oh, I'm too closed off with my musical genres, am I?" I said in a slightly mocking way.

Ruby started to laugh.

"Yeah, sorry, that did sound a bit pompous. What I meant to say is, there are other groups available besides The Smiths. You should open your eyes a bit wider."

"What's this Karen King like, then?

"Karen King?" Ruby let out a derisive laugh.

"What was she called again?"

"It's *Carole* King. Not Karen. My mum used to like her. I bet you've heard some of her songs. She was a prolific songwriter. I remember watching a documentary about her, and during her most creative period she was churning out hit after hit, for herself and other artists. It was like she was going to work nine to five and writing beautiful songs."

Ruby seemed to be a bit annoyed at me that I hadn't heard of Carole King.

"Was she friendly with Mike Spitz?" I mischievously added.

"Yeah, funny, Will."

"What is the album 'Tapestry' like?"

"It's a great, Will. If you get a chance, take a listen. You need to move away from The Smiths."

"I will. I promise."

It was so easy talking to Ruby now. The awkward silences were well and truly in the past. We were like two people who had known each other for years. She was funny too, and sharp. She was unlike anyone I had ever encountered before.

We weren't really sure what to do in Luxembourg. To be honest, I think it was a case of ticking off another country for bragging rights. I didn't know anything about Luxembourg, although it was referenced in a song, 'Ask', by The Smiths, where Morrissey paints a scene of wasting sunny days indoors, scribbling unsettling poetry to a girl in Luxembourg.

Luxembourg City, the capital, was much smaller than the other cities we had visited on this trip. We headed down to the old quarter and, en route, came across a McDonald's. It almost felt we were back in the UK. Ruby was running low on money, so I treated her to a Big Mac meal and a strawberry milkshake. I had the same.

"I'm meeting Tom next week."

"Oh, that's nice". It wasn't. It was terrible. I wanted to be the one meeting Ruby next week, and the week after, and the week after.

"Yeah, he's coming to see me in Birmingham."

"So why are you telling me this now, Ruby?"

"I don't know, really. Just thought I would mention it." To be honest, I would rather not know or think about it.

Outside, it had started raining. Really raining. The kind of rain that sends people running for cover.

"Are you looking forward to seeing him?" I reluctantly asked.

"Yes, I suppose I am."

"Well, that's good, then." It wasn't good. It wasn't good at all. Ruby was meeting up with Tom. And she was looking forward to it. She was looking forward to it. Looking forward to it. To it. I wanted to punch someone. Where was Jim Pepperman when you needed him?

"Shall we go back to the station? We can leave early for Brussels, if you like?"

"OK, then. I think the rain's stopped." My mood, like the pavements of Luxembourg City, had dampened. That would make a good Smiths lyric, I thought.

# Chapter 62

## Brussels

We headed off for the train station where we were quickly able to board an earlier train to Brussels, in the final new country of the trip: Belgium. According to the guidebook, Brussels was famous for chips and mayonnaise and strong beer. I was in the mood for a strong beer or two. I needed something to take the edge off. I needed to take my mind off the fact that Ruby was meeting Tom in a week's time and was looking forward to it.

It was about three hours by train to Brussels, and we would get there late afternoon, so we wouldn't have much time to explore the city. Again, Ruby sat opposite me on the train.

"You've gone a bit quiet, Will."

"Oh, sorry – I'm just a bit tired."

*Come on, Will, don't spoil the last day with Ruby. No sulking.* She may be meeting Tom in a week's time, but she was here with me now. *Enjoy the last few fleeting moments with her.*

"I know what you mean. I fantasise now about sleeping in a bed with a pillow."

"Oh, what I would give to be able to sleep in a horizontal position again."

"Ore use a toilet where my deposits flush away."

This made me laugh – despite the sadness I was feeling that these were the last few hours with Ruby.

"Or enjoy one of my mother's Sunday dinners."

"I dream about clean clothes."

"Television."

"Toilet paper."

"Solid stools."

This made Ruby laugh.

"A hot shower or, better still, a hot bath."

"Not carrying a rucksack around."

"But, then again, there are lots of things that I'll miss about the holiday," said Ruby.

"You start," I replied.

"Waking up in a different country."

"Feeling the sun on your face every day."

"I know soon it will be back to wind and rain again," laughed Ruby.

"It's still your go, Ruby."

"Strange food."

"Different cultures."

Ruby was silent suddenly, as if lost in thought.

"Come on, Ruby, what else will you miss?"

"Not seeing you every day, Will. I think not seeing you every day is what I'll miss most."

I was surprised to hear Ruby say this. We sat in silence for a minute as the train went through a tunnel, and the carriage went dark.

Light flooded into the train again as it emerged from the tunnel.

"And not seeing you every day too, Ruby. I think that is what I'll miss the most."

We both sat in companionable silence as the train sped along its way and over the border into Belgium.

Neither Ruby nor I had been to Belgium before, so we were both quite excited to see the city of Brussels. When we arrived at the station, Ruby wanted to phone her dad, so we found an international phone box nearby. There was no queue for the phone, and I sat on the platform to wait for her to finish. About ten minutes later she was back.

"Everything OK at home?" I asked.

"I think so. My dad seemed quite upbeat, which is unusual for him. He's looking forward to seeing me. He said he'd really missed me. Why don't you phone home, Will? I've got some spare coins you can use."

"Oh, OK. I suppose I better had."

I realised that, apart from sending the odd postcard, I hadn't phoned home as much as I should have. Ruby helped me with the number as there was a little confusion with the international dialling code. As the phone started to ring, Ruby stepped away to give me some privacy. My mum answered on the fourth ring.

"Hi, Mum, it's Will."

"Will, is that you?"

"Yes, Mum. I'm in Belgium."

"You're in Belgium?"

"Yes, Mum. Belgium."

"You sound so near."

"I'm in a phone box an the station at Brussels."

"In Brussels?"

"Yes, Mum. Brussels."

The conversation was going well. The money was going down rapidly. I put a few more coins in to increase the credit.

"How is everyone? How's Dad?"

"We're all fine, Will, thanks. Your dad has found a few more jobs you can apply for when you get home. He's cut out the adverts from the paper for you."

"Oh, eh, tell him thanks."

Great, I thought.

"Are you still all travelling together?"

"No, it's just me and Ruby now."

"Just the two of you?"

"Yes, Mum, just the two of us."

"So is Ruby your girlfriend now, Will?"

"No, Mum, she's not my girlfriend."

"Just a friend."

"Just a friend, Mum. Look, I've got to go. I'm running out of credit. I'll be back tomorrow, or the day after. Bye, Mum."

"Oh, OK. I'll tell your dad you rang. Bye, Will."

I put the phone back on its cradle, and again, for some reason, felt like I was going to cry. A big wave of emotion hit me. I wasn't sure what it was or what it meant. Was I feeling homesick? Was I just overly tired? Was it the fact that this the holiday and my time with Ruby was coming to an end? I walked over to Ruby and asked her to look after my rucksack as I needed to use the toilets in the station. My stomach still wasn't right, and I had run out of the brown tablets. I went into the cubicle, sat on the toilet, and burst into tears. I sat on the toilet for about five minutes, crying – and wasn't sure why. *Come on, Will. Snap out of it.* Whatever *it* was. Back on the station, Ruby was looking at me with concern.

"Are you OK, Will? You look a bit upset."

"No, I'm fine. I got something in my eye and had to wash it out."

"Everything OK at home?"

"Yeah, I spoke to my mum. She said my dad has been cutting out job adverts for me from the paper. That will be nice to come home to."

"It's nice he's looking out for you, though."

"I suppose – but it's my life, at the end of the day. I would like to have a say in my future."

"Well, you can, Will. It's up to you."

"I suppose. It's just difficult to know what to do. It's OK for you. You seemed to have your life sorted, a good job to go to."

"You'll have that, Will, too – don't worry, it may just take you a bit longer to find what you're looking for. Come here."

I walked towards her, and she hugged me.

"You'll be OK, Will – just you wait and see."

"I know I will. I've got you as a friend now, haven't I?"

"You certainly have, Evans, whether you like it or not."

# Chapter 63

## The Kiss

We only had a few hours in Brussels, so we set off to explore the city. We headed for the Grand-Place, which is the central square of Brussels. The guidebooks said that the Grand-Place was famous for its Gothic architecture and thought to be one of the most beautiful medieval squares in the whole of Europe. It was only a short walk to the square, and, feeling hungry, we bought some chips from a stall on the way. We tried the famous chips – or frites as they were called here – served with a generous serving of mayonnaise.

As we sat on a bench and ate the frites, I looked down the street and saw a man coming towards us. He looked like Jim Pepperman. *Please don't let it be Jim Pepperman.* He'd already put a spanner in the works once when Ruby and I were getting on well. *He can't be here in Brussels. Surely not.* How unlucky would that be? But when he walked past us, I realised he wasn't anything like Jim Pepperman. Same height, but apart from that the resemblance ended. What was the matter with me?

"Hey, Will – as it's our last day, shall we get a drink? We should have enough money for a few."

"Sounds good to me."

Finishing our frites, we walked on for a while until we found a bar with seats outside. A waiter came over quickly and took our order.

"Two beers, please."

Neither of us knew any Flemish, but the waiter spoke perfect English.

"What beer would you like?"

"Two Lambic beers, please," answered Ruby.

The waiter seemed impressed with Ruby's choice and left to get the order.

"Look at you, asking for Lambic beers. Know your beers, do you?"

"I've read about Lambic beers. Apparently, they use a longer brewing process and they don't use cultivated yeast in the brewing process."

"Who knew, and who is 'they'?" I said, laughing.

Unperturbed, Ruby carried on.

"Yes, the beer is fermented through exposure to wild yeasts and bacteria."

"As long as it tastes OK."

"It should do."

"Remember that day back in Swansea when I first met you?"

"I certainly do – it was well embarrassing."

"You'd had a few Lambrics that day."

"I know. I suffered after that."

"At least it brought me and you together."

"Wasn't all that bad, then."

The waiter reappeared, with the beers on a silver tray. The beer was served in a tall glass and had quite a sour taste to it.

"I've tasted better beers, to be fair. Not like my usual Brains Dark from the Cardiff brewery."

"Give it a chance, Will – that's your first sip. It's an acquired taste."

The sun had emerged from behind the clouds, and it felt good to feel the warmth. Ruby was right about the beer: the more I worked my way down the glass, the nicer it seemed to taste. It wasn't long before I felt that moment when the alcohol in the beer seemed to reach my brain. It was almost as if somebody had turned a light bulb on in me. I looked at Ruby; her face was slightly flushed, bathed in the Belgian sunlight. She looked beautiful. The more I drank the more attractive she became. Ruby had made a good dent in her beer too.

"After we finish this, let's try and find the Manneken Pis," said Ruby.

"The what?"

"The Manneken Pis – it's a famous statue of a little boy urinating. I don't think it's far from the Grand-Place."

"OK, sounds like another photo opportunity – not that I make a habit of taking photographs of little boys urinating."

"I should hope not," laughed Ruby.

We finished our beers and set off to find the statue. Ruby was right: it *was* only about a ten-minute walk away, though we did have to stop a lovely Belgian girl to ask directions.

"So what's the story of the Manneken Pis statue?" I asked.

"I'm not too sure. It's something to do with a little boy who urinates on a fire and saves the city from disaster. I read somewhere that the boy was hung in a basket in the trees as a good luck symbol, and from there he urinated on the enemies of the city too."

"Sounds like a resourceful little boy."

"Or Pete, after he's finished the Mumbles Run."

The statue was much smaller than I imagined, when we finally found it. It was dressed in a red coat, of some significance we weren't unaware of. Apparently, they change the costume on the statue regularly, with the costume changes posted on the railings around the fountain. We waited for a photo opportunity and asked a German couple to take a photo of us.

"Well, that was well worth the walk," I said, sarcastically.

"What shall we do now?" asked Ruby.

"More Lambrics?"

"Good shout."

We headed back to the same place we'd been to earlier, and even managed to get the same table. The waiter seemed amused to see us back.

"Hello, my friends. You come back for more beer?"

"Yes, please. Two more Lambrics."

The waiter smiled and went to get the beers.

"I can't quite believe that tomorrow we'll go back to our normal lives," began Ruby.

"I know. I think I'll have to make an appointment with the GP to sort my stomach out. I reckon I've lost about a stone in weight these last weeks."

"Yeah, you do look a bit skinny, you lanky string of piss. You need building up." Hearing Ruby say that made me laugh.

"Don't you start – though this will help," I said, as the waiter brought over more of the strong Belgium beers.

"What did you think of me when you first met me at that Swansea disco?"

"I fell madly in love with you," I said, smiling.

"But any girl could have fallen into your arms that night."

"And I probably would have fallen madly in love with her too."

"So it could have been anyone?"

"I suppose, yes." And we both started to laugh.

"Did you know Beth likes you?"

"Beth?"

"Yes, Beth. Don't play dumb."

"I hadn't realised. How do you know?"

"She told Pete, and he told me."

"Well, you can't believe anything Pete says. Didn't you learn that this trip?"

"Well, it could be true."

"It doesn't matter, anyway, because she's gone back to America. Though she's given me her address."

The alcohol was kicking in now, and my inhibitions were fading rapidly.

"Which reminds me," I continued. "Why didn't you ask me for my address at the end of term?"

"Well, to be fair, Will, I didn't know you that well. In fact, I only met you in the third year, if I remember correctly."

"I suppose," I reluctantly agreed.

"And you never asked for my address, either."

"I did get it, though – I asked Pete for it."

I hadn't realised. What were you like in the first two years of university?"

"I was a nightmare. To borrow Morrissey's sentiment, I had a crippling shyness that could come across as rudeness."

"You and your Smiths lyrics. What does that even mean?"

"To be honest, I don't even know myself. But shyness does stop you doing things you would like to do."

"Which was?"

"Talking to women, really."

"And you think you've conquered that now?"

"I'm getting better."

"That's debatable." This made me laugh, and a bit of

beer came out of my mouth.

"Oh, Will, that's gross."

"Well. stop making me laugh. then. What were *you* like in the first two years of university?"

"Well, I was a good girl, obviously," she said, and winked at me as she said it.

"I suppose I was a bit of a swot. I wanted to get a good degree, and worked hard," Ruby continued.

"And played hard?"

"Not really, though I did go a bit wild after my mum died."

"That's understandable. Were you shy too? You don't seem to be."

"Not really – shyness is a waste of time."

"I'm starting to think it is. But it isn't something you can easily control. Did you know that in my first year I used to sit on my own for all my lectures?"

"That's not too bad, though. I mean, you are there to make notes and concentrate, not make friends."

"Yeah, I suppose it would have been nice to have done both, like most people managed. It wasn't really a problem, except for those times when you had a gap in lectures."

"So what did you do then?"

"I used to go to the library."

"That's a bit sad, isn't it, Will?"

"Well, I didn't actually do any work in the library. At the back of the library was a staircase leading to a fire escape. I used to sit on the stairs. By myself."

"That's so tragic, Will. It's a shame I didn't know you then."

"It wasn't as sad as you think. I used to buy myself a bag of crisps as a treat and eat them on the stairs, and nobody even knew I was there."

"Cheese and onion?"

"No, always salt and vinegar – they were my favourites. I would eat the crisps and use the empty crisp bag to catch my tears. Then I would return to my lectures smelling of vinegar."

"I can imagine you were a bit sad. Though surely the bit about the empty crisp bag catching your tears is made up? I mean, what were you even crying about?"

"I suppose I did make that bit up! I wasn't crying into an empty crisp bag. I was a bit lonely then, though, that's all."

Ruby was looking at me in a strange way. It was hard to describe. A bit like a mother looking at her sick child. I hope it wasn't pity at my pathetic stories.

There was a jukebox inside the bar, and the music was projected outside by a pair of black speakers, one of which was above our table. Somebody had put some money in, and the music made us jump when it started.

"I can't believe it, one of my favourite songs. It's from *Tapestry* by Carole King. That album I was telling you about."

"What's the song?"

"My mum's favourite too, 'So Far Away'. She loved this song."

We sat in silence in the sun, sipping our beers and listening to the music. The music was making Ruby sad, and she tried to wipe away a tear from her face. Ruby was listening to the music intently. Carole King's words spoke of a longing to see a loved one at the door and the ache of their distance, pulling at Ruby's heart. I knew she was thinking about her mum. She looked like she was about to cry.

"I'm just going to the toilet, Will."

"No worries."

I needed to change the music so walked over to the jukebox and selected some other music. This one was bringing the mood down. I didn't want Ruby to be feeling sad on our last night. I chose 'Wake Me Up Before You Go-Go' by Wham, and 'Careless Whisper' – the song that had brought us together. Ruby was behind me now at the jukebox, just as my first selection began.

"Ha ha, didn't have The Smiths, did they? I do love this song, though. Come on, Will, let's dance."

Luckily, the alcohol was working its magic and my inhibitions and social anxiety were parked up for the day. Ruby grabbed my hand, and the two of us started to dance. She was a good mover. She had a good ear for the music, though I hoped she wouldn't start that nomadic, wild dancing and make off down the street. The track was over too soon and the saxophone opening of 'Careless Whisper' filled the air.

"They're playing our song," I shouted in Ruby's ear.

"What do you mean?" Ruby shouted back.

"Never mind," I replied, disappointed that Ruby was unaware of the significance of the song. The song that had brought us together.

Was it my imagination, or was Ruby holding onto me a bit more enthusiastically than was necessary? *Please don't be asleep.* It was almost as if time had turned back full circle. But Ruby wasn't asleep. She had her head buried into my shoulder and her arms around my waist now, and was pulling me tighter and tighter. As George Michael sang about how good they could have been together, Ruby lifted her head and looked directly into my eyes. She moved her hands up to the back of my head and pulled me towards her. And then she kissed me. By the jukebox, in the bar by the Grand-Place. She kissed me. And I kissed her back, as if it was the last time I would see her. It was probably the finest moment of my life to date, and I felt a surge of happiness course through my body. The kiss and the song finished too soon, and we returned to our seats. The moment had passed, but was likely to stay in my memory as the highlight of the holiday. I hoped Ruby felt the same, but remained unconvinced. She didn't mention the kiss. Neither of us did. Instead, she said that we should be leaving for the train station as we had to get the train to Ostend.

# Chapter 64

## The Last Leg

The trip from Brussels to Ostend was quick, only about an hour and a half, but the train was really busy, so I wasn't able to sit with Ruby. I was still thinking about the kiss and whether it meant anything to her and where it left me. I think it was just the alcohol. Or the surroundings, or maybe the fact that it was the last day of the holiday. Who knew? I would have to try and speak to her on the ferry.

As we boarded the ferry, I heard a familiar voice.

"Oi, you two!" It was Mothball and Pete.

I couldn't believe it. What were the chances of bumping into those two? First Jim Pepperman, and now another serendipitous moment. Though, thinking about it, the chances of meeting them were probably higher than I imagined. After all, our interrail tickets were due to run out at the same time. So the probability was higher than I could forecast. For some reason, I thought of a maths question. If six travellers had a thirty-day rail pass, what was the probability that four of them would meet on the Ostend to Dover ferry on the penultimate day? It was one of those impossible questions, like the ones I used to be clueless at in A-level maths. Usually about a bloke climbing up a ladder and he was halfway up, carrying a bucket, and what weight would need to be in the bucket for the ladder to collapse? Or something like that.

Ruby was hugging Pete and Mothball. It was only a quick crossing to Dover – less than three hours – and we headed to the bar. We pooled our money so we could stretch to a drink each. Mothball secured us a table. I was feeling a bit emotional. Pete went to the bar and came back with four pints of lager.

"I would just like to raise a toast to Pete," I said.

"What for, you dull bastard?" said Pete. Ever the wordsmith again.

"For organising this trip and, well, for inviting me. It's been incredible. I've had the best time."

Pete was looking a bit smug.

"You're welcome, Evans."

"Yeah, thank you, Pete," Ruby added.

"My pleasure. I'm thinking of organising another trip if anybody's up for it – probably next year now. But I'm thinking of going to Australia for a year. Probably get some work over there and do some travelling."

"Wow, sounds amazing, though I don't think I could get time off my job," said Ruby.

"What about you, Evans? Me and Mothball are already on board."

"I'll have to think about it. I haven't got any money left, and I suppose I'll have to think about getting a job once I get home, just to get some more money."

"Come on, Evans. Live a bit. You just said how much you enjoyed yourself this holiday – imagine what it would be like on the other side of the world."

"True. I'll let you know."

The few hours it took to get to Dover flew by and thankfully the crossing was calm after our previous ferry trips. Soon we were off the ferry and had arrived at Dover. We were back in the UK. Predictably, the skies were grey, and it was raining. We made our way to the train station, and soon we boarded the train to London Victoria, and we were back to where, four weeks earlier, I had begun my pursuit of Ruby. For some reason, the trip was no longer free on the interrail ticket in the UK, though we did get a fifty per cent discount. We were all tired on the train, and closed our eyes and attempted to sleep. Finally, we pulled into Victoria. From here, we would go our separate ways. Pete and Mothball were off to see Pete's favourite group, Marillion, tonight in London, and left on the Tube for their overnight accommodation. As I was going to Cardiff and Ruby was going to Birmingham, we would be going home on separate trains. We faced each other on the platform. We still hadn't mentioned the kiss, although I wanted to – but probably the time had passed.

"It looks like this is it, then, Will".

"Yeah, it's been fun. Thanks, Ruby. I've had the best holiday ever."

"Me too."

Ruby stepped forward, dropped her rucksack and hugged me. I hugged her back.

"Good luck, Will. Keep in touch."

"I will – if I ever get your address."

Ruby laughed. She reached into her side pocket of her rucksack and passed me a bit of paper. It looked like a note of some sort.

"Here you go, Evans. I've written you a note and my address. Though don't read it yet. Wait until I'm gone. Bye, Will."

And she kissed me on the lips and walked away for her train.

As she walked away, I knew I had one more question to ask. Otherwise, I would regret not asking. I dropped my rucksack by a bench and sprinted down the platform, catching up with her.

"Ruby!"

Ruby turned around, surprised to see me so soon.

"What is it, Will?"

"Did I ever have a chance with you, Ruby?"

Ruby hesitated, and smiled mischievously.

"I wouldn't say you ever had no chance."

"I don't think I ever fully recovered from the shower-head incident in Istanbul. There was no coming back from that, I suppose?"

"Your words, not mine. Bye, Will."

And with that she smiled, blew me a kiss and walked away down the platform.

"Bye, Ruby," I replied, my voice cracking with emotion. Tears were not far away.

I had to wait for an hour for my train and bought a paper and some chocolate for the journey. I did want a Bounty, but, in a show of solidarity with Ruby, I opted for a Double Decker. I was tired and emotional and, to be honest, was now looking forward to getting home. The train was busy, as the trains from London to Cardiff always were. They seemed more cramped than the trains I'd been travelling on all over Europe. I managed to get a window seat and put my rucksack in the overhead storage, after taking out the paper and chocolate I had just bought. I felt my trouser pocket to make sure I still had the note that Ruby had given me, and was relieved to see it was still there.

I waited until the train had left the station before I took out the note. I was surprised to see it was a letter. I had been expecting just an address. When had she had the time to write this, I wondered? I think she must have written it on the train from Brussels to Ostend, which was the only time we were apart after the kiss.

Dear Will,

I just wanted to say how much fun I've had these last few weeks, and I think most of that was down to you. You made me laugh so much and made those long train trips a breeze. I'll never forget this trip and our last night in Brussels. Don't overthink that kiss, Will. It was of the moment. I'm still racking my brains to think of an end to that egg joke, and I'll think of you every time I look at my green glass snails. Take care, Will. Good luck with the job hunting, or maybe you will decide to go to Australia. The world is your oyster.

Love, Ruby xx

Underneath she had written her address. And a PS.

PS: Don't forget to listen to *Tapestry* by Carole King. Track 7. And I did think of an end to the egg joke. When the women says to the man "Haven't you heard of the expression, don't put all your eggs in one basket?", the man replies, "It's OK, I was planning to make scrambled eggs anyway."

I read the letter again. The woman opposite me was looking at me with concern. I hadn't realised I was simultaneously crying and laughing. I quickly wiped away my tears and folded up the note and put it back in my pocket.

"Are you OK?" the concerned woman opposite me asked kindly.

I was embarrassed now.

"Oh, sorry. I'm fine. It's just hay fever, I think."

The woman smiled and carried on reading her book. Once I got to Cardiff, I would have to buy that Carole King album.

# Chapter 65

## Back Home

Finally, I was back in my hometown. It seemed a lifetime ago when I had come here to buy my interrail ticket. I headed out of Cardiff Central Station and walked up St Mary Street. I took a right turn though one of the arcades and came out into the Hayes shopping area. Near the corner of the arcade was my favourite record shop: 'Spillers Records'. It was quite a small shop, which would be a problem, what with me carrying a large rucksack, so I waited outside for the crowd inside to disperse a bit before I went in. The records were arranged alphabetically, and I had to wait for a pregnant hippy woman to move away from the 'C' section. I wondered if she'd end up with a C-section when it was time for her to give birth. I couldn't even find any Carole King records – maybe she wasn't as well known as Ruby had made out. I must have been tired, for I suddenly realised I should have been looking in the 'K' section for King, not 'C' for Carole. I finally came across the Carole King section. Ruby was right: she was one prolific songwriter. There were a number of her albums. I finally found *Tapestry* and took it to the counter, where a good-looking girl with purple hair took the album from me.

"Cool choice. I love this album," the purple-haired shop girl said.

"Thanks – it was recommended by my friend."

"She's got good taste."

"Not in men," I added.

"Sorry?"

"Oh, nothing."

I quickly paid for the record, which was put in the famous Spillers bag, red with big black letters. Outside the shop, I'd almost forgotten see what track seven was. I quickly took the record out of the bag to check. Number seven song on the album was 'You've Got a Friend'. I was anxious to get home and listen to it, in particular the lyrics.

I lived a few miles out of the city centre and found a phone box, to call home to arrange a lift. About an hour later, my dad pulled up at the top of Churchill Way in his orange Austin Maxi.

"Hi, Dad."

"Hi, Will, nice to see you. Wow, look at the colour on you! You must've had some sun."

"Yeah, to be fair, the weather has been great. I've seen a lot of sun these last four weeks."

I wondered how long it would be before he brought up my employment status, and it was even quicker than I'd anticipated. We had barely got to the bottom of the road before he started.

"I've found a few jobs you can apply for. I've cut out a few from the *South Wales Echo*. I've left them on the sideboard. There is a good one in the biochemistry laboratory at the University Hospital of Wales you could apply for."

"Oh, OK. I'll take a look. I may be going to Australia. though .with Pete and Mothball."

I knew I was playing devil's advocate when I said that.

"Look, Will, we can talk about that later. I know you're tired. But, to be truthful, Will, you can't go gallivanting around Australia now. I mean, you've just had a month on holiday, so you're already behind in your job applications. It's sad to hear, Will, but the party is over now – it's time to buckle down and join the real world. When I was your age, I was already engaged to your mother and working in two jobs, just to make ends meet."

I wasn't ready to buckle down and get my ends to meet. But I was too tired to argue now, so let it ride. My mum seemed more pleased to see me as I walked through the door and dumped my rucksack in the hall.

"Blimey, Will, you look like the wild man of Borneo!" she announced when she looked at me.

I didn't know who the wild man of Borneo was.

"I'm making a nice chicken and leek pie for your tea. Why don't you go upstairs and have a nice warm bath? It looks like you could do with one, and then you can tell us all about your holiday," she added.

That did sound like a good idea. I went upstairs to my bedroom and started to undress. While the bath was running, I quickly got the Carole King vinyl out of its sleeve and placed it on the turntable. I moved the arm of the record player so that the needle aligned with track seven on the album, and lowered the arm until the needle was touching the vinyl. I turned the volume up and waited for the static hiss to be replaced with the music.

The song was about love, I think, but the love of a friend. I suppose the clue was in the title. Ruby was basically saying, via the song, that if I was down and troubled all I had to do was call and she would come running to see me. It was a nice sentiment, but I didn't want Ruby as a friend. I wanted more.

I was still troubled, though, by my stomach. I wondered if I called and said I still had diarrhoea she would come running? It was more likely she would be running in the opposite direction. I did need to get my bowels sorted out, though, and told my mum about my 'troubles'. She called the doctor for me, and, because of a cancellation, I was booked in the following morning for an appointment.

I didn't sleep well that night. I thought I would sleep for hours, as I was finally in bed in a horizontal position, and I wasn't travelling as I slept. But I couldn't sleep. I kept thinking of that kiss in Brussels, and the note, and the album. But mostly the kiss. I had to try and think of something else. It was strange to wake up in the same place as where I went to sleep. No more different countries for me for a while.

I was pleased, the next morning, to see my appointment was with my usual GP, Dr Watkins.

"Hello, Will. Looks like your skin has improved. What can I do for you?"

I told him of my symptoms, and my travel exploits, and he said to bring in a stool sample as soon as I could, which he would send to the hospital laboratory, and he would take it from there.

Back in the house, it wasn't long before my bowels were off again. I wasn't sure how to collect the sample, but luckily my dad had given a sample recently. He told me to put a lot of toilet paper down the bowl on top of the water to catch any faecal matter. Oh, what joy. But it did work, and I was able to get a sample, which my dad dropped off at the surgery for me. A few days later, I had a call from the surgery. Dr Watkins wanted to see me. I was a bit worried when I told Mum, but she said it was probably nothing to worry about.

Dr Watkins looked pleased to see me.

"Well, Will, you've caused some excitement at the surgery."

"What do you mean?" I asked anxiously.

"We had a call from Microbiology at the hospital. Apparently, they had to pass on your sample to the London School of Tropical Medicine."

"Is it something serious?" I was starting to panic slightly.

"Well, no, don't worry, Will – you're in the right place. It was good you came to see me, though."

"So what did they find?".

"Well, Will, you have two infections going on at the same time: you tested positive for giardiasis and amoebiasis. Amoebiasis, better known as amoebic dysentery, and is the more serious of the two. It's caused by the parasite *Entamoeba histolytica*. Giardiasis is also caused by a tiny parasite."

"My stomach has been bad for a while. Is it treatable?"

"Yes, we can give you some medication, which should get you feeling better soon, although amoebic dysentery can be quite serious. In rare cases, if you don't get treated it can cause death."

My face must have turned white.

"But don't worry, Will. That's not going to happen with you. I'll prescribe some medication which you can pick up from the pharmacy and start taking today."

"How do you get that *amibe … amebee …*"

"Amoebic dysentery is normally contracted via the faecal–oral route."

"The what?"

"The faecal–oral route. Basically, at some stage of your holiday, you must have ingested contaminated faeces."

"That's horrible. Are you sure you catch it that way? Is that the only way you can get it?"

"I'm afraid so. But don't worry – in about two weeks you'll be feeling as right as rain. Just jump on the scales, though. I want to make a note of your weight."

I was shocked to see I had lost over a stone in weight in four weeks.

"So, start this medication straight away, and make sure you eat regular meals. We need to start building you up."

"I know – I've been described as a lanky string of piss," I said as Dr Watkins passed over a prescription he must have written earlier. He was laughing now.

"I wouldn't go that far, but I could write that in my notes if you like. And another thing, Will, before you go …"

"Yes, Dr Watkins?"

"Try not to eat any more contaminated shit. Other food sources are available." With that, he let out a big belly laugh, obviously amused by his own joke.

# Chapter 66

## Four Months Later

I had finally got my first proper job at the University of Wales Hospital in Cardiff. I was starting as a junior B medical laboratory scientific officer in the biochemistry laboratory. The pay was shockingly bad, but I was still living at home, so it shouldn't be a problem. Mum and Dad said they wouldn't charge me any rent for a while, until I found my feet financially. I was told that once you are trained up and qualified, your pay would go up, through out-of-hours work and unsocial hours payments. Though this would take a few years.

I'd had a letter from Ruby that morning, so I was feeling buoyant. We'd been sending letters to each other almost on a weekly basis. She was doing well in her new job and had some lovely colleagues and a good social life with work. Reading between the lines, I could tell she was still seeing Tom, but she kept any mention of him vague. She too had been to the doctor and had been treated for giardiasis, but unlike me, she didn't have amoebic dysentery as well. She wondered where we had picked that up from and expressed concern over my weight loss. She said she was pleased with herself for thinking of an end to my egg joke and also, unfortunately, had smashed one of the glass snails. The rest were still intact, though. She missed the holiday and said it was still the best experience of her life. I told her I loved the album Tapestry and played it most days, although I still preferred The Smiths. She said she still didn't like The Smiths. She asked if I was going to Australia. I said it was unlikely, though Pete had said he wasn't going until

September now, as Mothball had some 'family issues' to sort out. So I hadn't definitely ruled it out, though my finances had taken a big hit.

My first day at work was going well. It was a big, busy department, and I was shocked to hear the laboratory never closed. It was open twenty-four hours a day, 365 days a year, and a colleague said, "The light is always on." Some of the staff were only a few years older than me and were already on the housing ladder, as there were good opportunities to pick up extra shifts. We had an hour for lunch, and a lot of staff took advantage of the onsite swimming pool. I hadn't brought any sandwiches the first day and was told most staff buy food in the canteen and take back to the staffroom.

I followed the signs to the hospital canteen. Staff discount was offered on the food by showing your identification badge. As I queued to pay for my tuna baguette and a bag of beef and onion crisps – which had recently overtaken over from salt and vinegar as my favourite flavour – I looked over to see a group of nurses sitting at one of the tables in the canteen. I was surprised to see one of them was Cheryl. Cheryl Wilson, my old biology A-level school friend. I was too shy to go over and say hello, but after I paid for my lunch, her table of six nurses stood up to leave, and our paths crossed at the tray station.

"Hello, Cheryl," I said confidently.

Cheryl stopped, and turned to look at me. I wasn't sure if she was going to recognise me but, luckily, she did.

"Will Evans! You're a blast from the past. What are you doing here?"

"I started work here – today's my first day. I work in the labs here, in biochemistry."

One of the other nurses shouted over to Cheryl, to say they'd see her back on the ward.

"I can't stop long – I've got to get back to work. What time's your afternoon break? We could meet up later?"

"Yes, that would be great – it's at 3.30."

"OK, good. Want to meet up here?"

"Yes, that'll be nice. I'll see you later."

"OK – see you later, Will."

Cheryl was looking good in her nurse's uniform. She was just as attractive as I remembered her from school. I wondered if she was single.

The afternoon was really dragging. I wasn't really concentrating and kept looking at the clock on the wall to see how long it was until 3.30. I tried to stifle a big yawn, unsuccessfully.

"Boring you, am I?" asked the ginger-haired laboratory trainer called Tim.

To be honest, you are, Tim, I thought. *I mean, you're only a few years older than me. You could lighten it up a bit. Make this induction tour a bit more interesting. And, also, sort out your body odour, could you?* He did smell a bit.

"No, sorry – I'm just a bit tired after lunch," I hastily replied. My mind wasn't focused on the automation of the processing of GP blood samples – it was flitting between Cheryl and Ruby, and how different they were.

"Automation is the future," the ginger-haired bore continued. Yeah, yeah, I thought. Who cares? Not me, that was for sure.

"Workloads are just going to increase, and automation will be the key factor in improving turnaround times," Ginger Tim wittered on.

I wasn't even sure what he was talking about. What

was this turnaround time he kept going on about? I didn't like to ask, in case it made me look stupid – but, as the laboratory produced results for patients from the blood samples, I assumed it was the time it took to get the result back to the clinician or GP from the laboratory.

Finally, Ginger Tim finished his tour of the laboratory, and I was free to go on break. I rushed to take off my white lab coat, washed my hands quickly and made my way to the canteen. I quickly got myself a coffee from the automated coffee machine and sat at a nearby vacant table. There was no sign of Cheryl. I sipped my coffee slowly. It wasn't the best coffee I'd tasted, and it didn't compare to some of the coffees I'd drunk while interrailing. After about ten minutes, Cheryl finally entered the canteen. She waved to me as she queued for her coffee. Five minutes later, she was sitting opposite me.

"Sorry I'm late, Will – I had to take some bloods from a patient. I probably could have given them to you to take to the lab. They were for biochemistry."

"I wouldn't know what to do with them. I'm not trained up yet. It's only my first day, after all," I replied.

"So, Will, what have you been up to since I last saw you?"

I filled Cheryl in about my life over the last few years, going to university, getting my degree, going interrailing, meeting Jim Pepperman. I was talking quickly, as I was conscious there wasn't much time left on my break. I asked Cheryl what she'd been up to since last time I'd seen her. She told me about her training to be a nurse and how she had now left home and was sharing a flat with three nurses she had meet on the course. There was no mention of a boyfriend, and this piqued my interest. I had to move on from Ruby. I was still thinking about her too much. I decided there and then to ask Cheryl out.

"Eh, Cheryl, I was wondering – do you fancy going out for a drink with me sometime this week?"

"Oh, I wasn't expecting you to ask me out." Cheryl was blushing now.

"The thing is, Will, I have a boyfriend – one of the doctors on the ward. We've only been going out for about two months, but things are going well."

"That's great, Cheryl. Really great," I replied. It wasn't great. It wasn't great at all. "No worries. It was lovely to see you again, anyway. I'd better get back – don't want to upset Ginger Tim on my first day in work." I realised that this was the second time I'd asked Cheryl out, both with the same outcome. I was proud of myself for having the courage to ask her out, though. Again. Maybe it was a bit too soon, however. But Cheryl had blown it now. I wouldn't be asking her for a third time.

I was a bit dejected as I walked back along the corridor towards the laboratory. How long was this corridor? It seemed to go on for ages. Why were hospital corridors so long? Where was the laboratory? Would I ever get a girl to go out with me?

# Chapter 67

## Easter 1986

I was looking forward to Easter. I had a week off work and, to be honest, couldn't wait to get away from the place. The first few days of the job were OK, but as time went on I was starting to realise it wasn't what I wanted to do for the rest of my life, and I was already starting to get bored. And I was sick of Ginger Tim and his incessant training. I was waiting for the postman to come as I was hoping I'd have a letter from Ruby. I'd sent a couple of letters to her in the last month but was still waiting for a reply. I expected she was busy with work and exams and stuff. I looked out of the window as the postman was coming down the drive. He seemed to have a lot of letters in his hand, which was a good sign. My dad reached the letterbox before me and brought the pile of letters to the dining table to read with his morning mug of tea.

"There's three letters for you today, Will. Someone's popular."

He passed me the correspondence. They were all handwritten. I recognised one from Pete's handwriting and opened that first.

Evans, I'm now finally going to Australia in the summer. I had to delay the trip for a while as my dad had been ill. He had a heart attack. I knew all those years of smoking would catch up with him eventually. Anyway, he's doing OK, thankfully, so my trip is still on, although the thick bastard is still smoking. Mothball is still on board. He's been struggling to get a proper job and has been working in a factory, making aeroplane seats, but hates it. Let me know if you're still interested. You only live once.

Pete

I took my cup of tea to my bedroom to read the other two letters. I didn't recognise the handwriting on either. One felt like an invitation. I would open that last. I sipped my tea, which I'd forgot to put sugar in, as I tore open the second letter. It was from Beth.

Hi Will,

Are you missing me? I've been thinking about you a lot. Did you get together with Ruby in the end? Why haven't you written to me? I thought you would come and see me in New York. I am missing the UK, though not the weather! I'm working for a big company, in HR. I spend a lot of time in interviews as HR is a big part of the recruitment process. Get yourself over here. I could probably get you a job! Would love to show you the best city in the world. It would great if you could come. Write, please, Mr Evans.

Love, Beth xxx

My heartbeat had increased rapidly. Maybe Ruby was right. Beth did like me. I quickly read the letter again. She wanted me to come and visit her. I had written to her twice since I got back from interrailing, but she hadn't replied. So what was that about? I looked at the address on the letter, it was different to the one I had been using. She must have moved, and my letters couldn't have been forwarded. What were the chances, two letters on the same day, both invitations, one to go to Australia and the other to USA? Exciting times.

I still had one more letter to go. I decided to get another cup of tea, this time with sugar in it. Downstairs, my dad asked me who the letters were from. He was surprised to hear about Pete, and told me that wouldn't be an option for me as I had a good job which I couldn't give up and they were hard to find. He did say I could go on holiday to see Beth, and that was a good opportunity, to be shown around the city by a local. It wasn't up to him, though. I was anxious to see what the final letter was, as it felt like an invitation. Back in my room, I lay on my bed and tore open the final letter.

Tom and Ruby invite you to share in our joy as we get married on Saturday 15th June 1986.

Service at 12 noon at St. Peter's Church, Harborne, followed by a reception at Waters Head Golf Club for dinner and dancing.

RSVP

I couldn't believe what I was reading. She had barely mentioned Tom in any of our letters, and now they were getting married. I felt sick. In fact, I was going to *be* sick. I rushed to the bathroom, where I vomited into the toilet bowl. I stayed in my room for a while, trying to get my head round the invitation. I went downstairs, where my mum was peeling potatoes for lunch.

"Your dad said you had a few letters today, from Pete and Beth. What was the third one?"

"It was an invitation to Ruby's wedding."

"What, Ruby, the girl you went interrailing with?"

"Yeah, her."

"Oh, you liked her, didn't you?"

"Yes, I did, I mean, I still do. I can't believe she's getting married so quickly."

"When is the wedding?"

"In June."

"Are you going to go?"

"I think so. Yes. She was a good friend to me." I sat down at the dining table and stared out of the window. I felt like crying but couldn't do so in front of my mum.

"Are you OK, Will?" Mum asked, a look of concern on her face.

"Oh, yeah, I'm fine." But I think the emotion in my voice was saying the opposite. I wasn't fine. I wasn't fine at all.

And then my mum did something that really surprised me. She put down her potato peeler and dried her hands with a tea towel. She came over, put her arms around me, and gave me a hug. I couldn't remember the last time she had hugged me.

"Never mind, Will. What's the proverb, 'When life gives you lemons, make lemonade'?" I didn't know how to respond. My mum was more perceptive than I gave her credit for. But I didn't really understand what she was on about, with the lemon thing.

"Thanks, Mum," was all I could come up with in reply. I quickly wiped away a tear so my mum couldn't see that I was upset. But she knew. A mother's instinct.

# Chapter 68

## The Wedding

The only positive thing that I could think about the wedding was that all the interrail crew were invited. We would be on the 'friends' table. Pete came down the night before the wedding and stayed at my house. The plan was to get the first train up to Birmingham in the morning. We had booked rooms at the golf club where the reception was being held. Pete dropped his stuff off in what my mum was now referring to as the 'guest room', since my younger brother was away at university. After my mum had fed us both a comforting fish pie, we inevitably ended up at my local pub. We ordered a couple of pints, Brains Dark for me and Strongbow for Pete, and sat down at a small table near the toilets.

"Well, that's a surprise about Ruby getting married," began Pete.

"I know. A bit quick, don't you think?"

"Could be up the duff?"

"I hadn't even thought of that. Do you reckon she is?"

"No, I don't think she is. How are you feeling about it? I bet you're gutted. I did say you had no chance there. I'm surprised you're going to the wedding, to be honest."

"Yeah, you did, I suppose. Why did you keep saying that?"

"Well, nothing against you, Evans, but Tom Bellows is like a better version of you."

"What do you mean?"

"Well, he's better looking, he's brighter, he doesn't have acne, and he's also funnier than you, Evans."

"Kick a man when he's down, why don't you?"

"Sorry, Evans. Sometimes you've got to be cruel to be kind." Pete laughed in that annoying way again.

He was right, though: Tom Bellows was a better version of me. He would have thought of an end to that egg joke straight away, no doubt.

It was a beautiful, sunny day when we got to the church. It was also really hot, and most of the congregation were milling around outside, reluctant to go in. Tom was standing near the door of the church. I'd already gone over and shaken hands with him. Bastard looked immaculate, in his morning suit, with his freshly coiffed hair and perfect skin. The best man, who I recognised from university but didn't know, shouted for everyone to make their way into the church as the bride was on her way. All the friends were in the same pew. I was sitting next to Gwen, who was looking lovely in a simple olive-green dress, next to the aisle.

I was secretly hoping Ruby had put on loads of weight and would look uglier than I remembered. However, this wasn't the case, as I noted when the door of the church opened and her dad proudly and slowly walked her down the aisle. Her brown hair was curlier than usual and encased in a halo of fresh flowers. A long veil flowed from the back of her head. Her shoulders were bare, and her skin was beautifully tanned. The dress itself could be described as 'classic', in traditional white. She looked like a princess. She would have hated being described as that, but that was the only way I could describe it. Seeing her look so beautiful, it was obvious then that she was out of my league. I felt quite emotional as she walked down the aisle. As she came closer to me, she looked directly at me, gave me the most beautiful smile and very gently mouthed, "Hi, Will."

The service went quickly, and after about thirty minutes or so the bride and groom exchanged rings and became Mr and Mrs Bellows.

As the congregation gathered outside the church and waited to throw confetti, Gwen came up to me and put her arm around me.

"Doesn't she look beautiful, Will?"

"She does. She really does. It'll be you and Tigsy next."

"Ha ha, good one Will. I don't think either of us are ready for marriage just yet."

"Well, you're a lot closer to marriage than me."

"We're still young, Will. There's a big world out there, full of possibilities."

Tigsy had joined us and playfully punched me on the arm.

"It's game over, then, Will – not even any extra time. The only thing you can hope for now is a quick divorce."

"Alright, Tigsy, let's move on, shall we? Give it a rest, will you? Let's get to the reception, shall we? I need a drink – well, a few drinks. I need to take the edge off."

There was a coach for guests, to transport them to the golf club, and a welcoming drink of sparkling wine or orange juice. I took two glasses of sparkling wine and tried to drink one quickly, but the bubbles made it difficult.

"Drowning your sorrows, are you, Will?" laughed Pete.

"Give it a rest, Pete. I just told Tigsy the same thing. You should be the one drowning your sorrows. Didn't your Dutch friend give you the boot?"

"It was only a holiday romance, Will, nothing more. You should learn from me. Stop jumping in at the deep end. Paddle a bit in the shallow end first."

I didn't know what he was on about, but he was getting on my nerves. I wondered if our friendship would last, now that we had left university.

I briefly said hello to Ruby at the line-up and told her how beautiful she looked. I shook hands with Tom again and told him he was a lucky man. To his credit, he said he knew. The 'friends' table was near the back of the room, a long way from the top table. The food came out quickly, and there was a lot of wine on the table. I was drinking a lot, probably too much, and was starting to get drunk. Ruby's dad stood up and began the speeches. He spoke eloquently about how much they missed Ruby's mum and how proud she would have been today to see her daughter looking so beautiful. I could see Ruby was crying, and Tom passed her a tissue. Next up, it was Tom. Spitefully, I was secretly hoping he would make a mess of his speech. But, predicably, he had everyone laughing within minutes. He went on to say how he would look after Ruby and never let her down and how much he loved her. Bullshit, I was thinking – but deep down I knew what he was saying was true.

The best man stood up and delivered a typical best man speech. A few jokes about Tom and a rather inappropriate joke about a vacuum cleaner and lack of suction, which went down like a lead balloon. Finally, it was time to toast the bride and groom, and everyone stood up and raised their glasses to toast the happy couple. Everyone had expected the speeches to be over, but, to my surprise, Ruby got to her feet and said she would like to say a few words.

"Hello, everyone. Sorry, I know it's not traditional for the bride to speak at her own wedding, but I would just like to say a few words. I wish my mum could have been here today at my wedding. Me and dad miss her so much. She would've loved to have been here today. But I know she wouldn't want me to be sad. She always encouraged me to get as much out of life as possible. 'Don't put all your eggs in one basket,' she would say. She always encouraged me to try new things, travel and see the world. And she remains in my heart today and going forward. So, can I ask you all to stand up and raise a glass to my mum?"

Some people who had known Ruby's mum raised their glasses and said, "To Rachel." Others, who didn't know her name, myself included, just said, "To Ruby's mum." I was thinking about that bit in the speech, about putting all your eggs in one basket. Was that a subtle reference to the egg joke on holiday, or was I just overthinking again? Mothball, who was sitting next to me, interrupted my thought processes.

"So, Will, how's the job going? I heard you're testing shit and piss!"

"Well, yeah, we do a bit of that, but it's all in safety cabinets – and you're all gloved up and stuff, and you can't smell anything."

"Sounds gross."

"We mainly do blood tests, though."

"Sounds boring."

"To be honest, it is. I'm starting to question my life decisions."

"Have you made up your mind about Australia yet? I can't wait to go. Are you coming?"

"I'm still thinking about it. It is a big decision. My dad will freak out if I go."

"It's not up to your dad. You're a big boy now, Will,

do what your heart tells you. I'm not a fan of this wine, I'm off to buy a pint from the bar. Want a pint, Will?"

"What, Mothball, are you offering to buy me a pint?" I started to laugh.

"Well, no. I'll buy you a pint. and you buy me a pint later, Will. That's how rounds work."

"Ha ha, thought as much. Go on, then. I'll have a pint of lager."

Mothball got up to go to the bar, and almost immediately Ruby, who had been moving from table to table, speaking to everyone, sat down next to me.

"Hi, Will. Thanks for coming," she said, rather formally.

My heart started to race again. She could still do that to me after all this time. Looking at her now, in her wedding dress, with her immaculate hair and makeup and those big beautiful brown eyes, I don't think I had ever seen her look so beautiful.

"Hello, Mrs Bellows."

"Ha ha, that sounds strange. It is going to take a bit of getting used to."

I was quite drunk now, it so would probably only be a short time before I would probably say something inappropriate.

"Where's Tom?"

"Oh, he's at the bar, talking to his friends."

"You look amazing, Ruby. He's a lucky bastard."

"I know." And we both laughed.

"I liked your speech. Especially the bit about putting your eggs in one basket."

"That bit was for you, Will."

"I was hoping it would be."

"I really enjoyed our time together on holiday."

"Me too."

"So how are you enjoying your new job?"

"I'm not, really."

"Oh, that's a shame. Are you going to go to Australia with Pete and Mothball?"

"I haven't decided yet. Ruby, can I ask you a question?"

"You don't need to ask, Will."

"Why did you get married so quickly? I mean, I'd been writing letters to you, and you hardly mentioned Tom in any of your letters."

"I know. It was just, if I had, you would've stopped writing to me – and I liked your letters, Will. They made me laugh."

"I liked your letters too. I suppose now we can't really write to each other anymore."

"I suppose not, Will. I'm not sure Tom would be too happy about it."

"Yeah, I wouldn't be, if I was married to you and Tom was writing to you."

"It's a shame, though. At least I managed to finish your egg joke."

"Yeah, that was funny, I was struggling to think of an ending."

I felt like Ruby had something else to say to me. It was almost as if she was wrestling with her conscience – or was I just reading too much into it? Suddenly, Pete appeared, carrying three pints of lager. He was drunk. Very drunk. You could always tell by his eyes. They had a sort of hangdog appearance. He put the drinks down on the table and put his arm around Ruby.

"Broke his heart, you did, Ruby, getting married to Tom. Poor bastard didn't stopped crying for weeks when he found out you were getting married."

Ruby looked uncomfortable and tried to move away. But Pete wasn't letting her.

"Spent all those weeks pining after you. I told him he had no chance. But would he listen? He was like a dog with a bone."

I stood up to face Pete.

"Oi, Pete, give it a rest, will you? It's Ruby's wedding day. Stop making a tit of yourself."

"OK, Evans, lighten up. I was only messing with the pair of you."

Ruby was looking annoyed with Pete and looked over to the bar, where Tom was standing.

"I'd better go – it looks like Tom is calling me over. Take care, Will."

Ruby leaned over and kissed me on the cheek, and went off to find Tom. I was annoyed with Pete. He had ruined the conversation with Ruby. I stood up to go to the toilet. I watched as Ruby reached Tom and kissed him. For some reason, all I could think about was The Smiths' lyric from their song 'Hand in Glove', telling me a brighter life was out there, urging me to hold tight. But it was too late now: she wasn't staying on my arms, and she appeared to have found the good life with Tom Bellows.

I didn't speak to her again. I wouldn't be able to write to her again, in the way that we had been doing. I did speak to Tom again, though. He came over to my table and sat down next to me. He apologised for pushing me over in Corfu and said he felt bad about it for a long time. I accepted his apology and told him not to worry about it. It was water under the bridge. He said he'd been worried I'd been getting too close to Ruby, and it was a factor in him asking her to marry her, probably a little sooner than he had envisaged. I magnanimously said she only had eyes for him all along. He was a good bloke, I suppose. I grudgingly accepted that. *Time to close the chapter on Ruby now, Will. Time to move on.*

# Chapter 69

## July 1986

"Hi, Mr Fitzroy – can I have a quick word?"

Steve Fitzroy was the biochemistry laboratory manager. He was a big bloke, an unusual shape, in that he was both really tall and grossly overwight. He had started in the laboratory straight from school and worked his way up to manager of the department. I hadn't had much to do with him since I started, but knew of his reputation, which was strict but fair. He had a packet of chocolate digestives on his desk, and he must have just finished one as he surreptitiously wiped some crumbs off the side of his ample mouth.

"Oh, hi, Will. Yeah, take a seat. I've got a meeting at eleven, so I've only got a few minutes. What can I do for you, young man?"

"I was wondering – or hoping, really – if I could have some time off?"

"What do you mean, take some annual leave?"

"Well, no, not annual leave exactly. I wanted to take six months off work unpaid but keep my job open."

"OK, that's an unusual request – as a sort of sabbatical?"

"Yes, a sabbatical." That was the word I was looking for.

"Can I ask what for?"

"I would just like to go travelling for six months, but I don't want to give up the job. I've had an opportunity, which, if I don't take now, I may well regret."

"Well, Will, that's a big ask. I mean, my job is to keep the laboratory running smoothly. What would I do if

266

everyone came to me with the same request?"

"I know. I was just asking. To be honest, I wasn't really expecting a positive response I was just sounding it out, I suppose. Thank you, Mr Fitzroy."

I stood up to go back to the laboratory, where no doubt Ginger Tim would be waiting to train me up good.

"Sit down, Will. I haven't said no yet, have I?"

"Oh, sorry. No, you haven't."

"Cheryl told me all about you."

"Cheryl?"

"Cheryl Wilson. She's my niece."

"Oh, I didn't know that you two were related. She never mentioned it."

"Yes, she told me all about you, how you helped her with her biology A-level."

"Yeah, I couldn't have done a very good job – she failed it first time."

Mr Fitzroy laughed, a surprisingly high-pitched laugh for a man of his stature.

"Yes, Will, she did, but she persevered and passed it on the second attempt. And now look at her."

"Yeah, I know she's doing well. I met her a few weeks ago."

"I know, she told me about it. Didn't she turn you down for a date – twice, I hear?"

Mr Fitzroy was laughing now, which I thought was a bit unprofessional.

"Look, I think we're straying a bit off topic here," I said bravely.

"Sorry, Will, you're right. I'll tell you what I'll do. I'll have a word with HR and hopefully have an answer for you by the end of the day."

"Oh, OK. Thanks, Steve."

"It's Mr Fitzroy to you."

I don't know why I suddenly decided to call him Steve.

"Oh, sorry, Mr Fitzroy."

I returned to the laboratory. I was having training in laboratory reception this afternoon, or 'pre-analytical' as Ginger Tim described it in his presentation. There was only half an hour until home time when Ginger Tim shouted over to me.

"Hey, Will! Mr Fitzroy wants to see you."

"OK. Thanks, Tim."

I almost said Ginger Tim. I had to be careful: he was known to be very sensitive about his ginger hair.

"Good news, Will," Mr Fitzroy said as I stood in front of his desk. He didn't offer me a seat this time. Mr Fitzroy continued. "I've spoken to HR this afternoon, and they said a sabbatical is possible but ultimately it's down to the discretion of the manager. I don't think there's ever been another request in Pathology for a sabbatical. You are the first, Will."

"Oh, OK." I waited for Mr Fitzroy to continue. I think, secretly, he was enjoying making me sweat. That sweaty hospital manager had my destiny in his podgy hands.

"Well, Will, you should be delighted to hear I've decided to allow you to take a six-month sabbatical. I'll need you to complete an application form for me, which, when I approve, I'll send on to to HR for confirmation. Then, as they say, the jobs a good 'un."

"Oh, that's great, Mr Fitzroy. Thank you so much. It's much appreciated."

"But Will, don't let me down. You are young and have a good opportunity here at the hospital. Get this travelling lark out of your system, and when you're done get back to work. Who knows, Will – you too could be sitting at my desk as laboratory manager one day."

"Thank you, Mr Fitzroy."

I was staggered that he'd agreed to my proposal. Now all I had left to do was speak to my dad and phone Pete. And I already knew I didn't want to be sitting in Mr Fitzroy's seat any time in the future.

# Chapter 70

## The Decision

My dad wasn't very happy when I told him I had taken a break from work and was going off travelling for six months. I'd already told my mother.

"And work agreed for you to have a sabbatical?"

"Yes, Dad. Mr Fitzroy said it was at his discretion, and it would be OK."

"Well, I think it's a mistake. I mean, you've already done travelling. You spent the month in Europe not long ago, on the trains. Why do you feel the need to go racing around the world again? You need to grow up, Will, and get on with your life."

"I am, Dad – that's why I arranged for a sabbatical in the first place. I'll have a job to come back to, and it's only for six months."

"Well, it's your life, Will. I know your mother isn't happy about it."

"I'll talk to her now." Mum was in the garden, tending to her roses.

"Hi, Mum. I suppose you spoke to Dad about me taking a sabbatical, Dad's now saying you're not happy with me going?"

"Yes, Will, I did speak to him. But I didn't say that, Will."

"So do you agree with Dad that I shouldn't go?"

"To be honest, Will, I *don't* agree with your father on this one."

"You don't?"

"No, Will. I think you've got to take these opportunities when you can. I wish I'd had a chance to do something like that when I was younger."

"Does Dad know you feel like this?"

"No, Will. We do have secrets sometimes. We are two individuals, after all, not one unit. The thing is I've noticed a change in you Will. Since you went to that wedding you've been quite down, haven't you?"

"I suppose I have."

"It's like the lights are on but there's nobody home with you, Will, lately. It must have been hard for you to see Ruby get married. But listen, Will, get out there – enjoy yourself, and, if things don't work out, come home. Me and your father will be here to pick up the pieces."

I wanted to hug my mum there and then, but my sense of awkwardness kicked in, and all I could manage was, "Thanks, Mum."

Right, all that was left to do was phone Pete and tell him the news. I would wait until this evening, and decided to go for a run to clear my head. I didn't really like running, but occasionally, once you got past the first mile, you could get into the zone and lose yourself in a run. It was only a few miles to the beach at Lavernock, near Penarth, and when the tide was out it was a great place to run. I jogged down slowly, and when I got to the beach I started to run faster and faster on the sand. I was sprinting now, as fast as I could go, and it felt fantastic. To be out on the beach, on the sand, by the sea. I was young, I was getting over Ruby, and my life was moving on. The world was full of possibilities.

After I'd got home, showered and had tea – one of my dad's pressure cooker stews – I went to phone Pete. He answered on the third ring.

"Alright, Evans? Have you stopped crying now, after the wedding?"

"Alright, Pete. You were the one crying, Pete, when you had to pay your bar bill at the end of the night."

"Well, Evans, have you made your mind up? Are you coming to Australia with me and Mothball?"

"I'm not. Sorry, Pete. I'm not going to come."

"What do you mean, you're not going to come?"

"I *am* going travelling – I'm just not going to Australia."

"Where are you off to, then?"

"I'm off to New York, to see Beth."

"Beth? You hardly know her."

"Well, she's asked me to go over and stay with her for a while. She's sharing a flat, and they have a spare room."

"And you'd rather go to America to chase another woman than come to Australia with me and Mothball?"

"I would, yes."

"Well, it's your choice, Will. I reckon it's a big mistake. I mean, you haven't got a good track record in chasing women. You spent the best part of a month chasing Ruby all over Europe, and look where that got you. And now you want to do the same thing again with some American girl?"

"I know, but I had fun trying with Ruby".

"You know what I'm going to say next, don't you, Evans?"

"No, what's that?"

"You've got no chance with Beth. Don't waste your time, Evans. No chance."

I could hear him laughing to himself in the background. No doubt throwing his head back in that annoying way of his. But I would prove him wrong. My mind was made up. It was all systems go. There would be no looking back. I was off to America and my pursuit of Ruby – sorry, I mean Beth – was on.

No chance, Pete had said. Just you wait and see.

**The End**

## About The Author

Gareth Alun Thomas was born in Dinas Powys, just outside Cardiff but now lives in Blackwood in the Welsh valleys. He has worked for over 34 years for the NHS as a Biomedical Scientist and has recently retired and returned to work part time. Working less hours, Gareth finally had time to write his first novel, something that he always wanted to do. When his parents passed away Gareth and his brothers had to clear the house. He came across an old diary he had written when he went travelling with five friends across Europe on an interrail ticket. Using this diary as a template, Gareth finally wrote and completed his first novel, "No chance."

Gareth has been happily married to Amanda for over thirty years and they have three children together, two girls and a boy. In his spare time Gareth enjoys walking the dog, travelling and playing the guitar as well as cooking for the family.